MY LORD VALENTINE

"Honey, I have come to understand so much more about myself this week than I ever have before. Enough to know I want you. I need you."

Bron stood and gathered her up into his arms and held her close. He pulled her to him and lifted her chin. "Honey," he whispered. "I . . ." There were no words for what he was feeling, and so he claimed her lips, his body quivering with love and desire as her slender arms threaded around his neck and her slim fingers jammed into his hair.

"Don't you want me, too?" he murmured into her ear.

Tears trembled in her lovely aqua eyes. "I do. That is the trouble!"

"Then marry me, my sweet wild Honey. I have fallen deeply in love with you, and I never thought I could love any woman. Marry me!"

—from "Wild Honey" by Donna Simpson

BOOK YOUR PLACE ON OUR WEBSITE AND MAKE THE READING CONNECTION!

We've created a customized website just for our very special readers, where you can get the inside scoop on everything that's going on with Zebra, Pinnacle and Kensington books.

When you come online, you'll have the exciting opportunity to:

- View covers of upcoming books
- Read sample chapters
- Learn about our future publishing schedule (listed by publication month *and author*)
- Find out when your favorite authors will be visiting a city near you
- Search for and order backlist books from our online catalog
- Check out author bios and background information
- Send e-mail to your favorite authors
- Meet the Kensington staff online
- Join us in weekly chats with authors, readers and other guests
- Get writing guidelines
- AND MUCH MORE!

**Visit our website at
http://www.zebrabooks.com**

Valentine Rogues

Cindy Holbrook
Debbie Raleigh
Donna Simpson

ZEBRA BOOKS
Kensington Publishing Corp.
http://www.zebrabooks.com

ZEBRA BOOKS are published by

Kensington Publishing Corp.
850 Third Avenue
New York, NY 10022

Copyright © 2001 by Kensington Publishing Corp.
"A Valentine Dream" copyright © 2001 by Cindy Holbrook
"The Merry Cupids" copyright © 2001 by Debbie Raleigh
"Wild Honey" copyright © 2001 by Donna Simpson

All rights reserved. No part of this book may be reproduced in any form or by any means without the prior written consent of the Publisher, excepting brief quotes used in reviews.

If you purchased this book without a cover you should be aware that this book is stolen property. It was reported as "unsold and destroyed" to the Publisher and neither the Author nor the Publisher has received any payment for this "stripped book."

All Kensington titles, imprints and distributed lines are available at special quantity discounts for bulk purchases for sales promotion, premiums, fund raising, educational or institutional use.

Special book excerpts or customized printings can also be created to fit specific needs. For details, write or phone the office of the Kensington Special Sales Manager: Kensington Publishing Corp., 850 Third Avenue, New York, NY, 10022. Attn. Special Sales Department. Phone: 1-800-221-2647.

Zebra and the Z logo Reg. U.S. Pat. & TM Off.

First Printing: January, 2001
10 9 8 7 6 5 4 3 2 1

Printed in the United States of America

CONTENTS

A VALENTINE DREAM   7
  by Cindy Holbrook

THE MERRY CUPIDS   99
  by Debbie Raleigh

WILD HONEY   169
  by Donna Simpson

A Valentine Dream

by
Cindy Holbrook

One

> *"There is no such thing as coincidence."*
> —*Unknown authors, known authors,
> this author, and many others . . .*

Flames flared high around Pandora. It was uncomfortably warm, and she was a person who was fond of heat. She and Prinny, they always jested. Moans and shrieks sounded from all about her, but she could not assign a direction to them. She walked through a mud-brown landscape, the red gold of the flames the only color.

Women dressed in brown rags toiled amongst the rocks. Filthy and with blackened, chipped nails, they looked as if they hadn't bathed in decades or eaten in centuries. There was not a decent bosom amongst the toiling horde. There would be no need for corsets here. Or ribbons and lace. Or feathers and perfume.

"Madre di Dio. I am in hell! But how did I get here?"

"Because you help no one but yourself," a voice, thick with a Cockney accent, said from behind.

She spun. A woman with horns, long talons, and a forked tail watched her. *Santa pace.* At least she wore something other than brown—red satin, to be precise. Her gaze was insulting and derisive.

Pandora's heart raced. "Wh-who are you?"

"Cor, I'm the devil, love." She laughed. "My, but you are a slow top."

"The devil is a man."

"No, he isn't." She grinned evilly. "There are *no* men here. As I said, this is hell, ducky."

"Oh, God!"

"He isn't here, either, so don't you be thinking you can twist him around your little finger like you do the rest of them blokes."

Pandora fell to her knees and lifted clasped hands. "Please. I am too young. I cannot be dead. Please. Let me go."

The scene blurred out of focus for a moment, then returned. Hope surged through her. Could this be a dream?

"Very well. I will for now." The devil swished her spiked tail. "But you'd best change your ways, you selfish ninny. Help someone else, for fiend's sake and use your knowledge of men for someone else's benefit."

"I will. I will!" Pandora frowned. "But . . . how do I do that?"

A flash of lighting shot through the landscape. White. The brightness of it was a relief. A deep, cooling relief. Thunder rumbled.

"Oh, very well. I'll tell her." The devil crossed her arms and tapped a talon. "If this weren't a dream, I would give you a good piece of my . . ."

"This *is* a dream then?"

"W-e-ll . . ." Lightning flashed. The devil jumped and glanced up. "All right, all right. Confound it! For someone eternal, you are infernally impatient sometimes." She curled her lip and delivered a nasty glare. "I don't see why I need to tell you this. You'll be arriving here sooner or later, the way you live. I don't see why it can't be now and just have done with it." There was a sizzling sound, like that before a major thunderbolt. The devil grimaced. "I'm getting to it. Damn, but I hate these bloody dream appearances. Now listen well."

"I am. I am!"

The devil rolled her eyes. A crafty looked flitted across her face. "If you wish to save yourself . . ."

"I do. I do."

"You must help a poor, pitiful creature find her true love. And soon, mind you. Time is passing. Hell isn't." She shrugged. "*If* you succeed in that—and don't think it's going ter be just a snap of your fingers, mind you—you will be permitted to live out the rest of your trifling little life."

"Thank God!"

"Blast you." The devil visibly cringed. "Stop using His name in front of me. It is bloody rude of you, I vow."

"I am sorry."

"You will be, if you fail." A gray mist rose and swirled about them. The devil and hell became a blurred vision. "You will be mine!"

"But who is it I must help? How will I find the pitiful creature? How long do I have?"

"You have until . . . bloody hell, there it goes!"

The devil disappeared. Hell disappeared.

"No. Come back. I must know!"

It turned gray and silent. Then a girl's face appeared before her. She wore a mob cap and servant's dress and held a lacy, heart-shaped valentine to her chest. Then that image, too, disappeared.

Pandora slowly opened her eyes. Her heart pounded in fear. But her lovely pink satin tester greeted her eyes. She gripped smooth champagne-colored sheets to her. A fire crackled merrily in the fireplace—exactly where it belonged.

"*Che roba.* I am still alive." She sat up, inhaling a deep breath of gratitude.

The door opened and her maid entered. "Good morning, mum. Here is your chocolate." She carried a large silver tray across the room and set it down upon the table.

An eager smile crossed her face. "And a messenger delivered this for you."

The maid lifted something from the tray and walked over to her. She held it out. It was a lacy, heart-shaped valentine.

Pandora shrieked.

Jacklyn was dressed in a sapphire blue riding habit with a very dashing cut to it. Twitching a cuff embroidered *à la militaire* with black braid, she assessed her appearance as she strode by one of the pier mirrors encircling the octagonal entry, alternating with panels of tall windows. She paused and angled a jaunty black hat trimmed with a band of chinchilla that matched the fur trim on her lapels, then adjusted the scarf of blond lace that trailed from her hat to her waist. Excitement raced through her as she drew on her black gloves and walked across the large marble foyer toward the elegant outer doors. Never had she owned such a fashionable habit before. She chuckled. Indeed, never had she owned such a glorious town house before, either. Her father had been a stingy man in life, which meant he had left much behind in death.

She shook her head. She must not think upon that matter. It was time to cast off the gloom of the past. She had much to anticipate, after all. She was finally in London.

"Where are you going?" voice asked.

She turned. Mrs. Neville, her chaperon, stood behind her. Heavy black bombazine skirts rustled like a crow in flight as the small lady stepped forward. She still wore the darkest of mourning, though it was a full year and a half since Father had passed away.

"I wish to ride in the park."

Horror crossed Mrs. Neville's face. "My dear! You cannot."

"Why not?"

"It would not be proper."

"If you were to accompany me, it would be proper. Or perhaps the groom?"

"My dear, *nothing* is ever proper. Nor is it safe—never safe enough for a true lady. I have a famous notion. Do let us go into the parlor. We may start stitching those lovely samplers I sketched out."

"I do not wish to."

"Tsk. What would your father say?"

"What can he say? He is dead." She bit her lip.

"For shame! Do not speak in such a manner."

"I am sorry. I mean he has passed on to his reward, God rest his soul."

"What on earth are you saying? Your father is not dead. He is still living. You must await him. He will be arriving soon."

"What?" Jacklyn shook her head in confusion. "Th-that is impossible."

"No, no. You need only wait. You were always the impatient one." Mrs. Neville laughed. "But that is neither here nor there. You simply must wait."

"No. No!" Jacklyn spun, ran to the door, and jerked on the handle. It wouldn't open. Angry, she whirled upon Mrs. Neville. "Where are the keys?"

The older woman frowned. "Keys? There are no keys, my dear."

"There must be keys!"

"No. The house did not come with keys." She shrugged. "You do not need them. They are completely unnecessary."

"I must have the keys! I will not remain locked up here forever. I shall ask the solicitor." Jacklyn turned back to the door, reached for the handle—and realized the door was smooth. There was no handle now, nor a keyhole. Appalled, she ran to the windows. They, too, were smooth glass with nary a crack.

Outside, she could see a beautiful neighborhood. A carriage passed by with six shining horses. People happily strolled up and down the street. Couples in the square promenaded arm in arm. Children skipped along with their nannies. "But . . . but how do I get out? I—I must get out."

"Why, dearest, whatever do you mean?" Mrs. Neville looked astonished. "You do not get out." She walked over and peered out the window. "Isn't this a delightful view? I declare, what fun we shall have watching from here."

"I do not want to *watch!*"

"Tsk, tsk. You are such a teasing one. We came to London for that purpose, did we not?"

"No, I came . . . to do more. To go out! To meet people. To finally live."

"Go out?" Mrs. Neville shrieked and lifted her hands to her face. "Heavens, no. Proper ladies do no such thing, I assure you."

"But . . ." Jacklyn's heart sank. "Is nothing going to . . . to change?"

"Of course not, dear." Mrs. Neville walked up and put a bony arm about her charge's shoulders. "Things never change. You really must stop thinking such nonsensical things."

"But . . ."

"Dearest." Mrs. Neville's voice sunk to a whisper. "Do you really want to go out? You would not know how to behave. You never do. Your father is right, you know."

"I—I . . ." She halted and looked out the window with longing.

"My," Mrs. Neville sighed. "What a lovely time we will have watching it all go by."

"No! No! No!"

The entire scene turned black. She jerked awake, stunned and breathless. Thank God! It had been only a dream. Morning sunlight gleamed through the windows.

She looked quickly to the fireplace and sighed. No, there was no fire in the grate as yet.

A rap at her bedroom door sounded. She smiled. Her maid Betty was simply late. She wondered what the time was.

"Come in."

The door opened, and she felt a twinge of disappointment as Mrs. Neville entered. She was a small, spare woman. At least she wore lavender half-mourning instead of the black in Jacklyn's dream.

"Jacklyn, dear, are you all right? I heard you cry out."

"I am fine. I had a nightmare."

"I see. Sleeping in new places can do that to one. I vow I did not sleep a wink myself. So many noises. It is not at all like the country. I know you say this is the safest of neighborhoods, dearest, but I feared that we were to be robbed and slain in our beds last night, truly I did."

"We are very safe, Mrs. Neville, I assure you." Jacklyn held back a sigh. They had been in London a fortnight and Mrs. Neville still considered it as a new, strange place. Jacklyn shook her head and scrambled from beneath the covers. "Faith, but it is cold. I ordered Betty to make up the fires this morning. Where is she?"

"Oh, my goodness!" Mrs. Neville's hand flew to her mouth. "I am sorry, dearest, but when she came to my room, I told her she'd best cease what she was about. I was sure she had mistaken your instructions."

"I see."

"Forgive me, Jacklyn. But I never dreamed you would have ordered it."

She bit her lip in impatience. "I did. I detest a cold room in the morning."

"But what a frivolous extravagance!" Mrs. Neville looked scandalized. "Mercy, what would your father say?"

"What do you mean?" Jacklyn tensed. The terrible dream mocked her, confusing her sense of reality.

"God rest his soul." Mrs. Neville shook her head sadly. "I fear he would roll over in his grave if he knew what you intend to do."

"Thank God." Her common sense reasserted itself, and with it her confidence. Her father *was* dead. "I mean, God rest his soul."

"Madam, I fear we have a contretemps in the kitchen." Garman, Jacklyn's butler, who was generally efficient to the point of being frightening, strode into the parlor. His face twisted in alarm. "Please come!"

"Oh, dear." Mrs. Neville dropped her sewing. "Whatever could it be?"

"Yes, Garman. Whatever could it be?" Jacklyn sat forward a little too eagerly. Whatever had "flapped" her unflappable butler must be something to see.

"I fear the upstairs maid has barricaded herself in my pantry. She refuses to come out."

"Truly?" Jacklyn stifled a laugh. Garman's look of pained dignity was something to behold. "Why did she do that, pray tell?"

"Yes." Mrs. Neville rose, wringing her hands. "Why would she do such an odd thing? It makes no sense."

Garman cleared his throat. "A—a woman chased her into there, I believe."

"Gracious." Jacklyn's brows rose.

"Oh, no!" Mrs. Neville clearly trembled. "She must be a thief. One of those dreadful mohawks I have heard about."

"No, madam." Garman's face flushed to a bright red. "That is not what she is."

"Do you know her, Garman?" Jacklyn asked, intrigued by his reaction.

"Most certainly not, madam." Garman reared back as if she had slapped him. "I would never associate with the likes of her. Not that I could. She is extremely particular. Only the highest titles for that one. She is the most expensive . . . er, well, so I have heard."

"Really?" The morning was definitely looking up, in Jacklyn's opinion. "Let us not waste time, then."

"Where is this Miss Armstrong? She must talk to her maid. She must make that pitiful creature realize that I, Pandora Sabatini, am here to save her!"

The most dramatically beautiful woman Jacklyn had ever seen swept into the parlor. Hair of flame, eyes of glittering emerald, and a magnificent figure were merely the first characteristics that caught one's attention, but the woman's vibrancy actually overpowered those stunning features.

"Dear me." Mrs. Neville paled to gray.

"Are you the mistress here?" Pandora's finely shaped brows creased.

"Indeed, I am not!" Mrs. Neville drew her spare frame up to its full five feet. "Never would I be a mistress."

Pandora's green eyes darkened in sincere sympathy. "Yes, to be sure."

Jacklyn choked slightly. "I am Jacklyn Armstrong."

"Ah! I must talk to you."

"So I gathered." Hiding her smile, Jacklyn waved a hand toward the settee. "Do sit down, Miss . . ."

"*I* am Pandora Sabatini."

The lady said it as if Jacklyn should have known. Jacklyn looked properly apologetic. "Do forgive me. I have just arrived from the country and am quite green, I fear."

"I understand. You are a gapseed. Yes?" The pout disappeared from Pandora's lips.

"Er, yes." Jacklyn's mood lifted all the more as Mrs. Neville gasped. The small woman paced about in a small circle, refusing to join them. Garman was the opposite.

He appeared as if he wished to sit down and hang upon Pandora's every word. "Garman, perhaps you could bring us some tea?"

"That would be nice." Pandora turned her great green eyes upon the butler. "But I want the maid the most. Please bring her to me."

Jacklyn bit her lip. "Tea and the maid, then, Garman."

Garman nodded, but forgot to bow. He turned and walked dazedly from the room.

"I believe he will do his level best. Still, one should ask just so much of their servants."

"Yes. Many do not know that." Pandora cocked her head. The most charming smile crossed her face. "Ah, I have the famous notion. *Senz'altro* . . . ah . . . certainly, I need your help, yes? If you will give it to me, Miss Arms . . . Arm . . . pah! Jacklyn. That sounds much better. Armstrong. It is harsh. You are not so. Me, I can tell these things."

"Thank you." Jacklyn flushed with pleasure despite herself.

"I shall teach you . . ."

"Oh! Never!" Mrs. Neville scurried forward and back like a frightened terrier. "You shall not teach my sweet Jacklyn anything, you wicked, wicked woman."

"I beg your pardon?" Pandora's eyes widened. She looked at Jacklyn and frowned. "Who is this very nervous woman? *Per carità,* she is touched in the head, yes?"

"This is Mrs. Neville. She is my chaperon."

"No! That cannot be." Pandora shook her head. "That is most dreadful."

"She is not that bad, I assure you," Jacklyn said over Mrs. Neville's outraged shriek.

"You are too kind, Jacklyn." Pandora wagged a finger at her. "Much, much too kind. She wails so. She belongs in the opera."

"Oh, dear." Jacklyn sputtered on her laughter. Mrs.

Neville screamed even louder. Only morality plays were acceptable to the little lady. "You are in for it now."

"Be gone, you Jezebel. You—you . . ." Mrs. Neville broke into unintelligible gibberish.

Pandora leaned forward in a clear attempt to try and understand her. Her bountiful bosom strained even more from its low décolletage. Mrs. Neville squawked all the more.

"You must forgive her." Jacklyn sighed. "I fear she objects to your, ah, profession."

Pandora frowned in clear confusion. Then enlightenment dawned within her eyes. "Ah, no, but you are confused, little crazy woman. I am no doxy, yes? I am a courtesan. One of the greatest in the world. I am most respectable. I have had royalty to my bed."

Mrs. Neville flung up her hands and fled the room, babbling all the way.

"Per carità." Pandora shook her head. "Is she a relation to you?"

"No."

"That is good. But then why do you let her out in the public? You should hide her, yes?"

"Mrs. Neville is not exactly crazy." Jacklyn searched for the right words. "She . . . she is merely very sheltered and possesses the most delicate of nerves. She will revive once she spends some calming time within her chambers."

"Under her bed, yes?"

Jacklyn laughed. "Something like that. But at least she leaves when she is overcome with emotion. She does not *faint,* thank goodness."

"Bah! Those women who faint all over the place, I cannot abide them."

"Neither can I." Jacklyn felt the strongest charity for Pandora.

"In England, they faint for nothing. Now I have seen things to make a *man* faint back in Italy, yes. But here it is silly. They have the best of foods, the best of clothes, and still they fall to the ground. Me, I think they should loosen their corsets."

"Indeed." Jacklyn bit her lip. "Pray, do let us forget poor Mrs. Neville for the nonce. She will return within an hour, I make no doubt. You said I could help you. Why have you chased my maid Betty into my butler's pantry?"

A solemn look crossed Pandora's face. "I wished to talk to her, but she ran from me as if I—I were a monster. This I do not understand. Will you help me?"

"I shall most certainly try."

"It is a matter of life and death, Jacklyn."

"Heavens." Jacklyn started. "Whose death?"

Tears filled Pandora's eyes, large, glistening droplets. "Mine."

"Yours!" Jacklyn stared at her in both alarm and fascination. The fascination derived from the fact that Pandora's nose did not redden, nor did her eyes swell. Jacklyn never cried, but Mrs. Neville did, copiously. She was generally pathetic looking while doing so. Jacklyn shook her head to clear it. "How can this be?"

The tears continued to slip down, one diamond after another upon her porcelain cheek. "I found out only this morning."

"Y-you did?"

"I must help your maid Betty find her true love, else I will die. On Saint Valentine's Day, no less."

"Gracious."

"Tanto peggio. Worst of all, her true love is my lover."

"Indeed?" Jacklyn swallowed hard. She experienced the strongest urge to chase after Mrs. Neville and beg if there were a space left for her beneath the bed.

"Or he would have been. We have been in the negotiations, yes. He is the King of Hearts, you know?"

"No, I didn't." And Pandora had claimed Mrs. Neville to be cracked in the knob. Surely that was the pot pointing a finger at the kettle. Jacklyn's heart sank. She had been hoping for something to enliven her life, but a full-blown crazy Italian woman was not what she had had in mind. "The King of Hearts, you say? Just where does he rule, this King of Hearts?"

"Ah, I forgot. You are the gapseed. The King of Hearts is the Earl of Hart."

"Oh." Relief filled Jacklyn. At least he was an actual man. "Why is he called the King of Hearts?"

"Because he is the most famous of lovers with the ladies."

"He is a rake, in other words."

"Not just any rake, no. The premier rake, yes. Ah, me. How I wish he could be mine."

An indelicate snort escaped Jacklyn. She held no respect for rakes. They were the lowest kind of man, and men as a whole were exceedingly low. Jacklyn knew she conversed with a crazy woman, but she could not help but be drawn into the plot. "It might be . . . difficult to make a match of my upstairs maid with an earl, don't you think?"

"Yes." Pandora nodded. "I believe that is why the task has been given to me. Who else but Pandora Sabatini could do this? I am to use my special talents and great knowledge of men for someone else's benefit than my own, yes."

"To arrange such a mésalliance would require talent, to be sure."

"It will be spectacular and famous. Like the Gunning sisters, yes?"

As a baronet's daughter, Jacklyn had heard of the two Irish sisters of common origins who had stormed the town and claimed two titled men for husbands. In truth, it seemed a fairy tale to her. "Indeed?"

"That the task is so hard is only fitting. I am to save my life, yes? One does not save one's life by little chores."

Jacklyn drew in a breath. She might as well take the bull by the horns. "Why do you believe this, Pandora?"

Pandora's eyes widened. "I saw it in a dream. Just last night."

Relief overwhelmed Jacklyn. Pandora might not be as insane as she was fanciful and superstitious. She settled back in her chair. "Tell me about this dream."

"I was in hell." Pandora's beautiful face twisted in horror. "There are no men there. None whatsoever."

"No men?" Jacklyn lifted her brows. "That sounds like heaven to me."

Pandora reared back. "You cannot mean it?"

She appeared so shocked that Jacklyn relented. "Forgive me. But surely some men must go to hell?" She lowered her voice. "If not all of them."

Pandora frowned in consideration. "You are right. I only know that they were not there. They must keep us separated, yes. And the devil is a woman. I did not know this, did you?"

"Drat." Jacklyn shook her head. "That was what my father professed. I was determined he was wrong."

"It is no laughing matter, Jacklyn. Hell is terrible. Everything is mud. Brown mud."

"Gracious. How dismal."

"The devil told me I must do something to help a poor pitiful creature win her true love, else I would die and go to hell."

"Pandora, it was only a nightmare. You should not take it to heart."

"This was not a nightmare." Pandora crossed herself. "This dream was a portent. It is my fate. I dare not ignore it."

Jacklyn smiled gently. "Pandora, dreams are nothing more than images from our deeper consciousness. The mind becomes jumbled and draws visions and pictures from many hidden places within it. That is all. There are no such things as portents. Or fate."

Pandora crossed herself again and glanced heavenward rather apologetically. "You do not believe in God?"

"I do. Only I misdoubt his involvement with us." Jacklyn shrugged. "I cannot imagine God, who is mighty and magnificent, wishing to hover about and dabble in our lives routinely. Surely he has grander things to do? And as for popping into our dreams to . . . to let us know if we have missed the wicket or not? No. What you think of as portents are merely dreams. And fate is nothing more than coincidence."

"Coincidence?" Pandora appeared scandalized. "Bah! I have never understood this coincidence. There is fate, yes. Destiny, yes. Coincidence, no."

Jacklyn frowned. "Do you not think it rather prideful of us to believe God is so concerned with how our lives pass? Arranging an individual fate for each of us would be rather demanding, don't you think?"

"Why? God is mighty, yes? Me, I think he can do this most easily. And of course we should expect it."

Jacklyn gazed at the beautiful, confident creature before her. She could understand how Pandora might expect it. "Indeed."

"He made us, yes? Then we must be great, too."

Jacklyn sighed. "That is a charming notion."

"It is true. Why would God make us if He did not have a reason to do so? That is fate!"

"Perhaps." Jacklyn shook her head. She realized she should not expect logic from a woman like Pandora. "Are you positive you did not go to sleep feeling overset with something?"

"No. I had a late dinner with Lord Fortesque, which I enjoyed very much." Her gaze turned dreamy. "Lobster in clotted cream, sugared grapes, the sweetest marzipan swans, and . . . and iced champagne. Magnifico."

"Good gracious. That explains everything. You suffered a fantastical dream because of eating so late and such an odious combination of foods."

"Odious? No. I adored it." Pandora shook her head. "And I was not overset. I was very . . . er, happy when I went to bed. I had severed my relationship with Lord Fortesque with the greatest élan, which does not always happen, you know? The men, they can carry on so."

"Then you were feeling guilty for casting him off and dreamed of hell."

"I tell you, no. And how can you explain that when I asked the devil who I was to help, I immediately saw the face of a woman—a woman, mind you, I had never seen before." Pandora's gaze turned triumphant. "Until this very morning, that is. Then, when I rode out in my carriage, I saw her immediately, there before me, walking upon the street. It was your maid Betty! Explain that!"

Jacklyn stared. "You must have seen Betty at some time or another. That is why you dreamed of her."

"Never! I saw her in my dream because it was a sign." Pandora wagged her finger. "And what of the valentine, eh?"

"I do not know," Jacklyn said cautiously. "What of the valentine?"

"I asked the devil how long I had, yes? In my dream, Betty was holding a valentine to her heart. When I awoke, my maid immediately brought me a valentine from Lord Hart. It is still a month from Saint Valentine's Day, but I received it."

"You must have been thinking of Lord Hart. After all, he is the King of Hearts. That's why you dreamed of a valentine."

"The valentine in my dream was the same as the one he sent me. That is not coincidence."

Jacklyn shrugged. "All valentines look the same, do

they not?" She frowned. "But why on earth did he send you a valentine so very early?"

Pandora sighed. "He vowed he would win my heart and I would be his before Saint Valentine's Day."

Jacklyn snorted.

Pandora frowned.

Jacklyn schooled her expression. "That was quite romantic."

"Yes. But I must give him up to Betty. That is very obvious."

"Why?"

"Why?" Pandora looked at her as if she were daft. "I told you. Betty was holding Hart's valentine close to her heart in my dream. They are meant be together. I must bring them together before Saint Valentine's Day or I will die. It is very clear. I do not see how you could be confused. You appear an intelligent woman to me."

Jacklyn strove to hold her patience. "You are not going to die. You are reading things into a dream that are not there."

"Bah! I dreamed of your maid, whom I did not know. Then I saw her walking on the streets immediately after my dream. That is a portent."

"A coincidence."

"I dreamed of a valentine. I received it when I awoke. The very one which was in my dream."

"Coincidence again." Jacklyn lifted her chin as Pandora threw up her hands. "Coincidences can be freakish, I own, but they all have a logical explanation once a person pieces it together. And the logical explanation is *not* that it is God speaking to us from the heavens."

Pandora studied her long and hard. Sadness entered her eyes. "Ah, me. Are you one of those people who do not believe in love?"

"I believe in love." Jacklyn grimaced. "If one is lucky, one might escape it."

"Santa pace!" Pandora's gaze narrowed. "Have you never dreamed of love? Have you never dreamed of a man?"

Jacklyn shifted. "No. I—I haven't."

Pandora eyes lit and she crowed. "You lie! I know this, yes. You have dreamed of a man."

"Not exactly." Jacklyn flushed. "Very well. I have dreamed of a man."

"Tell me."

"He walks toward me in my dream."

"Yes? Yes? Then what?"

Jacklyn blinked. "That is all. He walks toward me."

Pandora's face fell. "He walks toward you. Nothing more?"

"I am sorry to disappoint you, but that is all."

"Ah me. How very tragic." Pandora shook her head. "I am fated to help Betty to win Hart. Destiny must not be ignored. But how I wish I had been fated to help you instead. I do not know your maid, for she ran from me . . ."

Jacklyn's lips twitched, as the vision became clear to her. "After you told her this story, no doubt?"

"No!" Indignation crossed Pandora's face. "She did not give me a moment, no, not one. I hailed her from my carriage. She turned, looked at me, and then ran."

"Oh, my!" Jacklyn couldn't help herself. She doubled over in laughter. "You mean you chased her in your carriage after you shouted at her? Just . . . just what did you say?"

Pandora's green eyes widened. "What else? I called out for her to stop. She was the pitiful creature I was to save?"

"And she ran?" Jacklyn subsided to a chuckle. "I cannot imagine why."

Pandora frowned severely. "You are very odd, yes. But as I was saying, I do not know your maid, but surely she does not need my help with love as much as you do."

"No, I do not, I pr-promise you. R-remember, Betty is your duty. Thank heaven."

Pandora pouted.

Jacklyn strove for a serious look. "And—and I will be pleased to help you with her, if I can. Will that redeem me within your eyes?"

Pandora tossed her head. "Perhaps, yes."

The parlor door opened and Jacklyn glanced up. Her mouth fell open. Garman entered with both tea tray and Betty. His smile was rightfully triumphant. "Here is your tea, madam. *And the maid.*"

"Ah Betty, there you are." Jacklyn strove for composure. "This is Miss Pandora Sabatini. Have you perhaps met her before?"

Betty, eyes wide, gulped and broke into tears. "I beg pardon, Mum?"

"It is all right. Do not cry."

"Ha! I told you I have not met her." Pandora rose. "You may tell her the truth."

"I—I have never met her, Miss Armstrong."

Pandora stretched out her hand. "Betty, I am here to help you win the love of an earl. The Earl of Hart."

"Cor!" Betty gasped. "Never say so."

"But I do. That is why I followed you here."

"Well, I'll be bumfuddled. Is that why? I thought . . ." Betty clamped her mouth shut, fright crossing her face. "I didn't know why you followed me, but I was that scared, I was."

"Yes." Pandora waved it away with her hand. "Would you like to marry an earl, Betty?"

Betty broke into a broad smile. "Cor. Wouldn't I just!"

"Good." Pandora nodded. "You shall. It is destiny."

Two

"So this Betty believes you and is willing to meet me?" Lord Hart peered out the window as his carriage came to a stop before an elegant town house.

"Yes, but only here at Miss Armstrong's." Pandora frowned. "She refused point-blank to meet you at my house."

"Indeed? I wonder why."

"Bah. Perhaps she is like that crazy Mrs. Neville who does not like it that I am famous." Pandora waved her hand. "It does not matter. What matters is that you and Betty fall in love by Saint Valentine's Day."

"To save your life I would do anything, my love." The earl grinned in good humor.

Pandora's eyes lit with passion. "Ah, how I wish you could have been my patron. But even for you, I will not give up my life." She shook a finger at him. "You are destined to love Betty, do not forget it. By Saint Valentine's Day you must be hers."

"Yes, sweeting." Lord Hart didn't see any reason to tell Pandora the truth. By Saint Valentine's Day *she* must be his. He opened the door and alighted, then helped the voluptuous Pandora down from the vehicle.

Gads, but she was a passionate and beautiful creature. Whatever game she required him to play to win her to his bed, he would. The woman clearly possessed romance within her soul. The fantasies she spouted no doubt stemmed from that very nature. He would gladly pander to any of her little dramas. He never doubted that in the end it would be well worth his while.

"Do not 'yes' me!" Pandora's green eyes glittered as he tucked her gloved hand into the crook of his arm. "You do not think it possible."

"With you, Pandora, anything could be possible." He chuckled as they strolled up the walk to the town house, then rapped upon the door.

"Do not tease me." Pandora sighed. "Destiny is against us."

The earl leaned over and whispered, "Perhaps I should have a talk with destiny—man to man, that is. He might have pity on me and change his decree."

"Aha!" Pandora's eyes narrowed. "You do not believe me any more than Jacklyn."

"Jacklyn?"

"Miss Armstrong." Indignation laced Pandora's voice. "She told me my portent came from my eating lobster with clotted cream and champagne the night before."

A laugh escaped him. "Did she?"

"Yes." Pandora nodded as the door opened. A thin-faced butler greeted them. "Good afternoon, Garman. We are here to see Betty."

"Yes, ma'am." Garman bowed. "Miss Armstrong begs that you join her in the parlor. Betty . . . Betty is not prepared yet."

"Very well," Pandora said.

Lord Hart frowned as they followed the butler. "Why is this Miss Armstrong helping you if she does not believe your dream?"

"She is a good woman." Pandora shook her head and sighed. "She makes me very sad."

"Why?"

"She does not believe in fate. Everything is a coincidence to her."

"Indeed? How unusual." He refrained from adding *for a woman*.

"She doesn't want love, either." Pandora's voice was scandalized as they stopped before the parlor door, Garman signaling for them to remain. He entered the room to announce them. "Only imagine."

"You are bamming me!" The earl could not help but be amused.

"I am not." Pandora's brow puckered in delightful confusion. "She hates men."

"A regular battle-ax, what?"

"She thinks heaven is where there are no men." Pandora sighed as Garman returned to escort them into the parlor.

Lord Hart broke into outright laughter as they entered the room. It died when his gaze fell upon its occupant. She was tall, with gleaming auburn hair drawn back smoothly from her face. Her features were regular, and not out of the ordinary. Her dress was sober and quite nondescript. Yet when he met her inquiring gaze of clear amber, the earl felt as if someone had belted him in the stomach. In that open gaze was an eagerness to share in the amusement, share in life.

He halted as the woman's eyes widened as if in recognition and shook his head to clear it. He had never met the woman before, he was certain, but she looked at him as if she knew him. Indeed, as if she had known him intimately.

"Jacklyn." Pandora rushed over to the woman.

"Jacklyn?" The earl frowned. *She* was the battle-ax?

"Permit me to introduce you to Westbrook Lockyear, the Earl of Hart, whom I have told you about, yes."

"*He* is the King of Hearts?" Jacklyn's gaze of recognition turned to one of dismay. Apparently she was as surprised to discover who Lord Hart was as he had been to learn who she was. His reputation was obviously not to her liking.

He forced a smile. He strolled over, feeling as if his approach was possibly the most important one he had ever made in his life, which was a ridiculous thought. He bowed. "Hello, Miss Armstrong."

"Hello, Lord Hart." Her voice was soft, yet her eyes were now guarded.

The earl stared down at her. It simply wasn't enough. Almost as if he could not control himself, he reached out and picked up her hand. A warm feeling invaded him. Her hand was soft and smooth, fitting into his palm perfectly. He clenched his teeth. Another idiotic notion. Pandora's flights of fancy were contagious. He bent and kissed Jacklyn's hand gently.

"Heavens!" a voice cried. "Unhand her, sir."

He straightened in astonishment. A tiny, drab little lady, nervous as a wren, was shaking her head at him, all the while she darted back and forth.

"This is Mrs. Neville, West," Pandora said. "She is crazy and of no relation to Jacklyn. Jacklyn, where is Betty?"

"She has lost her courage, I fear." She turned a cool gaze upon West. "Though I must agree with Mrs. Neville, my lord. I would like my hand back—if you would be so kind?"

West started. He had completely forgotten he held it still. He grinned and squeezed it before releasing it. "A thousand apologies."

Jacklyn drew her hand back, and he noticed she clenched it as she rested it in her lap. She looked to Pandora. "I have tried to bolster Betty's confidence, but I am afraid I have had no success."

"What?" West chuckled. "Does she think me an ogre?"

"No." Jacklyn looked at him, her face devoid of emotion. "You are her destiny. Who truly wishes to meet their destiny . . . personally, that is? It does add a brick to the load, I would imagine."

"I thought you did not believe in destiny."

Her brows rose. "I do not. But if there is a destiny, I am sure I would be on tenterhooks myself if I were forced to meet him face to face." For some reason, she flushed and looked away.

West cocked his head. "What is the matter?"

"Nothing!" She said it quickly, far too quickly. She squared her shoulders. "How did you know I do not believe in destiny?"

"I am omnipotent."

"That I do not believe. That you *think* you are God, perhaps, but not that you are truly omnipotent."

"Per carità! West, do not tease Jacklyn. She is being everything that is helpful, and I do not wish for you to set her back up." Pandora stepped forward. "I am going to find Betty. You remain here." She moved toward the door, then halted. She pointed a finger at Mrs. Neville. "You are the chaperon, remember that." She then swung her finger toward Jacklyn. "And you hate men, do not forget."

"I did not say I hated men." Jacklyn gasped as Pandora turned and left. "I did not."

West smiled. "But you do hate them?"

"No, I do not." Jacklyn studied him. "I can very well live without them, I must own, but I do not hate them."

"Jacklyn! A lady does not say such things to a gentleman." Mrs. Neville halted. An anxious look crossed her face as she glanced at West. "Well, you are not to do so as a rule. In this case, well . . . you should not encourage a . . ."

"A rakeshame?" West quirked his brow high. The woman had clearly insulted him. Coming on the heels of her charge's obvious displeasure, it did not sit well. "A womanizer?"

"Gracious!" Mrs. Neville's hand fluttered against her bony chest.

"Well? It *is* clear you think me less than a gentleman. You are thinking, '*My, what a loose screw he is!*' "

"Oh, dear!" Mrs. Neville blanched. "I—I . . ."

"That is enough, my lord." Jacklyn's voice was cool, but West heard the thread of laughter in it. "You know she could not think that. She doesn't know the term."

"No, she may confess it." West's good humor immediately reasserted itself. "I do not mind. I *am* a debauched fiend." He winked at Mrs. Neville. "Come here, you fetching wench, and give me a kiss."

"Eek!" Mrs. Neville threw up her hands and ran from the room.

West stared in shock. "Faith!"

"Now look what you have done. That was too bad of you." Jacklyn's expression was vexed. "I have been trying for two weeks to assure her London is not a wicked place, that not every man would wish to ravish us or murder us in our beds."

West experienced another thrill of surprise. "Then you are not frightened?"

"Frightened?" Jacklyn frowned. "Why should I be frightened?"

"Mrs. Neville has left us alone."

She smiled wearily. "I am quite accustomed to that. She often finds it necessary to seek safety within the confines of her chambers when the conversation becomes too warm for her. She is a woman of deep sensibilities, you see."

West laughed. "And you are not?"

"No, I do not think I am."

West could not resist. "What of passion?"

"No, you are beside the bridge on that one as well." Jacklyn said it with a pleasant smile. Her eyes darkened in consideration. "Have we ever met before, my lord?"

"Ah!" Satisfaction filled West. The woman had given him two different signals before this. Now she was openly showing him her interest. He moved quickly to sit beside her. She did not object. "I do not believe so, Jacklyn."

She frowned, but did not cavil at his impertinence. "I know it sounds ridiculous, but I am sure we have met before."

"You sound very confident." West smiled at her and slid his arm along the back of the settee. "Why do you say that?"

She looked down. "We must have met before."

West lowered his voice. "Perhaps we have met in our dreams."

Jacklyn stiffened. Her eyes flew to his, the emotion within those amber pools clearly tumultuous. "How did you know? How did you know I have dreamed of you?"

That was enough for West. He could not imagine why Pandora thought this woman hated men. She was clearly ripe for one. He knew very well what it meant when a woman talked of dreams in conjunction with him. He leaned close, breathing in the soft scent of lavender. "And I of you!"

"What?" Her eyes widened.

West lowered his head and kissed her deeply.

"Mm!"

Her lips remained clenched tight. Faith, she was a complete innocent. He had not kissed an innocent in ages, West thought in an eager haze. Pulling her closer, he nibbled her lips gently. He would both tease and teach her how to kiss him correctly.

"Whof?" Jacklyn lifted her hands to his chest, even as she slid her lithe body lower into the cushions.

"That's it, love." Excitement pulsed through West at her response.

He received a fierce thwack and shove. Jacklyn slipped

out of his stunned arms and off the settee, bumping to the floor with a yelp.

"What the devil?" West stared. Her actions were quite unexpected.

"Ouch!" Jacklyn sat sprawled. She lifted her hand to her mouth. "You bit me!"

"I did not!"

"Yes, you did." Jacklyn lowered her hand and glared at him.

"Good God!" Her lip was actually bleeding. West frowned. "I couldn't have. I didn't. You must have . . ."

"Oh, very well." Jacklyn scrabbled from the floor. She groaned and then walked stiffly away from him. "It could not be your fault, I am sure. It is all mine. Do, do forgive me."

"I did not mean that." Faith, he was appearing a bumbling coxcomb. "I might have accidentally bitten you. I did not expect you to slide away like you did."

"Why not?" Jacklyn's expression was pained.

"Well." West blinked. He realized in that second that his thought processes had been totally skewered and that his explanation would not sound reasonable to her. "You wanted me to kiss you."

"I what?" Jacklyn gazed at him as if he were the village idiot.

West promptly felt akin to one. "You talked about meeting me in your dreams. If that is not casting out a lure, I do not know what is."

"I was not casting out a lure or anything else! I didn't say I *met* you in my dreams. I said I *dreamed* of you. That is different."

"Is it?"

"Yes, it is." Jacklyn squared her shoulders and jutted out her chin. "It means I have met or seen you at some time or another in the past. It most certainly does not mean I wish for you to—to kiss me." She rubbed her posterior, clearly in an unconscious movement. "Ever again. I do not like it. Not one whit!"

"Do not say that!"

"I will say it!" Jacklyn's voice rose. "I did not like it! I did not like it!"

"You do not have to shout it to the rooftops, do you?"

"Forgive me." Jacklyn flushed. She frowned then, her gaze unadulterated accusation. "You said you had dreamed of me, too, did you not? That is proof we have met before."

"I lied." West rolled his eyes. "I thought you wished for me to be romantic. That is how men and woman talk when they are romantic."

Jacklyn's amber eyes flared. "Pandora was right. I *do* hate men. I truly do."

"Jacklyn, listen." West rose and stalked toward her. "I apologize . . ."

"Do not come near me!" Jacklyn grabbed up a figurine from the table close to her and hefted it high.

"Wait!" West stepped back.

"West, dear!" Pandora called out.

Jacklyn swiftly lowered her arm and hid the figurine behind her back. West spun as the door opened and Pandora entered. Her smile was one of anticipation. "I want you to close your eyes this very instant!"

"Pandora." West sighed in exasperation.

"Close them!"

"Very well." Pandora possessed a dramatic bent and there was no use in fighting it. West closed his eyes. The picture of Jacklyn with her cut lip and her hand tucked behind her back concealing a particularly ugly Sevres shepherdess seemed burned into his eyelids.

"Open them now, West."

West opened them. A blond maid, as buxom as Pandora herself, with cornflower blue eyes, dipped him a curtsy. "Hello, m'lord."

A VALENTINE DREAM

Her voice was husky, her gaze ardent.

"This is Betty!" Pandora's voice held sheer triumph.

"Hello, Betty." West drew in his breath. Betty displayed every sign of willingness and desire. Why he thought Jacklyn had lured him on was beyond him now. The difference between the two women's behavior was embarrassingly obvious.

"Perhaps there is a destiny after all." Jacklyn quickly slipped past him and hurried to the door. "I wish you well with her, my lord."

"Jacklyn!" West stepped forward, but she was already gone. Sighing, he looked at the beautiful and clearly hot-blooded Betty. Blast and damn!

"Are you sure this is the way I'm ter dress?" Betty plucked at a lovely butter yellow gown of India dimity flounced with white muslin. Disappointment stamped her features.

"Yes, I am positive." Pandora, herself dressed in a dashing frock of emerald lutestring with a shawl of white satin bordered with plaid silk, nodded as she popped a morsel of biscuit in her mouth.

Betty's eyes showed skepticism as her gaze ran over Pandora's ensemble. "I thought I'd get to dress like you."

Jacklyn stifled a chuckle as Pandora threw up her hands. She herself felt rather dashing in her fawn colored morning dress of fine French cambric set off by a pale ruby pelisse with a collar applique of cinnabar brown satin. That very morning, the three of them had gone to Pandora's modiste. Apparently Pandora had dangled the jaunt like a carrot in front of the fainthearted Betty's nose.

"You cannot dress like me. I am a courtesan. I—I attract the passionate love, yes. Now you, you must attract the true love. For true love you must dress properly."

"Really?" Jacklyn was fascinated with the concept.

"Ugh." Clearly Betty was not as intrigued.

Pandora looked sage. "West is a rake, yes. But he is also English. With an Englishman you must dress properly so he does not take you any way *but* properly."

Betty's eyes crossed in confusion. "You mean I can't have true love unless I'm proper? Cor, does that mean . . . oh, no! You mean I can't have any . . ." Her gaze flicked to Jacklyn. "Er, you know *what* with his lordship?" Betty's full lip pouted out. "If that's the way it is, I don't think I wants true love. I wants . . . well, you know *what*."

"And you will have it, only later." Pandora rolled her eyes. "Jacklyn. Please explain she must be most proper for the nonce."

"Why should I?" Jacklyn frowned. "I do not understand it myself."

"You do not?" Pandora's face fell. "I expected you to explain it to Betty."

"No." Jacklyn smiled dryly. "I'm afraid I know nothing about it. I am proper because I was taught to be proper. I had no notion it should lure a man into true love with me. In fact, I hate to ruin your lesson, but my mother was always very proper with my father, even unto the day she died. And there was a decided lack of any kind of love between them."

"You may be quiet now, Jacklyn!" Pandora reached for her tea and drank from it quickly. She pinned Betty with a sapient eye. "Do not listen to Jacklyn. She is an innocent. And too confusing. Now, this is what I know: True love is where a man marries you, Betty. For him to do so, he must understand he will not be getting, er . . . you know *what* . . . for free. Once he loves you, then he will get some—and only *some*—until he has married you. *A tutti i costi*. No matter what! You must be very, very proper. You must be unattainable to him. Even cold."

"Bloody hell," Betty wailed. "I'm suppose ter be cold to his lordship, and him so fine? How am I going ter do that? I melt just looking at him. If'n he were to . . . well, what am I ter do?"

"I don't know." Pandora's glance at Jacklyn showed desperation. "Surely you can explain that to her, yes? You were the cold one with West yesterday. How did you do that?"

Jacklyn stared in astonishment. Then she flushed. Apparently Betty and Pandora enjoyed you know *what* far better than she had. That they enjoyed being bitten was strange to her, but she didn't wish to say it. "I—I'm sorry. I do not know why I can be cold and you cannot be. I imagine it just—comes naturally to me."

"Not naturally, Jacklyn." Pandora sighed. "It is not natural for *you* at all, this I know. You would not have helped me, or Betty, if it was natural to you. Bah! It was your parents' fault, yes?"

"Do you think so?" Jacklyn cocked her head to the side in consideration. "Father *was* a recluse and demanded I be the same. With his passing, I felt free for the first time in my life. I would not wish to give that feeling up and . . . and a man would take that away from me, would he not?"

"Padronissimo. As you like." Pandora cringed and glared at Betty. "Why did I ask her? She dithers about giving things up! She does not know how wonderful it is when a man . . . well, *we* know what. It is a pity, but we do not have time to help her right now. We must tend to you first. What you must do is *act* as Jacklyn does. Do not think like her, but act like her, yes?"

Betty moaned. "I'll never be able ter act like her. She's quality, and they don't feel the same as we do."

"You only have to withstand West for a while. Let me see." Pandora tapped her cheek. "Saint Valentine's Day is four weeks from now. For half of that time, you must be proper with West."

"Two whole weeks? Cor."

"You want to have true love, do you not?"

"Yes." Betty nodded, though her expression was dubious. "I want ter be a countess."

Jacklyn froze. She knew nothing about true love, but those words did not seem right for the occasion.

"And so you shall. You shall be most happy, forever." Pandora turned severe. "But you must not give in to wanton desire. West must respect you. You will behave like Jacklyn when he arrives."

Jacklyn stiffened. She had been enjoying the day and the ladies' company so much that she had forgotten West was due to visit soon. She sprang up, alarmed. "I believe I shall leave you two now. Ah . . . I should see to Mrs. Neville. I fear she may never come out of her room."

"No!" It was a shriek from both ladies.

Pandora fanned herself. "You must stay, Jacklyn. You will be the chaperon for us, yes?"

"What?"

"We shall watch how you act, you see. Then we will act the same. Betty will be able to turn her shoulder cold with West. Me, I can learn from you as well."

"I . . ." Jacklyn clamped her mouth shut. She was supposed to act as chaperon for her maid and the most infamous courtesan in London?

A spring of pleasure welled up within her. It might well be the oddest thing to happen in her life, but it chased the dark dreams away. Jacklyn had purpose. She would not be left alone in this house with only Mrs. Neville. What Jacklyn's father would say if he were alive reeled through her mind. She smiled wickedly and sat back down. "Very well."

The door opened at that moment. Garman stepped forward and announced the earl. Jacklyn's heart sank as West entered. He was a stunning man. With his raven hair and tall, lithe frame, he was handsome in the classic sense. But, like Pandora, his looks were but part of his allure. Something else altogether made West Lockyear a famous lover of women. It was a certain something in the glitter of his blue eyes, something in the curve of his lips and in the timbre of his voice. What that something was, Jacklyn, inexperienced as she was, could not say. But it drew a woman and mesmerized her. It made her blood and her heart sing.

Jacklyn swallowed hard. Well, it did, that is, until he bit one. Now Jacklyn only experienced a queasy feeling in the pit of her stomach when she looked at him. Why, oh why, had she dreamed of this man so many times before? She had always wondered about the man who walked toward her in her dream. To discover he was none other than the infamous King of Hearts was unsettling, to say the least.

"Good afternoon, ladies." West smiled that charming smile of his. Jacklyn's mouth went dry, but a fatuous sparkle entered both Pandora's and Betty's eyes. Their breathy greetings caused Jacklyn to worry her sore lip. Just how was she to be a chaperon to two women who clearly liked they 'knew what'?

West strolled over first to Betty. "May I say, Betty, you are looking very fetching today. That dress is fine as five pence."

"Thank you, m-my lord." Betty almost toppled from the edge of her chair in her eagerness. "I was hopin you'd like it. You don't think it too dull?"

"Certainly not. And do call me West. I refuse to stand upon ceremony with the lady who is my destiny." The earl smiled and reached down to pick up Betty's hand, then bent and slowly kissed it. Jacklyn had all she could do not to snort with disdain.

"Cor! I likes that." Betty sighed and wiggled her outstretched fingers. "Do that again, West. Please."

"Ahem." Jacklyn coughed discreetly and shook her head when Betty finally turned a starry gaze to her.

Betty flushed. She jerked her hand back. "Er, thank you, West."

West's brows shot up. He paused a moment. Then, smiling, he strode over to Pandora. "Pandora, my love. How are you this afternoon?" He lifted her hand, too, only he turned it over and kissed her wrist quite warmly.

Pandora laughed deeply, even as a blush rose to her cheeks. "West, dear. Stop that. I can feel it right down to . . ."

Jacklyn gasped.

Pandora froze. She jerked her hand back and made a show of adjusting her skirts. Jacklyn looked away as Pandora then proceeded to arranged her bodice with great seductiveness.

"That ain't proper!" Betty hissed. "Not a bit."

"What?" Pandora spun, her green eyes indignant.

"Hm, yes." Jacklyn hastened forward. She pinned a polite smile upon her lips. "It is a . . . pleasure to see you once more, my lord."

"Do call me West." West grinned as he took her hand in turn. Jacklyn clenched her teeth as she, too, felt it right down to her toes. His lips brushed her knuckles in the most correct degree. His eyes, however, sparkled with devilry.

Jacklyn smiled coolly and nodded as he released her hand. Knowing all eyes were upon her, she waved her tingling hand in the direction of a solitary chair. "Do let us be seated. You may sit there, my lord."

"She ain't real," Betty huffed as she and Pandora were left to sit upon the settee, while Jacklyn took up the chair farthest from them all. Jacklyn heard West choke upon a laugh. She cast him a stern look. "Betty, would you like to pour Lord Hart a cup of tea?"

"Would I just? I mean . . ." Betty sat up straighter. She attempted a dignified tone, her imitation of Jacklyn's accents rather transparent. "I would be pleased ter do so, my lord."

She poured the tea. Picking up the cup and saucer, she sashayed across the room and bent over West far more dramatically than was correct. "Here you are, my lord. And would ye be wanting anything else?"

"You know I do, Betty." West's tone was fond, his gaze resting appreciatively upon Betty's well-positioned charms.

"And what could that be, my lord?" Betty squirmed.

"Some biscuits perhaps?" Jacklyn spoke quickly, fearful of what the outrageous man might answer.

"Yes." Pandora's face had grown strained. Her eyes snapped. "I could use more tea, Betty."

Betty stiffened. Frowning, she turned and walked over to Pandora. She took the offered cup, her voice sharp and angry. "Of course, Pandora."

"Thank you, Betty." Pandora's smile was sweet as the maid filled the teacup. When she returned with it, however, Pandora whispered, "You are acting like a trollop. I told you to act cold."

"I am!" Betty glared. "What more do yer want from me?"

"I want you to behave." Pandora snatched at the cup.

Betty didn't release it. Tea splashed out of the rocking cup, raining upon them both.

"Blimey!" Betty dropped the cup. Her face mottled to blue as she looked down at the stain upon her skirt. "Look what yer done to me new dress!"

"I did not do it. You did, you clumsy girl!" Pandora sprang up. "And I bought you the dress, don't forget."

"I ain't clumsy!" Betty balled her fists. "You did that on purpose!"

"Ridiculous!" Pandora tossed her head. "Why would I do it on purpose?"

"West was paying attention to me, not you. That's why."

"What? How dare you!" Pandora drew in a deep breath, all but bursting her stays. "You ungrateful creature. I am trying to help you . . ."

"Rot! You want West for yerself!"

"Quiet." Pandora slapped Betty.

"Tart!" Betty shrieked and dived at Pandora.

"Trollop!" Pandora smacked Betty's cheek with one hand while she jabbed her other fist into the maid's stomach. Betty, unprepared for such a lightning retaliation, shied one meager blow to Pandora's ear.

"Stop!" Jacklyn dashed forward. Famous courtesan or not, Pandora would be mopping the marble floors with Betty if she weren't stopped. "You mustn't—"

She received Betty's fist to her chin for her efforts. The maid was swinging wild, indeed.

"Ladies!" West stalked up, tall and proud. He raised his voice in command. "Cease this, now! Do you hear me? Now!"

Three

Jacklyn froze. Dread twisted in her stomach. West surely must be enraged. His command echoed through the room.

Her eyes widened in shock when neither woman paid him any heed. Betty nearly milled Jacklyn down as she tried to lunge after Pandora. Pandora jeered and taunted her from behind Jacklyn.

"Blast it! I said stop!"

Jacklyn almost fainted as West reached for Betty. Except then he laughed! He merely grabbed Betty around the waist and swung her about in a circle.

"Get out of the way, Jacklyn!" West called over his shoulder.

Jacklyn numbly obeyed. Pandora charged. West released Betty, who now harmlessly windmilled the air in the wrong direction. His long arm shot out and halted Pandora in her tracks. "Do you want to take me on, too, darling?"

Pandora wheezed from hitting West's barricading arm so forcefully. Her face worked with anger. Then the rage drained away and her eyes lit. "Oh, West! You are impossible."

"I return the compliment, *ma belle*."

Pandora flushed. She gazed past West. "Ah me, but I have a temper. I do not mean to, but I do. I am sorry, Betty."

Betty gasped as she finally came to reality. She lowered her fists and spun. "What?"

"Of course Betty will forgive you, Pandora." West cast a most approving look upon Betty. "She's not the type to hold a grudge—are you, Betty?"

Betty's eyes widened. She bit her lip. "That's right, I ain't that type. That is, if'n she don't."

"She won't. Now here is my favorite part. Everyone kisses and makes up." The ladies eyed each other warily. West grinned. "I'll go first." He bent and kissed Betty on the cheek.

"Cor!"

"Do go and change into another dress, sweeting. Your sleeve is torn." West patted her gently upon the shoulder, then turned to Pandora. He flipped a fallen strand of hair from her forehead and kissed her. "I am sure you would like to freshen up as well, darling."

"Santa pace, but yes."

"Do hurry. I wish to take you lovely ladies out for an ice."

Jacklyn stood in wonderment as the two brawling ladies broke into smiles and eager exclamations. Together, they rushed from the room.

West's smile was conspiratorial. "Now it is your turn."

"What?" Jacklyn shivered.

West's gaze darkened. "What is it, Jacklyn? What is the matter?"

Jacklyn tried to surface from her fear and shock. If any such scene had erupted in her father's presence, it would have ceased on his first command. Nor would he have laughed or kissed any lady involved.

No, indeed. If it had been her father, all three would have been sent from the parlor in utter disgrace and confined to their rooms for the next week with bread and water. "You are not angry?"

"No. Are you?" West's voice turned gentle. "You must

A VALENTINE DREAM 47

remember Betty and Pandora have been raised far differently from us. It is common for them to fight." He chuckled. "Pandora clearly hasn't forgotten how to take care of herself."

Jacklyn smiled hesitantly. "She is v-very efficient."

"She grew up in the streets, from what I know." He shook his head. "The lady is a spitfire."

Jacklyn stared at him. Pleasure bubbled up within her. With it came laughter, clean and pure.

West raised his brow. "You find that amusing?"

"Yes. Yes, I do." Jacklyn stumbled over to a chair and fell into it. She drew in a deep, liberating breath. "You are *apologizing* to me for their behavior?"

"Yes?"

"You are not angry at them one whit? Or me either?"

"Why should I be?" He shrugged. "Though I wish you had not been caught between them."

"No. In truth, I found it . . . exhilarating."

A gleam entered West's eyes. "Did you now, Miss Armstrong? Faith, what a deep and dreadful confession to make."

She flushed, but stared at him closely. "You like them, don't you? Truly like them."

"I do." His tone was cautious. "Is there a reason I should not?"

"No. No, there isn't." She beamed at him. "I—I simply think it nice. Very nice."

West frowned. "I still do not see what is so extraordinary."

"No." West was a rake and bounder, but he clearly liked women. To Jacklyn that was something unique. Hope flared within her. Whether she truly hated men or not remained to be seen, yet she had just learned one thing: Her father hadn't liked women. "But I do."

"You do not intend to wash your hands of us?" West walked slowly over to her.

"What?" Jacklyn glanced up. "What do you mean?"

"Come now. Do not try and gull me. It is clear that you are to be 'the chaperon.' "

"Why do you say that?"

"Do not misunderstand me. I will take you in lieu of Mrs. Neville any day." He narrowed his gaze. "Though I must admit, the notion of those two coming the proper ladies is rather fantastical. What has made them even try to do so? Another portent of Pandora's?"

Jacklyn swallowed hard. "D-do you object to proper ladies, my lord?"

"No." West grinned. "My mother is one, you know."

"Indeed."

"She prays for my reform every day, in truth." His gaze darkened.

Jacklyn smiled. "That is sweet."

"Isn't it?" West snapped his fingers. "So that is the plan!"

"I beg your pardon?"

"Pandora has told Betty she should keep me at a distance and act like a lady, hasn't she? Gads, she is playing this game seriously."

"I do not know what you mean."

"A man marries a lady, not a trollop." He shook his head. "I'll bet a monkey that Pandora has told Betty she'd better not have any—"

"You know *what*," Jacklyn supplied, before she realized it. She gasped in embarrassment.

West barked a laugh. "Exactly. And you are set as guard dog to make sure of it."

Jacklyn flushed. "You are not angry?"

"You really must stop thinking I will be angry at every turn. Life loses much of its amusement if one does not enjoy the obstacles set in one's way as well as one's successes."

"I am glad to hear that."

"And what a delightful obstacle you are." West sat down next to her. He picked up her hand and patted it. "The most toothsome guard dog I have seen to date."

Alarm bells clanged in Jacklyn's mind. She jerked her hand from his and rose, scuttling away. "Y-you are not supposed to do that."

"What if I cannot help myself?" West stood.

"No. Stay where you are!"

West frowned. He took one small step, clearly an exploratory one.

"I said stay." Jacklyn's heart thumped. "I—I will not have you mauling me about . . . just because w-we are alone for the moment."

"Maul!" West's brows snapped down. He studied her. His gaze turned solemn. "I have a proposition for you, Miss Armstrong."

"Proposition? No. Do not."

"Please hear me out." West's lips twitched. "This is it. I promise to behave most circumspectly around you after this if you will grant me one boon."

Suspicion flared in Jacklyn. "What is it?"

"Permit me to kiss you . . ."

"What?"

"Just once. I vow I will not make another advance after that."

"Why do you want to do that?" Jacklyn unconsciously raised her hand to nurse her lip.

"I have a reputation to uphold." West grimaced. "Besides, I have given you the entirely wrong impression of kissing. I would like to rectify the matter."

"I do not . . ."

"Think of it, Jacklyn. Just one kiss and you will be safe from my lecherous advances."

"That is blackmail."

"No. Saying that I will refuse to visit Betty would be blackmail."

Jacklyn frowned darkly at West. He presented the most guiltless face. She discovered she didn't wish to press the point. She felt as if she had found life in the past two days. Furthermore, pure feminine curiosity prodded her to discover why Pandora and Betty liked they 'knew what' better than she did. Sighing, Jacklyn closed her eyes. "Very well. But you must promise not to bite me."

She could hear West move. She knew when he stood close. The scent of tobacco and soap and male teased her nose. Her heart knotted. She then felt the warmest, softest kiss upon her cheek.

Her eyes snapped opened. She gazed up into West's own mischievous eyes. She swallowed hard, relief overwhelming her. And disappointment. "There. That is done. That is your one kiss."

"No. That was just a peck."

"A peck?"

"A kiss must be on the lips. A 'peck' is when it is not."

Jacklyn thought hard. She supposed it made sense. "Very well. Hurry up and kiss me."

"After one more peck." West lightly placed his lips to her forehead.

"All right."

"Or two."

"Ah . . ."

West didn't lift his lips from her skin, but trailed them to her temple. "You smell most delightfully. Lavender, is it?"

"Er . . . I think so." Jacklyn's heart thrummed. "That wasn't a peck, was it?"

"Sorry. It was meant to be." West's voice was warm, amused. He offered quick soft kisses upon her cheek, then upon the curve of her jaw, then upon the column of her neck. "Are those better?"

"Yes. I mean no!" Jacklyn clenched her hands. Tingles

and sensations of the sweetest kind were coursing through her. "You sh-should . . ."

"What?" His voice was low and husky.

"Just kiss me." Jacklyn whispered.

"Your wish is my command."

Jacklyn's eyes snapped open. *"My wish!"*

The glitter of passion and desire in West's eyes made her close her mouth just as his lips descended upon hers. The warmth of his kiss caused Jacklyn to sag against him. His hands curved around her shoulders, then moved to slide into her hair as he gently moved her head and lips into a more perfect alignment to his.

A gasp of wonderment escaped Jacklyn. West groaned and pulled back. Jacklyn leaned heavily against him, her knees weak and her desire strong. "Are you going to k-kiss me again?"

"No." He untangled his hands from her hair.

"A peck then?"

"Jacklyn." His face dark, he gripped her shoulders and pushed her away from him. "You are the chaperon. And you'd better start acting like one right now."

Jacklyn blinked. She was too in awe of the sensations coursing through her. She now understood why Pandora and Betty liked this sort of thing. She flushed. And this was only the first part of it. No one needed to tell her that. Her own body clamored for more. Her heart raced. And her wicked, wicked mind was growing curious as to what that "more" was.

Then a new thought arose. If she were not Betty's chaperon, then West and her upstairs maid would be doing this exact thing. Jacklyn choked. A terrible emotion whirled through her, one very unkind toward Betty. "I most certainly shall be the chaperon."

West dropped his hands from her. She looked at him in inquiry. His face was closed. "You'd better go and prepare yourself."

Jacklyn's eyes widened. "For what?"

This time West turned red. "We are going for ices. Remember?"

"Oh, yes." Jacklyn stepped back and walked dazedly toward the door. In truth, she could remember only West's kiss and how she felt—and that she was going to be a very strict chaperon where Betty and Pandora were concerned.

"I cannot believe it." Jacklyn shook her head as they strolled along, viewing the exhibits of the Royal Menagerie. Mrs. Neville and Betty were far ahead of them, peering and gaping like children. "How ever did you manage to coax Mrs. Neville into accompanying us?"

West laughed. Never would he tell Jacklyn that because she had refused to bend to Mrs. Neville's sensibilities, Mrs. Neville had been forced to bend to Jacklyn's insensibilities.

That, and he had chosen their entertainment with care. Any sight which would make a Londoner yawn he had shown them. Indeed, Pandora had not possessed the stomach to accompany them upon such innocent amusements. But then, there was also the issue that she and Betty could remain within each other's company for only so long without coming to blows.

"I am sure I had nothing to do with it. She has merely seen her duty and risen to the occasion."

"No, I am sure you had something to do with it." Jacklyn's expression grew wary. "I see why they call you the King of Hearts. You manage to sway women into doing your will with the greatest skill."

"Do I?" West asked wryly. It was obvious from her statement that she was not included in the group. He studied her. She might very well be his greatest challenge.

"Indeed. I thought Mrs. Neville an impossible case, but

here you have her so fearless as to wander about amongst wild animals."

"True. Though they are caged, which mitigates their possible danger, don't you think?"

"To be sure." A sadness entered Jacklyn's eyes. "I have no doubt that is why Mrs. Neville will tolerate them. They are properly confined."

"And what of you?"

Jacklyn looked away. "I fear I sympathize with the poor animals. Being properly confined is certainly not all it is touted to be."

West laughed. "Whenever you wish me to help you escape your cage, I will do so gladly. I would enjoy seeing the wild animal in you set free."

Jacklyn's gaze flew to his. There was no shock, no feigned indignity within her eyes. Only a solemnity and, perhaps, longing.

"Truly." West discovered himself saying it with sincerity. He had intended the comment to be a shocking advance, yet now he found he meant it with all his heart. In the week he had spent in Jacklyn's company, he had seen a woman come to life. It was more intriguing and captivating than a rose opening into bloom or a caterpillar turning into a butterfly.

"How odd." Jacklyn shook her head.

"What?" West frowned.

"The notion of a man setting me free rather than . . ." Jacklyn shrugged and clearly shook off a thought. Her amber gaze met his teasingly. "I thank you for your charitable offer, my lord."

West forced a smile. "Even if you wish for only small excursions from your cage, I'm your man. Perhaps a little jaunt now and then."

Jacklyn's lips twitched.

"Nor are large roars demanded of you. A small meow

once in a while would be nice, I own. Just so I know you are enjoying yourself."

Jacklyn broke into a broad smile. West's own heart did something unusual. It performed a leap, a leap like never before. Where or when it would land, he had no notion. He only knew that gaining her smile was worth everything.

"Meow."

It came out calmly, softly.

West stared and then roared with laughter. His heart landed then, deep into enchantment. He had been mistaken. *That* was worth everything.

"Aha!" West cast her an exaggerated leer. "I have you alone, at last!"

Jacklyn gurgled with laughter. "Only because we are lost, my lord."

West slapped his hand to his heart. "I, my dear, am never lost. I intended this all along, I will have you know. It is Mrs. Neville and Betty who are lost, not us. You are at my mercy. What do you have to say to that?"

"What should I say?" Jacklyn hid her smile. She glanced down the three different paths that lay before them in the maze. "Only, do you think it wise to attempt anything when someone would be sure to stumble upon us?"

"I do not care. Let them be surprised. Or shocked. With you I find I must seize every moment I can."

"Indeed?"

West cast her a minatory look. "You, Miss Armstrong, are a hardened case."

"Am I?" Jacklyn laughed. She didn't feel like a hardened case. She felt happy, comfortable . . . and beautiful. She had never imagined a man's company could be so very enjoyable. "I am so very sorry I am difficult."

"Wretch. You feel no shame at all." West grinned with good humor. "You toy with my heart."

"I most certainly do not." They turned onto another path. The wind swept along it, and Jacklyn shivered. "Gracious, but this is cold. I am glad you know the way, else we could freeze to death."

"Are you frightened?" West put his arm about her, grinning. "Fear not. I will protect you."

"From the cold?"

"Certainly, and from anything else." He winked at her. "I'll slay any dragons that need slaying and even protect you from ghosts and ghouls."

Jacklyn sighed. "And from those things that knock about in the night?"

"Yes." He smiled, but gently this time. "What did you dream about me?"

Jacklyn started. She quickly unwound his arm from about her. Before it had felt comforting. Now it felt intimate. "It was nothing."

"Nothing? I am insulted. Never before have I had a woman dream of me and say it was nothing!" Indeed, he looked offended.

"I must apologize again, I fear. In truth, I have only dreamed of you walking toward me."

"And?"

"And that is all. I wake up then, or the dream changes to another."

West cocked his head. "How long have you had this dream?"

"I cannot remember exactly, but I know I've had it for quite a few years." Jacklyn shrugged. "We must have met when we were younger."

"That might be. I traveled extensively when I was younger."

"But I have not. I have never been outside of Little Borehamwood before now."

"I do not remember visiting there." West grinned. "Admit it, Jacklyn. It is fate. You are to be mine."

Jacklyn trembled. It must have been another breeze. She forced a smile. "Have you been eating lobster with clotted cream and champagne, my lord?"

"No." West laughed. "Have you?"

"No." Jacklyn made a face. "I am sure that *would* have given me nightmares."

"I must be grateful."

Jacklyn lifted a brow. "Why?"

"You did not consider your dream of me a nightmare."

"Ah! But it could be. I do not know. The dream was never finished."

"I promise you, if you would only permit me, I would finish it for you. Indeed, you would think you had died and gone to heaven if you would permit me to direct the ending."

Jacklyn hid her smile and turned away. "You are incorrigible."

"I think you are taking it far too lightly." West frowned with mock severity. "The dream is a portent, don't you know? You have ignored the signs. Surely you will die . . . or something equally dreadful . . . if you do not love me."

"Love you?" Jacklyn spun back, astonished.

West looked as shocked as she was. "Did I say that?"

They stared at each other. Jacklyn swallowed hard. She dared not admit it. His gaze begged her not to. She raised a brow. "I thought you did not believe in portents."

Relief entered West's gaze. "No, I don't. But I think it unsporting of you not to. You are a woman. You should believe in them."

Jacklyn chuckled. "So I could be like Pandora? Going about doing fantastical . . ."

"And romantical . . ."

"Things? No, my lord. I met you sometime when I was young. That is the only explanation."

"I tell you it is too bad of you." West put his arm about her once more. "I am the man of your dreams. Admit it, *mademoiselle*."

"Hullo! Blimey, but this here maze is a pip." Betty paced toward them. Mrs. Neville trailed behind her.

West dropped his arm from about Jacklyn. "Blast."

Jacklyn chuckled. "No, my lord. You are the man of *her* dreams. Pandora has foreseen it."

West smiled with satisfaction as the leading soprano sang her last song before the intermission. It was not the clarity of her voice that made him do so, nor the excellent performance of the cast. It was the expressions that had played upon Jacklyn's face. He had known she would love the opera as he did.

A bored sigh huffed from behind them. West grimaced. Just as he had known Betty would not. Faith, but he wondered if Pandora had partaken of something more than just champagne the night of her dream. Opium perhaps?

Yet he would not complain. Pandora's wild fantasy had brought him into Jacklyn's sphere, where he never would have been otherwise. His pulse raced. Jacklyn was growing closer and closer to being his. He smiled and indulged himself in his own fantasy. She would be his greatest coup. Despite Pandora's proclamations and machinations, it was Jacklyn, not Betty, who would be his, and within the next week. She would be an early valentine gift to himself.

He shook his head wryly, remembering the valentine he had sent Pandora, the one which had caused all the commotion. Faith, how had so much changed within three short weeks? In it he had vowed Pandora would be his. Now it was Jacklyn he dreamed of possessing, Jacklyn whose passion and desire he must have for his own.

The theater lights went up and West schooled his face. He never doubted that Pandora observed them from her own box. She attended with the Marquis of Anton tonight. West did not intend to have her throw a spanner into his plans. Indeed, his scheme had taken on a grand design just to confound the courtesan.

West smiled at Jacklyn. "What do you think?"

"It is marvelous." Jacklyn's eyes were starry.

"Marvelous?" Betty's face turned indignant. "What do yer mean? The lot of them is wailing like scalded cats and don't even know the king's language. I didn't understand a word."

West coughed. "I am sorry you do not care for the performance, Betty. I had hoped you would." He turned to Mrs. Neville. "And what did you think of it, madam?"

"I am not sure." Mrs. Neville twitched. "Are you positive this sort of display is considered proper?"

"Most definitely." West said. "There is a moral to the story, I assure you. Of course, it is an Italian moral."

"But they are . . . are behaving with so much . . . excessive emotion."

"The best *ton* attends the opera. It is very proper."

"Hello," a light, feminine voice caroled just before the curtain at the back opened and the voice's owner entered.

"Witness that even my mother attends." West hid his surprise. He had not seen her in the audience.

The Dowager Countess of Hart, her blue eyes mischievous, smiled at him in a teasing fashion. "My dear Westbrook, I did not know you were to attend the opera tonight." She looked directly at Jacklyn. "Not that I ever know what my reprehensible son is about. And to be sure, I sleep better when I do not."

Jacklyn laughed. "I would imagine."

"Mother." West frowned. "Permit me to introduce Miss Armstrong. And . . ."

"How do you do?" Lady Hart nodded and immediately took up the chair closest to Jacklyn. "So you are the lady my son has been squiring about for two entire weeks?"

"What?" Betty glared. "Here now!"

"Mother." West gritted his teeth. "Please, you would not wish to embarrass Jacklyn with questions too personal in nature, would you?"

"Why wouldn't I?" Lady Hart waved airily. "Is it not a mother's duty to meddle in her son's life when he doesn't wish her to? So just who are you, my dear? You are quite the mystery lady."

Jacklyn's eyes twinkled. "That is because I am a nobody, my lady. The *ton* would not know me from Eve."

"Jacklyn!" West frowned.

"Truly? Lady Hart leaned forward. "And yet you have captured my son's attention. There is a story here, I vow."

"I would not say that, my lady."

"I would." Lady Hart grinned. "Which means you cannot be a nobody."

"I fear I am. My father was a mere baronet. I have lived my entire life in Little Borehamwood."

"Armstrong?" Lady Hart's brow wrinkled in contemplation. West groaned. His mother was a wonderful woman, yet when it came to the peerage and the greater and lesser families of England she possessed a mind stronger than an iron trap. She tapped her finger to her lips. Then her gaze widened. "Why, my dear, you are Sir William Armstrong's daughter, are you not? He is a recluse, and is extremely wealthy, if I am not mistaken."

"He was, my lady. He has but recently passed on to his reward."

"I am sorry, my dear." Lady Hart raised a brow. "And . . . and how did he leave you?"

Jacklyn laughed without affectation. "Very well, my lady. Very well, indeed."

"My, my." Lady Hart looked at West. "Miss Armstrong is being far too modest. She has some fine connections, Westbrook."

"Mother." West sighed in exasperation.

Jacklyn shook her head. "I thank you, Lady Hart, for your kind efforts, but you need not try to puff up my consequence. I have none."

"My dear." Lady Hart's smile turned small and secretive. "You are the first respectable lady my son has paid attention to within the past few years. I would like you for that reason alone. Though I like you simply because I like you. I watched. You cried exactly where I did the first time I saw this opera. I shall puff up your consequence as much as I can."

"Please do not." Alarm crossed Jacklyn's face. "It is not necessary. I do not seek . . ."

"Cor!" Betty's eyes widened. "She ain't to be the one."

"One?" Lady Hart's brow rose and she turned to study Betty.

"She ain't going to be a Gunning sister." Betty's eyes narrowed into slits. "I am."

West cleared his throat. "This is Jacklyn's . . . ah . . . companion."

"Really?" Lady Hart rose promptly. With that one word, she turned her attention back to Jacklyn. "You *are* an original. Very democratic, to say the least. However, I can tell you are special. I wondered why Westbrook had decided to host a masquerade ball so suddenly. Now I know. Of course, he generally entertains in a hubble-bubble manner." She leveled a stern look upon West. "Nor did he see fit to invite his very own mama."

"Mother!"

Lady Hart made a moue of displeasure. "I will bet my diamond brooch he has invited *you*, Miss Armstrong."

"Blast it, Mother!" West leveled a stern look upon her. "You just lost your brooch and stole my thunder at the same time. I was just about to ask Jacklyn."

"Thank heaven, Westbrook. I knew I hadn't raised a slow top for a son." She winked at Jacklyn. "You are going to attend, are you not? Since it is only one week

A VALENTINE DREAM

before Saint Valentine's Day, you may consider it a Valentine's Ball—thrown in your honor at that."

"Mother . . ." West shifted uncomfortably. Betty's face was darkening to a very ugly color.

"Very well. I shall leave." Lady Hart laid her hand lightly upon Jacklyn's shoulder. "He is a delightful man, my son, regardless of his many faults. But you can reform him, my dear. His father was the same when he was young. A shocking rake. But he was the best of husbands and I the most fortunate of women."

Lady Hart waved and departed. West rolled his eyes heavenward. Was ever a man so taxed? His mother had just auctioned him off as a husband to the very lady he had intended to seduce, but certainly not marry. "I am sorry, Jacklyn."

"Do not be." Jacklyn smiled. "She is a lovely person. She called me democratic, but surely she must be so. She is also quite deluded, I fear."

West lost his smile for a moment. He stared at Jacklyn. Was his mother truly the deluded one, or was he?

The curtains opened one more time and Pandora entered. Her look was such that West knew he'd best take measures to allay any suspicions. "Hello, Pandora. My mother was just here, and I fear she told everyone of my surprise. I am giving a ball this Thursday."

Her eyes narrowed. "Why?"

West reached over and clasped Betty's hand. "It is a masquerade. I thought Betty would enjoy it. You, of course, are invited."

"Blimey. I would just." Betty cast Jacklyn a cold look. "His ma was wrong. That ball is for me, not you!"

West would not and could not look at Jacklyn.

Four

"You want me ter do *what* to m'lord!" Betty's eyes popped open wide, as did her mouth, since she was dressed as Cleopatra of the Nile, one would have expected a far more queenly manner.

"You must seduce West tonight." Pandora was appropriately garbed as Venus. In the midst of winter, her Grecian robes appeared rather insubstantial. However, her words possessed the substance her dress did not.

Pandora had informed both Betty and Jacklyn that she would pick them up in her carriage and they would go in tandem to Hart's masquerade ball. She had declared she would have final instructions to impart. The Goddess of Love did not play around when she said she had instructions!

"Jacklyn, you need not play the chaperon tonight. You may go and find a nice man for yourself, yes?"

"Y-yes?" Jacklyn's heart twisted cruelly. She was dressed as a pastoral milkmaid in a round gown of blue dimity and a flounced organza apron. Of the trio, she was the least seductive in fashion. She swung up her shepherd's crook with its cascade of pink satin ribbons. Of course, Mrs. Neville had fled to her room, declaring it wicked to dress as anything other than a proper young lady.

"Why am I supposed ter seduce him now? Why tonight?" Betty asked. "Can't it be . . . tomorrow night?"

"No. Tonight is the night." Pandora's eyes glittered. "You have won West's respect, yes. He gives this ball for you. That is good. Now you must secure his passion."

The oddest look crossed Betty's face. "I—I don't know . . ."

"You hesitate? Why? I thought you would be happy! *Bell'affare!* You have been crying and sighing because I would not let you touch him before this. Now is your moment. What could be the matter?"

"I don't know." The woebegone Cleopatra gnawed on her lower lip. "I th-think I waited too long fer it. I've kind of lost me enthusiasm."

"Che roba!" Pandora flung herself back against the seat and crossed herself. "I can't believe it. Betty, Betty. You must not fail me now. I will die!"

"That's it right there!" Betty's expression grew harried. "A girl can't be enjoying nothing when so much is depending on it. Blimey, it ain't easy ter be romantic when one's always thinking about becoming a grand lady and you dying if'n I don't!"

"Ah! I understand." Pandora grabbed up Betty's hand. "It is the feeling I get with a new patron. The performance must be everything, yes? Do not worry. It is only the nerves. West is your true love. I have dreamed it, have I not?"

"All right." Betty lowered her gaze.

"He waits for you. He wants you. Remember that." Pandora sighed. "Ah, if only . . . no, no. Think what a lucky girl you will be. West told you he was wearing the red domino, yes? He told you this just last night, did he not? He has a special reason, yes. He is the King of Hearts. Tonight—tonight will be the most important evening of your life."

Jacklyn sat in the corner of the large ballroom, very much alone. She tried to not watch. Still, her gaze would stray to Betty, who now danced with West. Jacklyn had seen him only once, when they had entered the ballroom. He had greeted them and apologized that his duty as host must occupy him for a while, but that he would certainly join them when he could. Until then, he hoped they would enjoy the festivities.

Pandora had been claimed by the marquis, who was dressed like a monk. Betty had giggled and swirled off with a white knight. Jacklyn had promptly secured a chair at the back of the room. She almost wished Mrs. Neville had attended to keep her company.

Jacklyn wouldn't then have such a wealth of uninterrupted time to observe Betty waltz about in West's embrace. Tonight was their special night. Red-hot jealousy flared through her. She tamped it down. It was ridiculous. She could not feel anything for West.

She expelled a ragged breath. She did, though. She felt everything for him. In such a short time, all had changed. He had entered her life and tipped it upside down and then righted it to a more perfect angle. She didn't hate men. She loved them. Or, to put it succinctly, she loved him.

Jacklyn smiled wryly. She could even confess it to herself without torment. She knew her love for West was hopeless. Nothing would happen because of it, though her heart bled a little, to be sure.

Meeting West's mother had done that. She was so charming. And she had acted as if Jacklyn could be a viable candidate for West's hand. It had been like a glimpse of heaven which common sense had promptly blighted. Jacklyn knew better, even if West's mother didn't.

"May I have this dance, madam?" West's voice asked.

Jacklyn jumped, looking up in astonishment. A tall man in a green domino and mask stood before her. She peered at the dance floor where Betty still danced with West. She shook her head. Faith, she was hearing West's voice in her head now. "N-no, thank you."

"Come, Jacklyn, do not turn me down. I have done much to be able to hold you in my arms and dance with you without Betty or Pandora or Mrs. Neville overseeing us."

"West? Is that you?" Jacklyn frowned. "But . . . who is . . ."

"The man in the red domino? He is a friend of mine who has promised to act as—forgive me—the red herring tonight." He laughed. "I did not expect him to rub along with Betty so well, but all the better. He's doing an excellent job of steering clear of Pandora, I've noticed." He held out his hand. "Please, dance with me."

Jacklyn's heart leaped. "But . . . I do not know how to dance."

"And you never will, unless you try." West's eyes glittered behind his green mask. "Come with me."

"Yes." Jacklyn placed her hand in his. The fierce emotion which shot through her with just that one touch stunned her. She could barely breathe as West led her into the dancing throng. He had arranged everything in order to dance with her. He had wanted this magical moment as much as she did.

Jacklyn found her breath again when West put his arms about her. Indeed, it came out in quick gasps. How anything could feel so right and so dizzying at the same moment was beyond Jacklyn.

"Will you permit me to lead you?" West whispered it in her ear. His voice was deep, asking far more than his words.

"Do I have a choice?" Jacklyn attempted nonchalance as he swung her about with strong arms.

"No." West grinned. "I have been waiting for this evening far too long to let you say no."

Jacklyn's eyes widened. She could not pretend his

advances were a mere pleasurable game any more. He had openly declared it. He did not want Betty or Pandora. He wanted her. "My lord . . ."

"Please, for once, call me West. You have no one about for whom you must set an example now."

"West . . ."

"Ah. It is music to my ears! I can die a happy man." His gaze darkened. "Almost."

Jacklyn shook her head. "You are impossible."

". . . West?"

Jacklyn laughed. "Yes, West."

"Yes?"

Jacklyn blinked. "I forgot what I was going to say."

"Good." West grinned. "I had a feeling I would not have liked it. You are to offer me no objections tonight, my dear. Merely gaze at me with those beautiful eyes of yours and dance with me until . . ."

Jacklyn flushed. "Now I remember . . ."

"West," West supplied.

"I . . ."

"What the devil?" West muttered.

"What?" Jacklyn started, wide-eyed. His tone was anything but romantic.

"What infernal luck. Do not look now, but there is another red domino making his way toward Betty."

"Truly? Is that bad?"

"You might as well look now. Pandora has. I fear we have been bubbled."

"Oh, no." Jacklyn looked to where West indicated.

A red domino clad figure was approaching Betty, who was dancing with another man in a red domino. Pandora, who was nearby, had halted, causing both the marquis and the dancers about her to stumble. Even from across the room, her expression showed suspicion.

The dancing red domino apparently had seen the other red domino. He whispered something into Betty's ear, and together they hastened from the floor. The approaching red domino came to a halt, obviously stumped. Pandora apparently called out to him. He turned, saw her stalking toward him, and promptly took off in another direction. Pandora slowed, suffering a moment's indecision, then picked up her Grecian robes and spun to give chase to Betty and the first red domino, who had made excellent time in their exit from the ballroom.

"Good. We have a chance after all." West dropped his arms from about Jacklyn. "Hurry. Let us make our own escape."

"What?" Jacklyn's heart jumped. "Where?"

"I'll show you." West's eyes sparkled.

Jacklyn's natural instincts set up its alarms. She couldn't pretend to herself that going with West would be either proper or safe. "I . . ."

West stood quietly, his eyes steady upon her. "Pandora will be back once she finds out the ploy."

Jacklyn's new instincts of love muted the old alarms. Tonight could be hers and West's if she would but take a step in that direction. She never doubted that after tonight, things would change. Pandora would not need Jacklyn's support. Betty would be after him in earnest desire.

Jacklyn would be no match against either of them. Though that would not matter, for after tonight, or after next week, West would surely be casting his gaze upon another woman. Life for Jacklyn would turn gray again. She would be standing with Mrs. Neville, watching the world go by from the window as in her dream.

That would be *after* tonight, Jacklyn vowed. She smiled and placed her hand in West's grasp. "We must hurry."

West's eyes flared with both pleasure and passion. "Come."

* * *

West led Jacklyn down the hallways. He could not wait until he had her alone. Dancing with her, knowing no one had recognized them, that they could be totally alone, had thrilled him. Now it did more than thrill him. It made his blood run hot.

"Where are we going?" Jacklyn gasped.

"To the library." West did not mention it was already prepared for them according to his prior instructions.

"Your house is magnificent. It is no wonder Betty wishes to become a countess."

Jacklyn's words were tinged with derision. It struck at West. "And you would not?"

"I do not believe in fairy tales." Jacklyn's voice took on the oddest tone.

West glanced back quickly to define her mood. Jacklyn's face was clear now. She smiled. "Despite the Gunning sister stories."

"Those are true." West raised a teasing brow as they stopped before the library and he opened the door. "And their father was not even a well-to-do baronet like yours, Mistress Cynic."

"They certainly set their sights high enough, then." Jacklyn entered the library. "I would not have dreamed of attempting such a feat."

"You hold yourself too low." West bit it out. "My mother accepted you, and she should know."

"Your mother is a true romantic." Jacklyn smiled. Then her eyes widened in obvious enlightenment. "And that is why you are so adept at dazzling and bamboozling us ladies. You must have learned how to get around your mother at a very tender age."

West halted. Memories flashed through his mind. "I believe you are right."

"Aha!" Jacklyn grinned and turned to study the room.

"But Mother is no fool, either. You think too little of yourself. And that has come from your past."

"Gracious." Jacklyn walked slowly up to the large fireplace, where a fire blazed within. A lace-covered table sat before it. Upon it was a bottle of champagne and several tasty desserts. "How beautiful."

"Do you like it?" West moved toward her.

Jacklyn looked at him, her gaze filled with innocent awe. "Is every room in your house prepared like this one? You are the most discriminating host, to be sure."

West paused. His plans had been rushed and he hadn't primed Jacklyn correctly. They were to have danced the evening away. He'd planned to whisper seductive things in her ear and tease her, until she came here willingly, without illusions. "Not exactly. I had it arranged just for you. Do you like it?"

Confusion crossed Jacklyn's face. Then understanding came, and with it embarrassment. "I see." She turned away and moved toward the table, her head bent. "Yes. Yes, I do like it."

West bit back a curse. His gaze flitted over to the corner of the room, where a daybed was prepared as well. Satin sheets and rose petals bedecked it. He stifled a groan. God, he hoped she wouldn't see it. It appeared depraved now. "I am glad to hear it."

Jacklyn lifted the opened bottle and poured the champagne into the two glasses. She picked them both up and turned. A spark of some kind flashed within her eyes. She offered the glass to West.

He took it with a strained smile, uncomfortable for some reason. "Here is to . . . you and me."

"Here is to the evening." Jacklyn nodded and promptly quaffed her drink. West stared as she moved to refill it.

"We have plenty of time, Jacklyn."

"Do we?" The spark in her eyes was growing. "We can never know. Didn't you say we should seize every moment?"

"Certainly." Faith, it wasn't as amusing to have his own lines turned back upon him.

"Let us have another toast." Jacklyn raised her glass.

West could not ignore what lay within her eyes now. It was wildness. His pulse raced accordingly. He lifted his glass and didn't even consider his words. "To dreams!"

"I do not believe in dreams, you know that." Laughing, Jacklyn quaffed that glass as well. She turned and set it down with a studied precision. When she looked back at West, her face held an appealing mixture of mischief and passion. She walked toward him with fluid grace. "You may set me free from my cage now, West."

"May I?" West quaffed his champagne. He should have known when Jacklyn decided to do something, she would do it wholeheartedly. He had the oddest feeling, as if he had fallen far behind without even knowing it. He stepped past her and set his glass down upon the table.

Drawing in a breath, he strode over to the door and locked it. He had learned that valuable lesson long ago. The excitement of being caught was highly overrated, in his opinion. He'd rather know he had all the time in the world to enjoy himself, especially with Jacklyn. Grinning, he turned.

Jacklyn had acquired another glass of champagne. She stood within the fire's glow, her eyes brilliant amber as she watched him. She had to be the most beautiful woman West had ever seen in his life.

Ridiculous, his mind objected as West approached Jacklyn. He had been in the company of diamonds of the first water . . . toasts of the *ton* . . . incomparables. He stopped before her and gazed at her steadily.

"What is the matter?" This time Jacklyn sipped from the champagne glass. Her breathing was irregular.

West closed his eyes tight, then opened them. He shook his head and gently took the glass from her. "You are still the most beautiful woman I have ever seen."

"Thank you. That is a very nice thing to have said."

"You do not believe me?" West quaffed the rest of the glass.

"Of course not." Jacklyn smiled. Her voice held no bitterness, which in turn made West bitter for her. She stepped close, looking up at him. An entire new world flashed within her eyes, a world open for West's discovery. She lifted her lips. "Would you please kiss me, West?"

"You never have to say please with me, darling." West tossed the champagne glass down.

He did not hear it shatter as he drew Jacklyn into his arms. He kissed her upturned lips. They trembled. So did he.

"West." Jacklyn all but blended into him, wrapping her arms about him, molding her body to his, kissing him with open need.

West was set aflame. He growled and deepened the kiss. Jacklyn did not draw back, but met his kiss with a growing ardor. He ignored the sense that it was a kiss laden with innocence.

The fire roared through West all the more. But then he heard Pandora's voice murmuring in his head that he was aflame because he was going to hell. He tore his lips from Jacklyn's. "Are—are you sure you wish . . ."

"Yes." Jacklyn did not let him finish. Lips glistening and eyes blazing, she kissed him. Passion coursed through him as he held her close, her clothing teasing him.

Then his mother's voice drifted through his raging heat. *Why, my dear, she is not a nobody.* He groaned. Blast, what was the matter with him? How could such voices be in his head at a lustful moment like this? Hoping to chase them away, he jerked back. "Are you certain?"

"Oh yes!" Jacklyn kissed him.

West returned her kiss hungrily—but he had seen something in her eyes just before her lips had claimed his. It was uncertainty.

Need spurred West on. His old instincts for winning resurfaced. He trailed his lips to her ear. "You are special, Jacklyn. Very special."

"Thank you." It was a sigh of desire, not an acceptance of what he'd said. Jacklyn's fingers slipped into his hair and inexpertly played with it.

Her exclamation of delight racked West with his own shiver of delight. "You are!"

"Hmm, yes."

West's fingers expertly unfastened the back of her dress as he kissed her wildly, drawing a moan from Jacklyn. He should have been pleased, only frustration dampened it. Blast it, but Jacklyn held herself in too low esteem. Did she not know he was seducing her virtue away, stealing from her any chance of a proper marriage?

West slid the sleeves of Jacklyn's dress off her shoulders. Wanting to see her beauty uncovered, West drew back. Her bared shoulders were smooth and white. The valley between her breasts, their full curves only half exposed, beckoned with promise. West groaned from his want. "Are you sure?"

The passion in Jacklyn's eyes shattered. "Stop asking me that!"

West shook his head to clear it. What kind of gudgeon was he? "You are magnificent."

"Yes?" Relief filled Jacklyn's eyes.

She wanted to escape the question he had asked. That was normal for a woman. That was why a man seduced a woman, so that she had no time to consider it. Castigating himself, West turned his gaze back upon Jacklyn. In a moment, she would be totally revealed to him.

Jacklyn leaned in to kiss him. Shock rocked West. Jacklyn was seducing him as much as he was seducing her! *Seducing you away from any chance of marrying her.* The words hissed through his mind. He tried to push them away.

What was the matter with him? This was clearly what he expected, was it not? He was no moonling. He knew what he was doing. Tonight Jacklyn would be his. Yet she was a lady. In the morning she would be ashamed of what she had done as sure as the sun would rise. Then she would be lost to West. That was, unless he seduced her again . . . and again. But never would she marry him.

"Are you certain you want to do this?"

Jacklyn jerked back. "Why, why are you asking me that?"

West blinked. "I . . . what did I say?"

"You asked me if I were certain. Again!"

"My God." West had not realized that he had spoken. Worst of all, he had the terrible suspicion that he had been questioning himself.

Tears glistened in Jacklyn's eyes. "Now I—I can't!"

Her wail was sheer pain. She jerked her dress up and let out a small sob.

West stood frozen. He was an utter cad, yet he dared not move to soothe her. Or seduce her.

Jacklyn, flushed and clearly mortified, ran to the door. She jerked at it.

"No. No!" Her voice held fear. Then she discovered the key within the lock and turned it. She was gone within a moment.

West stumbled to a chair and fell into it. Why the devil had he asked her that infernal question again? Rather, why did he have to ask *himself* aloud? Frustrated desire ebbed away slowly, painfully.

Yet relief slipped in behind it. West groaned. Oh Lord, he was actually relieved. Relieved that he hadn't followed through with the seduction. Relieved that he had failed to take Jacklyn's virtue from her. He laid his head back upon the chair and sighed. There was no doubt about it. Jacklyn had unmanned him, unmanned him completely.

"Aha, there you are!" Pandora entered through the open

door. She frowned in clear exasperation. "What has happened to you?"

"I should ask you the same question." West raised his brow. Pandora's white flowing robes were no longer white. Rather, they were muddied and besmirched.

The strong smell of horse invaded the room as the enraged Goddess of Love stomped up to him. "I have been looking everywhere for you, Lockyear!"

Her slippers were well nigh unrecognizable and oozed sludge. West noticed her hem was also dank. "Where did you look, dear? Over hill and glen?"

"It is not amusing." Pandora's eyes glittered with menace. "You are in a green domino now. Why?"

West sighed. "I tore the red domino and was forced to change it."

"What! Why did you not tell me?"

West feigned confusion. "Why should I? I did not consider it of any moment."

"But it was of moment. Great moment!" Pandora flung out her hand in a dramatic fashion. "I thought you were in the red domino, and for that I have suffered greatly. I followed you—or thought I followed you. Bah! You do not know. For you I even entered the stables."

"Indeed? Why did you do such a tottyheaded thing? As if I would ever frolic in the stables."

"I thought it queer, but you were with Betty . . ."

"And you thought I was trying to make her feel at home?"

"I—" Pandora clamped her mouth shut. The woman was no fool. She cast him the most aggrieved look. "Then I thought I saw you in the gardens."

"Ah." West grinned. "Did you enjoy my ornamental pond?"

"Beast! I did not!" Pandora placed her hands upon her full hips, then groaned. "Ah, me, but I am wounded. And all because of that most stupid pond of yours. I tripped.

A VALENTINE DREAM

If I had not been so quick footed and turned in the fastest way, I would have been drowned, yes. I alone saved myself. It was no thanks to you or . . . or Betty . . . or whoever that fiend was in the red domino."

West laughed loudly.

"What? You dare to laugh at my misfortune?"

"Yes, I do. That will teach you to try and spy upon me, sweetheart. I should be angry, but it appears you have been punished enough."

Pandora's eyes widened in outrage. Then large tears welled in their depths and rolled down her cheek in bright and beautiful droplets. "But . . . but I only want you to be with your true love."

"Yes. Because you think you will die if I am not."

"I will!"

West chuckled.

Pandora glared at him. Then she sniffed and shrugged. "At least there is champagne."

She limped over to the table and poured the champagne out into the one glass. In the dim light, she did not see it had been used. Nor did she notice the broken glass upon the floor.

"I shall die and . . ." She froze. Her eyes narrowed as she peered across the darkened room. "What? Aha!"

West groaned. Pandora had spied the daybed. "Pandora, do not . . ."

"How lovely it is!" Pandora tottered over to it and stared. "Ah, West, darling, you are the most wonderful man." She sat down upon the silken sheets and sighed. "Does that silly twit Betty know what she is missing?"

"I gather not." West hid his relief. He might very well escape a scene yet.

"Madre di Dio. You do love her, do you not? That is why you prepared this wonderful bed for her. Ah, but we think much alike."

"Yes, we do, my dear."

Pandora gazed at him. She sniffed. Evidently that was her last tear. A slow smile crossed her lips and she stretched herself languidly over the daybed. Desire filled her eyes. "Come to me, darling."

"What?" West sat up, shocked. "Pandora, you are not . . . not offering me a slip on the shoulder, are you?"

"I need comfort. It has been so long." Pandora's lip pouted out. Then she smiled. "And now that I know you truly love Betty, it will be all right."

"All right. Why would it be all right? If I have found my true love, it would mean I cannot have a liaison with you."

"Why not?" Pandora wagged a playful finger. "I know you, West. You are a man of appetites. You will give your true love to Betty, but you will need another, yes? These appetites have nothing to do with the love."

"No!" West sprang up, anger coursing through him. "Would you act that way with your true love, Pandora?"

Pandora's eyes swam with tears again. Only this time, they did not glisten. Indeed, her eyes turned frightfully red and swollen. "No. Me, I would be faithful forever. But my true love . . ." She broke into a wracking sob and tears flowed, the type which would make a strong man cringe and dart for the door. They lacked art. "I—I have no true love."

"Ah, sweetheart," West strode over, and sitting down, gathered her into his arms. He received a good whiff of stables for his kindness. "Do not cry."

"Once, when I was young, I thought . . ." Pandora buried her head upon his shoulder. "But he was not! I have no true love." She wrapped her arms about him and trained her large green eyes upon him. "Please . achoo!"

"Bless you."

"Thank you. Make love to me, West. It will be all right. Betty will understand, I assure you. She is more like you and me than I thought." She pressed her bosom against him. "Make love to me."

West stilled. Desire rose, but rather as an old habit. It was not filled with the passion or thoughts Jacklyn had aroused. Instead, his body was responding to the beautiful body of a woman, as it had done so many, many times before.

West gazed into Pandora's brilliant eyes. They would both be able to indulge in bed sport, understanding exactly what it meant and didn't mean. He sighed. It would be so easy to lose himself in the physical passion. He would know Pandora's responses. She would know his responses. Experienced, they knew the games so well that there would be no embarrassing surprises.

Jacklyn.

His heart whispered it. Quietly. Yet it shocked West so much that he sprang up.

Pandora stared at him.

"I must . . . go." West spun on his heel and strode to the door. "I must."

"No! West, do not leave me. Achoo! Where are you going?"

"Away."

"What? Where away?"

"I don't know."

West's mind asserted itself. Stifling his heart's desire, he began planning his escape route, considering place after place. He didn't know where he was going. He only knew it would be far, far away.

Five

Jacklyn alighted from the carriage. In the dusky light, she stood a moment gazing at the Earl of Hart's town house. Her courage waned. She was tempted to turn tail and run. Yet she had built up her courage all day long.

Then the memory of her dream came to her. She grabbed the leash of her courage, lifted her skirts, and walked up the town house steps. She employed the knocker soundly.

It was almost twelve, the eve before Saint Valentine's Day. Would anybody answer? Had West already left for France, as he had written Pandora he would? She prayed he had not. There was no reason he shouldn't be on the high seas by now, yet in the wake of her dream, Jacklyn believed he was still in London.

The door at last opened. West's butler greeted her as if it were the bright light of day. Neither surprise nor concern showed in his countenance. "What may I do for you, miss?"

"Could you please tell me . . . has Lord Hart left town?"

"He has not, miss."

"Thank heaven."

"No, miss, you'll best thank the ship's captain, who became so tap-hacket he couldn't sail." The butler smiled. "My lord was forced to unearth him at the captain's doxy's place. He will have him sacked, I make no doubt."

A VALENTINE DREAM

"Oh, dear, I should hope not." A chuckle escaped Jacklyn. She had at last caved in to believing in fate. Now she was sure this fate at least possessed a sense of justice. "He would be casting stones, I fear. Not a good thing to do, I am starting to believe."

"Certainly, miss." Now the butler did look concerned.

Jacklyn shook herself. She was dithering. "Er . . . might I come in and wait for him? Ah . . ." She dragged in a deep breath. "Perhaps in his chambers?"

The concern actually disappeared. The man appeared comfortable once more, as if back to familiar territory. He bowed. "Indeed. If you would please follow me."

Jacklyn trailed behind him in amazement as he led her through the residence directly to a large suite without either comment or condemnation. He waved a hand when they stood in the center of a plush Axminster carpet in hues of celadon and gold. Two huge leather wing chairs flanked an elegant fireplace paneled with a deep green Italian marble. Gold velvet drapes were pulled across the window. The room was elegant, yet comfortably masculine. "The wardrobe is over there. I shall have champagne iced and sent up directly. Would you care for anything else in particular, ma'am?"

"P-perhaps w-water?" Jacklyn squeaked, her mouth turning to cotton.

"Indeed?"

He said no more, but left Jacklyn promptly. He appeared perplexed when he returned to discover her patiently sitting in one of the leather chairs. "Madam, are you not going to take off your . . . ah, your cloak?"

Jacklyn flushed. "No. No, thank you."

When he left, she quickly grabbed up the water glass and drank from it.

"Jacklyn!" West exclaimed.

Jacklyn choked and sputtered. The glass slipped

through her fingers and tumbled to the carpet. "Oh, dear. I am so sorry."

West didn't answer. He stood gazing at her, his look a cross between pleasure and fear. "I wondered if it were you." His normal sangfroid returned and he laughed. "Lambert was completely confounded. He begs your forgiveness. He thought you were . . . one of those ladies who are accustomed to making themselves at home in a gentleman's boudoir with . . . well, with wickedness on their minds."

Jacklyn's heart sank. She was clearly not original in her scheme. "He need not beg my forgiveness . . ."

"You are kind, as usual."

"I *am* here with w-wickedness on my mind."

"What?" Astonishment washed over the earl's face. His firm jaw dropped open.

"You see, West, I—I had a dream last night." Jacklyn reached up and unfastened her cloak. She permitted it to fall to the floor, standing as bravely as she could in a glowing, deep burgundy satin gown. If Mrs. Neville had seen it, the good woman would surely have dug herself into the floorboards beneath her bed. The modiste who had so skillfully addressed the fashion needs of Pandora and others of her cut had assured her it was indeed most improper.

West stared. "And I am having a dream now."

Jacklyn expelled a breath—and with it her fear. She smiled, walking to him. "I love you, West. I want to be with you as . . . as only lovers can be."

West stumbled backward. "That must have been some dream."

"It was." Jacklyn stepped closer.

West lifted a staying hand. "Stop! And . . . tell me what it was first!"

Unaccountable tears prickled in Jacklyn's eyes. "Do

you remember when I said I was positive I had met you before?"

"Yes. Did you remember where we met? Is that it?"

"No." Jacklyn smiled wryly. "I have given up that notion. I now know there is only one place I have met you. And that place *was* in my dreams, West. You were right."

West clearly sucked in a breath. "Truly?"

"Truly. Last night I finally saw the rest of the dream." The warmth and joy of it still filled Jacklyn. She sighed. "Before, I have only seen you walking toward me and nothing more. But last night, you didn't disappear. You continued to walk up to me. You took me in your arms, and . . ."

West's eyes darkened. He stepped toward her. "And what?"

"You kissed me. You called me your darling. And you laughed. You vowed that even after all our years together, my kiss could still make you randy. Then we . . ." Jacklyn halted to gain her breath.

"What?" His gaze was urgent. "What did we do, Jacklyn?"

"We turned toward a beautiful manor house. It was far off in the distance, but it . . . it was magnificent. Its stone was golden, and it had turrets and . . ."

"Yes." West nodded. "Go on."

Jacklyn blinked in hurt. "I . . ."

"It is Harthaven. My country seat. Go on."

A shiver coursed through Jacklyn. "We turned and walked toward it. Flowers bloomed everywhere, fields and fields of them."

"It was spring, then. Mother has pastures of flowers worked into her landscaping."

"Your mother sat upon a stone terrace. She was watching three children playing upon the lawns." Jacklyn smiled. "West, we were so very happy. I was so very happy."

"Children?" West backpedaled.

Jacklyn frowned. "Yes, children. Why?"

West's face darkened. "You dreamed that, yet you have come to me tonight looking like that! Just what are you thinking, Jacklyn?"

"I—I was thinking that I love you, West." Jacklyn shook her head in hurt bewilderment. "I—I want to be with you."

"Well, you aren't going to be!" West looked frightfully angry.

A numbness invaded Jacklyn. "I—I'm sorry. I—I thought . . ."

"No, you haven't thought, sweetheart. We'll not do that to our children, by God."

Jacklyn blinked. "Our children?"

"The three children in the dream, Jacklyn."

"Good gracious." Jacklyn gasped. "You—you think those were our children?"

"Of course." West frowned. "Whose did you think they were?"

"I don't know. Your brother's or sister's, perhaps?"

"I am an only child, Jacklyn. Did no one tell you that?"

"No, of course not. But . . ."

West barked a laugh. "I will lay you any odds you want, Miss Armstrong, that those are *our* children, and I'll be hanged if they are going to be bastards." He crossed his arms and lifted his head in a fair imitation of a miffed woman. "Fie, Mistress. Do not think you can seduce me in such a manner. I'm not that kind of chap! It will be marriage for me or nothing else, I'll have you know."

"West!" Jacklyn gasped. "We cannot . . ."

"That is right. We cannot bed until we are married." West smiled slightly, his gaze warm. "Didn't I say you must be the chaperon for us? I do not mean to pull caps with you, dearest, but you are making a right mull of it." His smile broadened and the warmth in his eyes flared to open love. "However, I will forgive you if you will marry me."

Jacklyn's heart leaped. "I—I . . ."

West shook his head, his voice cozening. "Think, Jacklyn. There will be no dream unless you marry me first. I'll not permit it. I'll not let you hold yourself so cheaply, or our love so cheaply."

"Then . . . then you love me?"

"With all my heart." He smiled wryly. "You may be the keeper of our dreams, darling, but I insist we live them as well. Will you marry me?"

"Yes. Yes, I will." Jacklyn laughed. Then a blush covered her. Gracious, what had she been thinking? Her attire was far too seductive, and completely out of place for a proper proposal of marriage. Pandora would have told her so. She dived for her cloak. "Dear me."

"Exactly." West grinned. "Now get the blazes out of here, my love!"

"Yes, West." Jacklyn struggled into the cloak's concealing folds. She laughed, both mortified and exultant. "Thank you so much for the proposal, my lord. I do hate to accept and run, but I must."

"I understand." West blew her a kiss from behind the safety of the opposite chair. "I will see you in the morning. No, I will see you for tea. I have a few important matters to attend to first. Tell Mrs. Neville she must be present. She may soothe her sensibilities with tea, brandy, hartshorn, or whatever she chooses. Just warn her that she dare not fail us! I can reform only so much at a time!"

Gripping the missive in his hand, West ran from the house and clambered into his carriage. He shouted for his driver to take him to Miss Sabatini's and to spring them.

He reread the missive.

West,

I am with Pandora. She is very sick. I fear she is dying. Please come to us.

Jacklyn

"Blast and damn Pandora's portents!" West clenched his teeth. He should not have said that. He would never have met Jacklyn if not for Pandora and her wild fantasies.

He exhaled slowly, attempting to control himself. It made no sense, the overpowering fear that assaulted him. He told himself it was merely more of Pandora's dramatics, nothing else. People did not die from failing to meet a dream's demands. That was so much superstition.

The carriage slowed before the courtesan's town house. West was embarking from it before it had even stopped. He leaped up the steps and pounded upon the door, opening it before the butler could. He greeted that stunned personage and commanded that he be taken directly to Pandora's room. The butler offered him no resistance, but scurried ahead to show him the way.

West halted upon the room's threshold. Faith, just a month ago he would have paid greatly to have the pleasure of entering. Now he detested the thought.

Pandora lay in a large bed that was the focal point of the room. Jacklyn sat upon her right side and Betty on her left. West's heart twisted. "Jacklyn."

"West." Jacklyn looked up, pain in her eyes, then rose and ran to him.

He enveloped her in his arms. "What is this all about, darling?"

She stiffened and stepped back. Clearly, she fought to contain herself. "I—I don't know. Pandora can't breathe and she can't move."

"My lord." Betty sprang up and rushed over to him.

Her face was swollen from crying. "I—I will marry you. I will marry you today, if you will."

"Oh. Oh." A low moan came from the bed. Pandora's face, wan and lost amongst a tumble of red curls, showed fever and fear. "Thank you, Betty. Thank you."

"I am sorry, Betty. But I fear I am already taken by another." West said it as gently he could. He cast Jacklyn a loving smile. Then his breath caught. He could see it in her eyes. "Jacklyn?"

"I—I cannot marry you, West."

"Jacklyn. No, you must." West held her tight. "I love you."

"And I love you." Jacklyn clung to him. "But . . . but it cannot be a true or good love if . . . if it is at the expense of Pandora's life."

"You cannot believe this superstitious rot!"

"She is dying, West. That is all I know."

"But what of your own dream?" West almost shouted.

"Yes." Her gaze was level. "How can I choose my dream over hers? Why is mine right and hers is not?"

"Which dream is that?" Betty's eyes widened. "Have you had a dream, miss? Are you going to die, too?"

"No!" West roared it. "She's not going to bloody die. Nor is Pandora." He stomped over to the large bed. Yet he was brought to a stand, emotion paralyzing him. He hardly recognized Pandora. Her vibrancy and spirit were a mere shadow. "Pandora?"

"West, my dear." Her eyes were large and dilated. "I—I am dying. Help me. I am dying."

"No, you are not dying."

"Please. Bring me . . . bring a priest. I—I must make my confessions. I must make my peace with God."

"No!" Betty wailed. She ran to the bed and fell to the ground in a heap. "I'll marry his lordship. I will. You gots to live."

"Ah, me. It is too late. I cannot move. I am dying."

Pandora reached out and gripped West's hand. *"Per carità!* Bring me a priest. The best you can find. I must make my confession. If I make confession I might go to purgatory instead, yes?"

"You are not going to . . ."

"Cease. I have failed. I did not help Betty to marry you. This is my dying request. You must hurry." A spark of the old Pandora returned. *"Santa pace,* but my confession will be long. It will . . . it will require much time, yes?"

"Please, West." Jacklyn moved to stand beside him, her eyes tormented. "Do something."

West gazed at Jacklyn. He saw his future in her eyes, yet it was fading. If Pandora died and Jacklyn believed it was her fault, there would never be any happiness for them.

He stiffened. It would not turn out that way, by God. "I will get the bishop."

West hauled Jacklyn into his arms and kissed her firmly. He set her away. "And the best of doctors, too. Prinny's physician himself, I vow. Pandora will not die and you shall marry me. That is final."

"But . . ."

"I love you, Jacklyn. I have found you at last. And you cannot say I haven't sought through enough women to do so. I will not lose you now. We are meant to be together." He laughed, though it was hoarse. "It is fate. And destiny. Coincidence be hanged." He turned to Pandora. Bending down, he kissed her hot forehead. "Believe this, Pandora. You are not going to die. I am going to bring you your bishop, and I am going to bring you the Regent's physician. Between the two of them, they should be able to heal you. Believe in that. Not your portents." He strode over to the sobbing Betty. "Betty, I appreciate that you would marry me, and Pandora does, too. But I do not think it would be a happy union for us."

A VALENTINE DREAM

"N-no, my lord." She gulped and sobbed. "I—I am s-sorry. It is all my fault."

"Nonsense. That is ridiculous." He crouched down and kissed her cheek. "It is not your fault."

West rose and stalked from the room, grim with determination. He would find Pandora her bishop and the Regent's doctor. They would save her, body and soul. She would live! He and Jacklyn would marry and have those three children, confound it, and the flowers would be in bloom all the time.

He focused on that dream and prayed.

The night shadows invaded the room. West had been gone for hours. Pandora had subsided into a dazed slumber. She coughed and moaned often. Jacklyn sat, watching over her. Betty sat across from her, crying heartbrokenly. "I can't stand this no more."

"Hm? What?" Pandora sputtered awake.

Betty wrung her hands. "I need ter confess. I just gots ter confess!"

"Is the priest here?" Pandora struggled to sit, only to fall back.

"No," Jacklyn soothed. "He is not. It is Betty who says she must confess."

"What?"

"It is my fault you are dying." Fear filled Betty's eyes. "West said it was ridiculous, but it ain't. You see—I lied to you."

"What do you mean?" Pandora struggled back up. She moaned, but remained sitting.

"I knows his lordship is supposed ter be my true love. And . . . and I wanted him ter be. Truly. I have tried." Betty choked and sniffed. "But . . . but I can't forget me Horace."

"Horace?" Pandora shrieked. A paroxysm of coughing

wracked her. Her green eyes glittered upon Betty. "Who is Horace?"

"He is your butler." Betty's eyes widened. "Didn't you know?"

"My butler?" Pandora frowned. "You mean Rundle?"

"Yes." Betty blushed. "But Horace is his Christian name."

"Y-you are in love with my *butler?*"

"Yes." Betty nodded. "I—I never thought there could be anything between us, being Horace is so far above me touch, him being a butler and me just an upstairs maid."

Pandora gurgled and Jacklyn feared she would expire upon that moment. "You thought him above your touch? What did you think West, then?"

"Well . . ." Betty shifted upon her chair. "I—well, you turned me head, you did! It was that fine story about those Gunning sisters that made me start thinking. And . . . and you said you had dreamed it." Tears of shame ran down Betty's face. "I—I figured if you dreamed it, it was sure ter happen. And . . . well, wot girl is going to sniff at marrying an earl? I couldn't tell ye nay. But . . . but now you are dying 'cause I—I can't love his lordship. I only wants me Horace. But . . . he won't look at me nohow 'cause I threw him over for an earl."

"Bah! It is only right that a woman looks out for her best interests." Pandora huffed, clearly distracted. "How dare he frown upon you!"

"I should have told you afore when you chased me down." Betty sobbed into her hands. "Only I was too frightened to tell yer. S'truth, I thought you was chasing after me 'cause you had caught Horace and me the night before and had just remembered it. Or that you had figured out I had spent the night with him and was but going home. That's why I hid in the pantry. And . . . and then I—I would have done anything rather than getting Horace or me sacked."

A VALENTINE DREAM 89

Life filled Pandora for a moment—angry and indignant life. "He was at the ball with you, wasn't he? He wore the red domino and masqueraded as West!"

"I'm sorry. It was my idea. I—I thought it would be our last time together."

"Wait . . ." Jacklyn held up her hand.

"You trollop! I entered the smelly stables because of you. I fell into a pond because of you . . ."

"Hold!" Jacklyn shouted so loudly that Pandora jumped. "What do you mean Pandora caught you and Horace the night before?"

"You little sneak, you . . ."

"Pandora." Jacklyn's voice cracked. "Let Betty explain."

Betty sniffed. "Thank you, Miss Jacklyn. The night before, Miss Pandora had come home with Lord Fortesque. She caught me and Horace er . . . er, flirtin' in the foyer."

"Flirting?" Pandora narrowed her fevered gaze.

"All right. We was kissing and more, we were."

"Doxy." Pandora spat. She frowned. "But I do not remember this."

Betty hung her head. "You—you was a bit on the go that night, if I do say so myself. I thought you were going ter ring a peal over me head and Horace's, but then Lord Fortesque grabbed you and started crying and begging for you to stay with him. Horace and me, we slipped out when you was, er—comforting his lordship."

Pandora nodded. *"Santa pace.* But I hate it when a man cries."

Jacklyn stiffened. A jubilant howl escaped her. It was unladylike, but she could not help herself. She howled.

"Jacklyn! Do not screech so." Pandora covered her ears. "Have pity. That is no way to behave upon my deathbed."

"Pandora. Do you not see?"

"See! Yes, I see? Betty lied to me. Me, the great Pandora Sabatini, must die because this jade lied to me."

Betty shrieked.

Pandora cringed. "There is quiet in purgatory, yes?"

"No." Jacklyn grabbed Pandora's hand in excitement. "I asked you in the beginning if you had ever seen Betty. You said no. She said no. But you *had* seen her, only you had . . . had too much champagne." She laughed. "And lobster with clotted cream."

Understanding dawned upon Pandora's face, and hope. "Ah, me! You think . . ."

"That is why you dreamed of Betty that night. That is why you recognized her the next day upon the street."

"Madre di dio!"

"They weren't portents, Pandora! It was just a bad dream."

A nervous silence fell upon the room. Betty's swollen eyes looked from one lady to the other. She gulped. "Does that mean she ain't going ter die?"

Jacklyn broke into a grin. "It does!"

Betty broke into a responding grin. "I don't have ter marry his lordship?"

"You most certainly shall not!" Jacklyn said sternly.

Betty sprang up. "I—I . . ."

"I am saved. It was just a dream." Pandora looked at Betty. "Go. Go to Rundle. Beg his forgiveness. That sin shall not be upon my head."

"Thank you." Betty sprang up and sprinted to the door. "Thank you."

Jacklyn laughed as the maid disappeared. She smiled at Pandora. "How are you feeling now?"

Pandora stretched her arms out. "I believe . . ."

"I have returned." West strode into the room. A man with a black bag followed behind. He was dressed in formal evening attire and clearly cross as crabs. "I have found the physician."

"West!" Jacklyn rose and hurried to him. "You will never imagine . . ."

"I found him at a soiree . . ." West snatched up her hands and kissed them.

"I was not at merely a soiree. It was a diplomatic dinner hosted by the Italian ambassador." The doctor stalked over to the bed and slammed his bag upon the table. "Nor did he 'find' me. He crashed into the dining room, dragging three servants behind him and rousting me from the fourth course as if I were but a lackey. I have never suffered such indignities in my life. I only came because I did not wish to make more of a scene than he had already caused."

"That and I threatened to carry him out bodily." West smiled. "I also have the bishop coming. The good doctor here was a charm compared to the bishop. Yet he promised once he finished the Mass he would attend you, Pandora."

"Oh, dear." Jacklyn bit her lip.

"You'd better be dying, Miss Sabatini," the doctor growled as he opened his bag. "Or, by God, I . . ."

"But I am not dying!" Pandora cried.

"What?" West exclaimed.

"It was only a bad dream, West." Jacklyn gripped his hands. "She had seen Betty before, but didn't remember because she had too much champagne. In fact, Betty is in love with Pandora's butler."

"I beg your pardon? What tomfoolery is this?" The doctor glared daggers at West. "My lord, I vow I shall have you brought to court for this!"

"But . . ." West blinked.

"I shall prove it to you!" Pandora, her eyes alight, flung the covers back. Her voluptuous body, garbed in a clinging silver satin, was revealed. The doctor gurgled to a halt.

West's brows rose in amusement. "That is the finest deathbed attire I have ever seen, Pandora."

"Thank you. You see! I was wrong. Jacklyn was right.

It was only the lobster, clotted cream . . ." Pandora swung her shapely legs over the bed's edge and pushed herself up from the mattress. She danced across the room, her arms flung wide. ". . . and the champagne. It was nothing but a bad dream!"

"See, West!" Jacklyn clapped her hands together.

"Ah!" Pandora shrieked. She toppled over like a puppet whose strings had been cut.

"Pandora!" Jacklyn gasped.

The men shouted even as Pandora screamed. The three hastened toward her.

"Ma belle!" an anguished voice cried as if from nowhere.

They all skittered to a stop.

A man loped into the room. He knelt down and dragged Pandora into his arms before anyone could move.

"Antonio!" Pandora cried.

"What?" West recovered first. He stepped forward, only to rear back again in surprise as Pandora flung her arms about the man and kissed him with a vigor and passion that was rather phenomenal for a dying woman. Jacklyn's mouth dropped open.

"Egad!" The doctor shook his head. "Well, I never."

"My Pandora," the man breathed. He was an older gentleman, his hair graying. He, however, returned Pandora's kiss with a fervor that showed his age did not matter one jot. "That man, he said you were dying. You cannot, my beloved. You cannot. I could not bear it."

Jacklyn squeezed West's hand and whispered into his ear, "Who is he?"

"I do not know."

"That is the ambassador." The doctor, his voice hushed, came to stand beside them. "It was his dinner party you so rudely crashed."

"Ah!" West nodded. "I didn't meet him."

"Of course not. You were too busy browbeating me."

"Antonio!" Pandora breathed. "You are here. I never thought to see you again. I—I never . . ."

Antonio drew back. His own eyes glistened with tears. "But I have always known of you. I have known of your rise to fame. I—I have watched your fantastic career, your great advancements."

"But . . . but why?"

"I have always loved you, Pandora."

"But you sent me away, Antonio." The wretchedness in Pandora's voice tore at Jacklyn. "Y-you married that lady and sent me away."

"I was young. I was a fool."

"I only wanted to be your lover." Pandora's voice was soft. "I—I never would have stood in your way."

"My family forced me to give you up. The lady's family was very strict. And she was . . . ah, I will not speak of her cold and unnatural nature. Those years were long. And lonely."

Pandora lifted her hand to his cheek. "My poor Antonio. Ah, me."

"You do not hate me?" Antonio's gaze exuded pain. "C-could you . . . ever forgive me?"

Pandora clung to him. "Why have you never come to me?"

"After my wife died . . ."

"She died?"

"Five years ago."

"And you knew where I was?" Pandora's eyes flashed. "You did not come to me?"

"I did not deserve you. I sent you away. I knew you could not forgive me. How could you? And you . . . you had risen to such fame and glory. I—I am still but an ambassador. My title and estate are not great . . ."

"How could you ever believe that of me?" Pandora wailed it out with high drama. She slapped her hand to her bosom. "Ah, me. How tragic, yes. Now I *shall* die, knowing that my only true love thought . . ."

Jacklyn gasped. "No. Oh no!"

"Yes, yes." Pandora's tears welled up. "He thought so little of me."

"Darling . . ."

"Pandora, your dream was true." Jacklyn's entire world capsized and then righted itself. Love told her the truth and she wouldn't draw back, no matter how fantastical it was. "Your dream *was* true!"

Pandora stiffened, her eyes stunned. "Jacklyn! You are cruel."

"No. Think, Pandora." Jacklyn went and knelt beside her. "You told me your mission was to help some poor pitiful girl to find her true love."

"Yes. But I failed."

Jacklyn shook her head. "No, you didn't."

"Jacklyn, you are right." West came to stand by her. "She helped you to find me, and me to find you. But you are *not* pitiful."

"No, I was. We are all rather pitiful without love." Jacklyn looked cautiously at Pandora. "But I did not mean me. I meant Pandora!"

"Never!" Antonio cried. "My Pandora is not pitiful. She is magnificent. From the first moment when I saw her in the streets, when she was but a poor peasant, she was magnificent. No rags, no dirt, could ever hide her beauty, her spirit. Ah, she was a gaunt one back then. Skinny, like a boy, yes. But always I knew she was the woman."

"Pandora." Jacklyn laughed gently. "Do you still not see? You were supposed to help yourself find your own true love. And you have. Now, forgive him, do. We have only a few more hours until the end of Saint Valentine's Day."

"But . . . but I was to use my knowledge of men for someone *else*, not me."

West chuckled. "You have been upon intimate terms with almost every political figure in England, Pandora. I have no doubt you could help Antonio excessively in that direction."

"Here, now," the doctor objected. "That sounds like treason to me."

"Bah!" Pandora waved her hand, though the slightest smile twitched at her lips.

"Your dream was right," Jacklyn persisted. "You only read the signs wrong."

"Sh! Sh! I must have silence." Pandora declared. Jacklyn clamped her mouth shut. Everyone watched with bated breath. She turned solemn eyes upon Antonio. "I ask you to marry me, Antonio. You will, yes? Or I shall die."

"Caschi il mondo. My darling, I will marry you. That would be a dream come true!"

"Miss Pandora!" Betty entered at that moment. Her eyes widened as she took in the scene of Pandora on the floor, embracing Antonio. "Cor, you must stop that, Miss Pandora. I can understand you wanting ter have one last . . . er, well, you know what . . . but the bishop is here. He says he will hear your confession and try to save your soul, but he won't be coming up to your boudoir."

Jacklyn giggled. West howled with laughter. Then he choked to a halt. He clasped Jacklyn's shoulder. "Confound it, forget the confessions. We can apply to him for a special license. And Pandora and Antonio need one, too."

"Cor." Betty clasped her hands together. "Can Horace and me ask fer one, too?"

* * *

The bishop closed his eyes, burrowing into his feather tick mattress. What a strange night. He hiccuped. Never would he tell another living soul the story.

He had been called to hear the deathbed confessions of the famous courtesan Pandora Sabatini. Indeed, *that* would have been a feather in his cap. Instead, when he arrived, he found a house full of bedlamites lying in wait for him.

Miss Sabatini, dressed most scandalously, had pounced upon him with far too much spirit for a dying woman about to be given her last rites. Instead she had begged of him to give her a special license to marry the Italian ambassador. Faith! That would clearly rock the political world. As for what the Vatican would say, the bishop didn't wish to consider.

Then Westbrook Lockyear, the Earl of Hart, had begged a special license to marry a Miss Armstrong. The bishop was kept informed of everyone in the *ton*. Miss Armstrong was clearly a nobody. Lord Hart had vowed she was a baronet's daughter, as if that were a great thing. How in good conscience, could he have given them a special license?

He cringed. None of this could bode well for his career. Worse, next the serving maid and butler of the household had begged for a special license, as well. They had acted as if it were reasonable for those of the common order to demand one from a bishop. The maid had kept blathering something about the Gunning sisters.

The bishop shook his head as he drifted into sleep. Had he actually permitted them to lure him into dining with them? He wouldn't have accepted, but the Regent's physician, Sir Merton, had, and he did not wish to appear churlish. Also, he didn't want the doctor telling any tales out of school, so to speak.

It was most extraordinary. The doctor had actually appeared to enjoy himself. He had quizzed Miss Sabatini about her illness, finally declaring she had naught more wrong than a vexing cold in the chest—the doctor had leered rather lasciviously at that—and an injured back. Imagine, a bishop called from Mass for nothing more than a cold!

And the meal had been ghastly. Who but a courtesan would serve lobster, clotted cream, and champagne to a bishop? Worse, he had been forced to listen to three raving couples offer him the most fantastical reasons why they should marry. The words *fate, destiny* and *love* had abounded, though "love" surely had been spoken the most profusely.

You can save us all if you will permit us to marry. Think of it. Six souls lie in your hands.

Lord Hart, that disgraceful rakeshame, had actually said that to him, b'gad. Only a heathen would have sought to barter like that with a bishop. Just what did he think he was about?

Suddenly a woman appeared in front of him. Well, not a woman. She possessed a forked tail, talons, carried a pitchfork, and wore bright red satin. She glared at him. "Ah, bloody hell, not again. I hate these here appearances."

"Who are you?" the bishop started up. He opened his eyes from sleep. Still she remained standing at the foot of his bed.

She rolled her eyes. "I'm the devil, dolt. And don't argue. I'm not in the mood. Now you'd best listen close like, 'cause I'm a busy woman, don't yer know? I . . ." Lightning, white blue, shot through the room. The devil jumped. "All right." She sat down at the foot of the bed, swinging a shapely talon. "You see, bish', there's this matter about you giving those poor souls special licenses and letting them marry. I've got to tell you, if you don't give the licenses to them, you'll be coming my way."

The bishop shook his head in suspicion. "Why are you t-telling me this?"

" 'Cause I'm a gambling woman, I am." The devil smiled. "It's your choice, and I'd like to discuss it with you,, you see . . ."

The bishop cried out and pulled the sheets up over his head. He was not a gambling man. He would marry those three couples off tomorrow posthaste. A command from the Pope himself wouldn't deter him. The devil was a woman, and he'd not take a chance with his fate, not even one small jot.

His stomach roiled. Nor would he ever eat lobster, clotted cream, and champagne again!

The Merry Cupids

by
Debbie Raleigh

One

"Oh, look Mama, 'tis the Wicked Raven."

A wide-eyed maiden sighed as she leaned out of her carriage to gaze at the tall, well-dressed gentleman with black hair and midnight eyes. Her heart skipped a magical beat at the sight of his absurdly handsome countenance. What lady could possibly resist such temptation? It was little wonder he was the constant center of attention throughout the *ton*.

"Melinda, turn about," her mother scolded. "I will not have you joining every other sapskulled maiden in tossing yourself at the feet of a disreputable rake. Mr. Ravendell might possess a certain charm, but he has no interest in anything beyond his own pleasure, and he has broken more hearts throughout England than Byron. Indeed, it is said that the Duchess of Salsville went so far as to . . . well, let me just say he is well deserving of his name. Wicked. Quite, quite wicked."

Clearly unable to recall her own fanciful youth, the elder woman was unaware she had just ensured her naive daughter's fascination with the elusively dangerous gentleman, along with most of the maidens throughout London.

"Do you suppose he will be at Lord Wesly's tonight?" Melinda sighed.

Indifferent to the longing gaze that followed his well-molded form, currently encased in a pearl gray coat and breeches, Guy Ravendell entered a drab building. He was far from pleased at being called from his bed at such an ungodly hour, especially when his head was still thick from his revelry of the previous evening. But the note he had received had been impossible to ignore and, reluctantly, he had forced himself to rise and travel to the somber neighborhood.

Now he passed through the narrow hall and pushed open the far door. Stepping inside, Guy grimaced.

The office possessed little to recommend it. Like many other solicitors, Mr. Stanton possessed the unfortunate presumption that cramped, starkly functional surroundings induced a sense of confidence in his clients. But the deliberate severity and musty silence sharply reminded Guy of Ravendell Manor and his grim-faced grandfather, memories that did nothing to ease his current ill temper.

Bloody hell. He felt as if he were again a lad being called to his grandfather's library for yet another lecture. The old boy had been a great believer in drilling into his heir the importance of duty and responsibility.

But he was no longer a lad, he sternly reassured himself, and those days of gray unhappiness were in the past. Now his life was filled with all the pleasures he could discover.

With an effort, he conjured up his familiar nonchalance and turned toward the short, rotund gentleman who was busily stirring the fire he had laid in deference to the damp January weather. As if sensing he was no longer alone, the gentleman abruptly turned and regarded Guy with obvious relief.

"Ah, Mr. Ravendell." The solicitor bustled forward, running pudgy fingers over his thinning gray hair. "Thank you for coming so promptly."

"Your message did say it was most urgent that you speak with me," Guy reminded him in dry tones.

"Yes, well, I did feel it incumbent upon me to do something before it was too late." The lawyer's pudgy fingers dropped to nervously pat his starched cravat. Despite the chill in the air, a sprinkling of sweat beaded his forehead. "You must understand it is always difficult when dealing with elderly clients. You can never be quite certain if they are entirely . . . stable."

Guy lifted his brows in mild reproach. "Surely you are not referring to me, Mr. Stanton?"

The solicitor widened his eyes in alarm. "You? Certainly not, sir."

"Then I can have no notion why you would insist upon this meeting. I thankfully have responsibilities to no one but myself."

"It concerns Miss Windmere and Miss Millie Windmere."

"Ella and Millie?" Guy abruptly frowned. He had been honest when he had assured the solicitor he possessed no responsibilities. Since his grandfather's death, he had deliberately kept his life uncluttered. But while he was not the legal guardian of his two elderly aunts, he was genuinely attached to them. His visits to Claremont had been the only brightness in his secluded existence. "What is wrong?"

Mr. Stanton waved his hand toward a wooden chair. "Please, will you have a seat?"

Impatient, Guy lowered his long frame onto the uncomfortable chair and waited for the solicitor to settle his bulk behind the desk.

"Well?" he prompted.

The solicitor fiddled with the papers on the desk before at last coming to the point.

"I thought you should be made aware of the fact that last week I received a message from your aunts requesting a change in their wills."

Guy felt a flare of exasperation. This was why he had been called from his bed? A fool's errand.

"Is that all? I suppose the old pusses have decided to

dump the lot on some tedious charity. I assure you, Stanton, I have no expectations from that quarter. I possess a more than adequate income. Let them play the Ladies Bountiful if it pleases them."

The pudgy face became stern at Guy's flippant tone. "The will has been altered in favor of a Miss Stone."

Stone? Guy gave a startled blink. "Who?"

"A young woman currently residing with your aunts in Kent."

"A relative?"

"No. She was a distant neighbor."

"Ah, an old friend of the family."

Stanton grimaced with obvious distaste. "I doubt your aunts would have had the occasion to be upon intimate terms with Miss Stone."

Guy's momentary relief was rapidly fading. Although the solicitor was clearly a fussy type of gentleman with a pretentious belief in his own importance, his genuine concern was undeniable.

"Then why is she staying at the estate?"

"She was recently hired by Miss Windmere to become her companion."

"A companion? What the devil would Ella want with a companion?" Guy gave a shake of his head. Although Ella had passed fifty more years than she would admit, she had always been a fiercely independent woman. Guy had only to suggest that his aunts move to London so he could keep a firm eye on them for Ella to crisply reply she was perfectly capable of managing her own life. "She has Millie, not to mention an entire regiment of servants."

Mr. Stanton leaned forward. "My sentiments precisely, which is why I took the liberty of investigating Miss Stone."

Guy was unnerved by the solicitor's bland confession. His own life would hardly bear up well beneath the scrutiny of investigation. Still, he was not the one charming his way into the lives of two innocent old women. With an effort, he thrust aside his distaste at the devious tactics no doubt used by the solicitor.

"I presume this investigation has something to do with your summons?"

"I thought you should know that Miss Stone's connections are of the most unsavory nature." Mr. Stanton gave a superior sniff, his beefy lips thinning. "Her father was a known rake and gambler who managed to lose his entire inheritance before he was shot during a hunting accident last year. Her only aunt eloped with an actor years ago and disappeared to the colonies. And the cousin who recently inherited the family estate is reputed to be involved in smuggling."

"Good God." Guy was taken off guard in spite of himself. A gambler, a tart, and a smuggler. Hardly the type of connections that inspired confidence. "What of Miss Stone?"

The solicitor shrugged, obviously regretting the fact he did not possess an equally shocking vice for the young lady.

"Very little is known of the young lady. She seems to have lived a sheltered life at the estate, with few acquaintances. Certainly I cannot prove any criminal activities."

Guy furrowed his brow as he pondered the disturbing news.

"And you say Aunt Ella has mentioned this woman in her will?"

"Both Miss Windmere and Miss Millie Windmere have left everything they possess to her. When they die, God forbid, Miss Stone will be a very wealthy young lady. Quite an accomplishment for a penniless maiden with few prospects."

His ominous tone was not lost on Guy. Damn. The last thing he desired was a dreary trip to Kent in the midst of winter, especially when he had his attention set on a lovely opera dancer fresh to town. But he could not deny a sharp sense of unease gnawing the pit of his stomach.

How could he possibly allow this woman to remain in the home of his vulnerable aunts? The very fact that she had managed to bewitch or bully them into changing their wills was enough to prove she was a devious jade. No, he would obviously have to drive to Kent and settle the matter himself. He could only hope the delicious opera dancer would be unattached when he returned.

Rising to his feet, he squared his broad shoulders. "Perhaps it is time I paid my aunts a visit. It has been far too long since we were last together."

"An excellent notion, Mr. Ravendell."

Claremont was, not surprisingly, a reflection of its owners—a whimsical jumble of Grecian and Gothic architecture. It made few attempts at sophistication. There was, however, a romantic frivolity to the sprawling wings and the tumble of balustrades and terraces. The grounds possessed a charming combination of wood and lawn, with a formal walk that led to a large lake.

Guy, however, gave little heed to his surroundings as he dismounted from his carriage and vaulted up the wide staircase. Instead, his mind was occupied with discovering the swiftest means of ridding his aunts of Miss Stone so he could return to London, a desire made even more intense by the dismal weather.

Upon reaching the heavy oak doors, Guy was greeted by the ancient butler, who offered him a stiff bow.

"Mr. Ravendell, welcome."

"Thank you, Lowe. I wish to see Aunt Ella."

"Certainly, sir."

Turning about, the silver-haired butler led the way through the vaulted corridor to a back salon. Guy took care to ensure the Van Dyck still hung over a pier table and that the rare Grecian vase was still in its shallow alcove. Everything appeared intact, he acknowledged with relief.

Upon entering the crimson room with its ebony lacquer furnishings and Chinese pottery, Guy discovered his two aunts seated beside a comfortable fire.

As always, the two elderly ladies were elegantly attired, their gray hair pulled atop their heads. But while Millie had grown progressively plump over the years, with a tendency to drift in and out of her own world, Ella remained unfashionably thin, with a shrewd intelligence that could at times be unnerving.

At the moment, both were placidly stitching on bits of linen, but at his entrance, they glanced upward.

"Guy," Millie chirped. She smiled in pleasure. "Ella, just look who has come to visit. It is Guy."

Ella set aside her stitching with an expression of mild surprise. "Yes, so I see. What an unexpected pleasure."

Guy offered a practiced leg. Straightening, he smiled with boyish charm. "Ella, Millie. You are even more beautiful than the last occasion we met."

Ella regarded him with dry amusement. "Always the scoundrel, Guy."

"Oh, I like scoundrels," Millie sighed, leaning forward to regard Guy with soft brown eyes. "Tell me, Guy, is it true you seduced the Duchess of . . ."

"Millie," Ella sternly interrupted before turning to her amused nephew. "What brings you to Kent?"

"Perhaps I simply wished to visit my two favorite aunts."

"In the midst of winter?" Ella demanded. "I find that difficult to accept."

Millie nodded. "You hate the country. You have always hated the country."

Ella's gaze narrowed. "What is it, Guy?"

Realizing that these two women knew him far too well,

Guy gave a rueful smile. He might as well come to the point. "I came because I was concerned for you."

"Concerned?" Ella gave a tinkling laugh. "Why ever for?"

"Your solicitor, Mr. Stanton, contacted me last week and claimed you have hired a companion."

A silent, rather queer glance was exchanged between the two sisters before Ella favored him with a guarded expression.

"How very odd. Why would he contact you?"

"Because he has discovered that this companion possesses several very unsavory connections." Guy paused for dramatic emphasis. "Perhaps even criminal connections."

Expecting dismay, even horrified disbelief, Guy was caught off guard when Ella gave another laugh.

"You foolish boy. I am well aware of Bianca's connections."

"Indeed? Then you should realize she is thoroughly unsuitable to be your companion."

"Ridiculous," Ella countered. "Bianca is a delightful child."

"Oh, yes, quite delightful," Millie added.

"Most villains are delightful until they decide the best means to take advantage of you," he pointed out.

"That is a horrid thing to say, Guy," Ella chastised.

"Horrid, but true."

"You know nothing of Bianca."

"I know all I need to know."

"And what is that?"

"That her father was a gambler and her cousin a known smuggler. That isn't even to mention an aunt who disappeared with a common actor. She is clearly unsuitable to be in this house."

A short, brittle silence fell at his words.

"That is enough," Ella at last said. "I will not hear

another word against the dear girl." Her expression was unrelenting.

Guy felt a twinge of irritation. For goodness sakes! He had abandoned his numerous entertainments in London, traveled through the detestable weather, and ruined a perfectly good pair of Hessians in the mud, all to warn his aunts of their danger. But rather than gratitude, both were eyeing him with growing disapproval.

"My only concern is for you and Millie."

"There is no need to be concerned."

"No, indeed." Millie gave a loud sniff. "You are being most unkind, Guy."

"What is unkind in speaking the truth?" Guy demanded in exasperation. "This supposed lady comes from a family that is clearly untrustworthy. The chit is quite likely to . . ."

"Guy."

Guy frowned at the sharp insistence in Ella's tone. Both women had turned to glance toward the connecting door. He slowly shifted to view the tiny maiden with a halo of golden curls and wide emerald eyes who was regarding him with icy distaste.

"Please continue, Mr. Ravendell. Likely to what?"

Two

Bianca had never intended to eavesdrop. She had been on the point of entering the room when she had overheard her name and realized the beastly man was attempting to convince Ella and Millie she was some devious charlatan.

Now she trembled with fury. How dare he presume to judge her? She had not been the one to recklessly gamble away her inheritance or to risk scandal by smuggling French brandy. Indeed, all she had ever done was attempt to keep the family estate from tumbling into ruins—until her cousin had abruptly decided he wished to set up residence in the country and demanded she vacate at once.

"Oh, Bianca, please come in." Ella interrupted her dark thoughts. "Do you not look lovely this morning?"

"Quite lovely," Millie added, her gaze drifting over the simple lavender gown that had been altered to fit Bianca's small frame.

Bianca hesitated. Reluctantly she stepped further into the room. For a moment she refused to glance toward the gentleman who had so sharply wounded her pride, but a sudden determination not to give him the satisfaction of knowing he had struck a nerve made her slowly turn her head to meet his dark gaze.

Her heart halted.

If life were fair, he would be a decrepit old rogue with a large paunch and yellow teeth. He should at least possess a pair of horns and a tail.

Instead he was ... perfect. From his glossy raven hair to his midnight eyes and sinfully handsome features, he was every inch the legendary Wicked Raven.

Against her will, Bianca felt a tingle race down her spine as that disturbing gaze swept over her. She felt as if every fiber of her being was seared by that piercing scrutiny.

"Bianca, may I introduce our nephew, Mr. Ravendell?" Ella absurdly made the introduction as if unaware of the sizzling tension filling the air. "Guy, this is Miss Stone, my companion."

Guy gave a stiff nod of his head, his expression unreadable. "Miss Stone."

"Mr. Ravendell," she grudgingly muttered before turning back to Ella. "Perhaps it would be best if I return later."

"Do not be silly, Bianca," Ella stated in firm tones. "You must not mind Guy. He has always been frightfully overprotective of Millie and me."

Bianca remained blatantly unimpressed. "Indeed?"

"Yes," Guy intruded without a trace of apology. "It is shocking how easy it is to take advantage of two trusting and rather naive ladies."

Bianca's emerald eyes glittered with a dangerous light as she whirled to confront him.

"And you think I am here to take advantage of them?"

He shrugged. "That is what I have come to discover."

"Tell me, Mr. Ravendell, are you always so suspicious of others, or is it simply me and my"—her mouth twisted—"unsavory connections?"

"I would hardly be a dutiful nephew to ignore the unfortunate gossip that has reached my ears."

Why, the rotten hypocrite.

"Dutiful? You?" She gave a sharp laugh. "Fah."

A raven brow arched upward. "Do you find that amusing, Miss Stone?"

"I find it absurd, Mr. Ravendell," Bianca readily retorted, momentarily forgetting the two ladies regarding the stormy encounter with avid attention. "I have been at Claremont for six months. In all that time, you have never visited nor even corresponded with your aunts. Perhaps if you were more dutiful, they would have no need of a companion."

Color bloomed beneath his prominent cheekbones. "My relationship with my aunts is none of your concern," he gritted.

"And any unfortunate gossip surrounding my family is none of your concern, Mr. Ravendell. I would never harm anyone, especially not two of the dearest ladies it has been my pleasure to know."

His expression hardened. "I would find your plea excessively more believable, Miss Stone, if you had not managed to convince Ella and Millie to change their wills in your favor."

Bianca took a sharp step backward at the ugly accusation. "What?"

He regarded her with a hint of impatience. "Do you wish me to believe you were not aware of your extraordinary stroke of fortune?"

"Certainly not," she denied, slowly turning to the women on the couch. This had to be some horrible misunderstanding. "Ella?"

The elder woman smiled with a strange satisfaction. "I firmly refuse to discuss such a tedious subject before tea."

"But . . ."

"Here is Mrs. Cadbury with the tray now." Ella waved the housekeeper toward a low table. "Bianca, will you pour?"

Rising early the next morning, Bianca made her way to the greenhouse to choose the flowers for the front salon.

It was a task she enjoyed. More importantly, it led her far from the main hall and Mr. Guy Ravendell.

Really, the gentleman was unbearable. It had taken every scrap of willpower she possessed to maintain a brittle composure through tea and later dinner. Only her genuine attachment to Ella and Millie had allowed her to suppress her ready temper. She would far have preferred to toss every available object at his arrogant head.

How dare he accuse her of such dreadful behavior? Ella had come to her as she had prepared to leave her family estate and insisted Bianca consider coming to Claremont to become her companion. Indeed, Bianca had every intention of declining the invitation until her already unpredictable life had taken a dramatic turn for the worse.

Desperation had forced her into her current position. Certainly she had never desired or even dreamed the two elder ladies would change their wills in such a fashion.

It was absurd. Thoroughly absurd.

Placing the last of the pale pink roses in her basket, Bianca reluctantly prepared to return to the main house. She could not hide here all morning, she firmly told herself, no matter how tempting the thought.

Still distracted by her dark thoughts, Bianca turned about only to give a startled cry as she spotted Guy Ravendell's large, masculine form standing just a few feet away. The basket slipped to the flagstone path, spilling out the roses.

"Oh . . ."

His dark eyes swept over her pale features with unnerving intensity. "I am sorry. Did I frighten you?"

Oddly disturbed by his presence, Bianca sank to her knees to retrieve the maltreated blooms. She was simply unaccustomed to being loomed over by a decidedly large gentleman, she reassured herself. The fact that he was astonishingly handsome had nothing to do with the tiny tingles in the pit of her stomach. "Not at all."

Without warning, he knelt beside her. "Here, allow me."

"No, thank you." She hastily attempted to gather the remaining roses, only to stab her finger with a sharp thorn. "Oh!"

"Let me see," he commanded, his slender fingers clasping her hand so he could view the tiny prick of blood staining her white skin.

The shock of his warm skin in such intimate contact with her own made Bianca instinctively attempt to pull away. The tingles became flutters.

"For goodness sake, hold still." He easily halted her struggles and wrapped a crisp white handkerchief about her wounded finger.

He was so close she could see the dark hint of gold in his eyes and smell the clean scent of his skin.

"That is not necessary." Her voice was oddly breathless, and she chastised herself for being a fool. This gentleman might be the most magnificent male she had ever encountered, but he was also the ill-mannered cad who had branded her a common thief, if not worse.

"I am simply attempting to be of assistance," he pointed out with exaggerated patience.

"I do not need your assistance, Mr. Ravendell."

"What if I tell you I came here to apologize, Miss Stone?"

She stilled, stabbing him with a glittering gaze. "Apologize for what, Mr. Ravendell? For insulting my family? Or for presuming I would willingly harm Ella and Millie?"

"Both," he promptly replied, seeming to forget he still held her hand. "I possessed no right to make accusations without even meeting you."

She refused to be swayed by his smooth words—the Wicked Raven at his most charming. "No, you did not."

"I assure you only my concern for my aunts led me to such rash assumptions."

"And now?"

He gave a faint shrug. "Now I am willing to give you the benefit of the doubt."

Her expression hardened as she firmly pulled her hand free. She could not concentrate when those odd tremors were traveling through her body.

"Meaning you were unable to convince your aunts I am a villainous blackguard determined to steal their fortune," she concluded, well aware he was as convinced as ever of her evil intents.

"Meaning that my aunts convinced me I was overly hasty," he corrected, his impatience mounting. "They seem to believe you are a paragon of virtue. We will soon determine the truth."

Her eyes widened with dismay. This was a turn of events she had not expected. "You are staying?"

"Of course." His gaze probed deep into her own, as if searching for her secret—a secret she had every intention of keeping hidden. "Does that bother you?"

"Not at all." With an effort she controlled her absurd flare of fear and rose to her feet. She had no reason to fear this man. No reason whatsoever. "I am simply surprised."

He slowly rose to his own feet, standing far too close for comfort. "Surprised?"

Her chin unconsciously tilted to a defiant angle. "Surely you will find being confined in the country a tedious bore?"

He lifted his brows as if startled by her audacity at questioning his own private affairs. Clearly he felt free to thrust his nose into her life, but did not appreciate being treated in kind. "Why should you presume I will be bored?"

"My family is not alone in being the center of gossip, Mr. Ravendell," she informed him in clipped tones.

"And what gossip have you heard, Miss Stone?"

She hesitated a moment before shrugging her shoulders. If he wished to know, why should she hold her tongue? "There are few in Kent who have not been entertained in excruciating detail with your madcap dares, your outrageous wagers at the faro table, and your preference for ladies of dubious reputation."

"Is that so?"

"Yes." She met his glittering gaze squarely. "Indeed, I cannot conceive how you dare condemn my relatives when you so eagerly follow in their footsteps." Having relieved herself of the sense of injustice that had haunted her since she had first overheard his accusations, Bianca gave a small toss of her head. Ignoring his narrowed gaze, she offered him a stiff smile. "Now you must excuse me. I promised Ella I would read her the paper."

Three

Several days later, Guy slowly made his way down the long flight of stairs. It was far earlier than he was accustomed to rising, but he discovered himself oddly restless.

And it was entirely Miss Stone's fault, he thought with wry exasperation. How the devil was he supposed to sleep when his dreams were haunted by wide emerald eyes and unruly golden curls?

It was all supposed to be so simple, he reminded himself as he moved through the empty rooms. He was to arrive at Claremont, inform his aunts of their imminent danger, and sweep back to London, satisfied with having performed his duty. But everything had gone abominably wrong.

First he discovered that, far from being innocent victims, his aunts had been well aware of Miss Stone's sordid connections. It had even been at their urging that she had come into their home at all.

And then Miss Stone had overheard his accusations and managed to put him on the defensive by forcing him to admit he had nothing more substantial than gossip and innuendo to back up his suspicions.

Even now, he could recall the wounded darkness of her eyes and vulnerable quiver of her lips, a memory that brought a stab of remorse in its wake.

Still, he was not a gullible, trusting sort of chap. He had known more than one lady who could cry on cue, and only a greenhorn was not aware that the face of an angel could easily hide the heart of a cutpurse. He was far from convinced Miss Stone was as innocent as she pretended to be.

Now he was effectively trapped in Kent, unable to leave until he uncovered the mystery of Bianca Stone.

Not an easy task, he acknowledged. She was a complex mixture of defiance and maidenly confusion, of cool intelligence and gentle kindness, of sudden laughter and hidden pain—a woman he found himself watching with growing fascination.

Shaking his head at his odd behavior, Guy moved through the library and into the front hall. He halted as he caught sight of the well-rounded housekeeper busily arranging flowers on a satinwood table inlaid with ivory.

"Good morning, Mrs. Cadbury."

"Good morning, sir." The housekeeper straightened and smiled cheerfully. "Delightful day."

"Yes, indeed," Guy agreed, although he had paid scant attention to the pale sunshine warming the wintry countryside. His mind was centered on a golden-haired scrap of a girl. "Have you seen Miss Stone?"

"No, sir. It is Wednesday. She always has the day out."

Day out, eh? Favoring her with his most charming smile, Guy casually leaned against the oak paneling. "I suppose she goes to visit her cousin?"

"On that I couldn't say, sir, although I would be proper surprised if that were the case." The housekeeper regarded him with growing curiosity. "Is there anything amiss, sir?"

"I was simply curious as to how Miss Stone was settling in," he hastily improvised. "It can be dreadfully dull for a young maiden in the country."

The housekeeper shrugged. "Miss Stone does not seem to mind. She is from these parts, you know."

"So my aunt tells me. Do you know her family?"

"Fair lot of scullions if you ask me," the woman promptly replied.

Guy gave a startled blink. "Indeed?"

Mrs. Cadbury nodded her head vigorously. "Her father came from a good enough family, but after Mrs. Stone died he was never the same. Took to drinking and gambling and never gave thought to the poor lass he left at home. Miss Stone had to raise herself with no one but the odd servant or two."

It was much the same tale his aunts had revealed. Guy discovered himself wondering what sort of gentleman would abandon his child in such a manner. "Hardly the environment for a decent lady."

As if sensing a hint of criticism in his tone, the housekeeper gave a faint sniff. "Mayhap not, but you'll not find a finer lady than Miss Stone. We were all quite disappointed when that dastardly cousin returned from the Continent and demanded she leave. If it had not been for Miss Stone, he wouldn't have had an estate to come home to—and not even so much as a thank you for her troubles."

"A pity." Guy was swiftly beginning to realize the staff was as blindly loyal to Bianca as his aunts were. Had they all been taken in by a clever charlatan? Or was she indeed such a remarkable young lady? "At least she was fortunate to have my aunt to depend upon. It must have been a great relief to come to Claremont."

Mrs. Cadbury surprisingly gave a sharp shake of her head. "Oh, no, sir. Miss Ella went to ask Miss Stone to come to Claremont, but Miss Stone said she preferred to find a small cottage on her own. Then she suddenly changed her mind and decided she would come. It has been a right pleasure to have her here."

"Yes, so I am beginning to realize," Guy drawled, his smile wry. "Thank you, Mrs. Cadbury."

Resigned to the fact Miss Stone had managed to bewitch the entire household, Guy turned and made his way out the front entrance. He would discover nothing from Mrs. Cadbury beyond the fact Miss Stone appeared to be a virtual angel.

Of course, he reminded himself as he crossed the front courtyard and headed toward the stables, he had discovered that Miss Stone had originally declined Ella's invitation. Had she simply had an honest change of heart? Or had Ella's insistence made her realize she could easily take advantage of the two elderly women?

More questions with no answers. What he needed was a few hours away from Claremont and Miss Stone to clear his tangled thoughts.

With a determined step, he completed his trek to the stables. A ride to the nearby village was what he needed for a well-deserved distraction.

It was late afternoon when he returned to the estate, yet he found himself avoiding the house and instead circling to the back gardens. His visit to the village had done nothing to ease his building restlessness. Perhaps a vigorous walk would be more effective.

He wandered along the pathways with little thought to his destination. Then the sound of a sweetly familiar voice made him glance toward a nearby meadow where Miss Stone was quietly speaking with a young, well-dressed farmer. Narrowing his gaze, Guy carefully regarded the intimate manner with which the unknown gentleman held Miss Stone's arm and how she leaned toward him to speak in low tones. At last they halted and, after a brief conversation, the farmer turned to make his way back across the meadow.

When Miss Stone neared the copse of trees he was effectively hidden behind, Guy abruptly stepped onto the path.

"Ah, Miss Stone." He offered a small bow, careful to observe the startled dismay that rippled over her delicate features before she hastily regained her composure.

"Mr. Ravendell."

"A lovely day for a walk."

"Yes."

He smiled with seeming innocence. "May I join you?"

She paused as if she longed to refuse his request, then gave a resigned shrug. "If you wish."

Together they moved up the path, Miss Stone taking special care to keep as much space as possible between them.

"Was the gentleman an acquaintance of yours?" he asked in a casual manner.

"I am acquainted with most of the people in this neighborhood."

Her tone gave nothing away, but Guy did not miss the tension in her profile. "Did you spend the day together?"

She abruptly stabbed him with a glittering gaze. "This is my day out, Mr. Ravendell. I do not have to account for my whereabouts to you or anyone else."

"I was simply attempting to be polite, Miss Stone."

Her lips thinned. "That I very much doubt, Mr. Ravendell."

He couldn't prevent a sudden chuckle. Damn, but the chit had spirit. "All right, Miss Stone. I must admit I was curious, but, as you so justly pointed out, you are free to do as you wish today." He sternly thrust aside his odd annoyance at seeing Miss Stone with the unknown gentleman and instead favored her with an enticing grin. "Might I impose upon you to spend at least a portion of your day walking with me?"

Her expression became wary. "Why?"

"I wish to become better acquainted," he smoothly retorted. "You accused me of having no right to judge you without even knowing you. I wish to satisfy myself that you are to be trusted with my aunts."

The conflict was etched on her delicate countenance as

she battled the urge to damn him to the devil. "If you insist."

His smile widened as he bravely risked life and limb and grasped her arm to lead her down a nearly overgrown path. "This way."

She stiffened at his familiar manner, but merely punished him with a forbidding frown. "Where are we going?"

"Do not fear, Miss Stone. You are perfectly safe, despite my tarnished reputation."

"I am not afraid. I just have never been this way before."

Guy held aside the overgrown limbs, caught off guard by the vivid memories of his youth that rose to mind. "This used to be my favorite path when I was but a lad."

She glanced up in surprise. "Did you spend much time here?"

"Unfortunately, no. My grandfather only allowed me to visit a fortnight during the summer. But they were magical days." His expression unconsciously softened. It had been years since he had allowed himself to recall those carefree days. "I would run through these woods like a savage, yelling at the top of my voice, and come home covered in muck and with my short pants invariably torn. But Ella and Millie never complained. They seemed to realize a boy needs to be a boy on occasion—a fact that never seemed to occur to my grandfather."

"He did not approve of your behaving as a boy?"

Guy grimaced. "My grandfather was a great believer in discipline of the mind and body. As his heir, I was expected to behave in a manner befitting my station."

Quite unexpectedly Miss Stone's gaze lost a hint of its frost. "That must have been very difficult."

"Not many would think so. I was, after all, surrounded by luxury and given the very best tutors."

"But you were lonely."

Startled by her insight, Guy regarded her closely. He was unaccustomed to anyone seeing beyond his image as the Wicked Raven. "Are you always so perceptive?"

A hint of color flooded her cheeks as if she regretted her words. "I simply know what it is like to grow up too swiftly."

Stopping in a small clearing, Guy gazed down at the tiny face that was becoming strangely familiar. "Yes," he said softly, "I suppose you do."

Bianca abruptly turned away, as if disturbed by his piercing regard. "What is this?" She pointed toward the battered trunk nearly hidden in the tall grass.

He gave a wry smile at her obvious unease. "My pirate treasure."

She wrinkled her thin nose. "Treasure?"

"It seemed so at the time."

He moved forward to kneel next to the trunk. Lifting the lid, he revealed a tumble of old clothing, used candles, bits of rope and sticks and, on the top, a delicate gold locket. With his slender fingers, Guy carefully plucked the necklace out of the rubbish.

"That is nice," Bianca murmured.

"My greatest treasure."

"From an admirer?"

"My mother."

His answer appeared to disconcert her. "Oh."

Guy studied the locket that glinted in the pale sunlight. "After my parents died, my grandfather had their belongings packed away. This was all I had left of my mother as a child."

"I am sorry."

Realizing he was revealing more than he'd intended, he gave a small shrug. "Don't be." He gently returned the locket to the trunk and instead grasped a battered stick. "Ah . . . my faithful sword."

She gave a small blink. "Sword? That is no sword."

"It is apparent, madam, that you are no pirate," he protested as he rose to his feet and held the stick aloft. "I have battled any number of oak trees, lilacs, and the ever devious rosebush with this sword."

"Quite the swashbuckler," she said in dry tones.

"Indeed." Lowering the stick he searched her emerald eyes. "And now, Miss Stone, it is your turn."

"Turn? What do you mean?"

"We are to become better acquainted, are we not? I wish you to tell me of your own childhood."

Four

Bianca took an abrupt step backward as his dark gaze probed her eyes. What was the matter with her?

She did not want to think of Guy as a lonely, vulnerable child—a child who, like herself, had no one to depend upon but himself. After all, he was the despicable cad who was determined to prove she was not to be trusted.

Had he not devoted the past week to shadowing her every movement as if he feared she might attempt to do away with his aunts beneath his very nose? And had he not been skulking in the gardens waiting for her return this afternoon? Her heart had nearly stopped when she realized he had spotted her with Bob Carter.

Still, it was far easier to dislike him when he was playing the role of the Wicked Raven. The Guy Ravendell she had glimpsed with his aunts and occasionally encountered when he forgot she was the enemy was far too enticing for her peace of mind.

Turning away, she determinedly conjured up a calm demeanor. "There is not much to tell."

Not surprisingly, Guy did not accept her vague dismissal. "Were you close to your father?"

"I barely knew my father." Bianca felt a familiar stab of regret. "He far preferred London to the country, and only visited when the moneylenders were pressing him for payment."

His dark head tilted to one side. "So you were left on your own?"

"I had Nurse," she retorted, unwilling to confess just how alone she had felt in the empty manor house. "She ensured I was tutored when I was young and taught me how to manage the estate."

"Did you not have any relatives who could have taken you in?"

An unconscious grimace rippled over her pale countenance. "Papa possessed the habit of expecting friends and relatives to support his extravagant lifestyle. They eventually cut him out of their lives."

Surprisingly, a dark frown of disapproval marred Guy's wide brow. "Your father should at least have ensured you had a proper chaperon," he retorted.

Bianca felt oddly vulnerable beneath his dark gaze. Ridiculous, of course. Mr. Ravendell was in no position to judge her father. Did he not live his own life for pleasure with no thought to others? But somehow the hint of reproach in his tone touched wounds that had never fully healed.

She averted her gaze from those all-too-knowing black eyes. "I was content."

He made a sound deep in his throat. "You were abandoned in the midst of the country."

"I preferred my independence."

He moved to stand next to her, close enough that the sleeve of his greatcoat brushed her arm. "Even though it meant you were not given a proper introduction to society?"

"I have no interest in society," she promptly denied. It was true. On the few occasions when her father had entertained, she had found the guests to be frivolous fools with more interest in the turn of a card than a sensible conversation. Even the handful of assemblies she had attended had done little more than reinforce her opinion she had little in common with the far more elegant young maidens.

"You are remarkably forgiving."

"I am sensible," she denied. "My father was a weak man with no interest in rearing children. There is no use wishing he had been otherwise."

Forgetting herself, Bianca glanced up, only to lose herself in the midnight of his eyes. For several long moments, neither spoke. Then Guy slowly nodded his head. "Yes," he breathed softly.

A sudden, sharp heat speared through her body and Bianca caught her breath. What was occurring? She had always prided herself on being a calm, utterly rational creature. She did not indulge in nervous spasms or panic at the least hint of difficulty. But since encountering Mr. Ravendell, her emotions refused to behave. She seemed to tumble between anger, bewilderment, and a strange tingling excitement at the blink of an eye. All in all, it was most discomforting.

"We should be returning," she muttered, taking a hasty step backward. Unfortunately, her boot caught on a half-buried rock and she tumbled backward.

With startling speed, Guy reached out to wrap a steadying arm about her waist. "Careful."

"Oh . . ." Bianca had never been so close to a gentleman. She shivered at the feel of the strong muscles of his arm pressed into her lower back.

"Thank you."

Expecting him to pull away as she regained her balance, Bianca glanced up to discover Guy regarding her with an odd fascination.

"What amazing eyes you possess, Miss Stone," he said in low tones. "As clear and intriguing as a kitten's."

The husky edge to his voice only increased the shivers racing through her body, and Bianca struggled for her wretchedly elusive composure. "Please release me, Mr. Ravendell."

A small smile curved his firm lips. "You are trembling. Do I frighten you?"

"You make me angry," Bianca insisted, although the delicious tremors racing through her blood were not anger.

His dark eyes narrowed as he lifted his hand to gently stroke the soft skin of her cheek. "Such a strange combination. Defiance, mystery, and such seeming innocence. I am uncertain whether to bundle you into the nearest carriage or . . ."

Lost in the sensations his fingers were creating, Bianca was unprepared as Guy swooped his head downward to claim her lips with shocking intimacy. Instinctively she stiffened. She was no gullible miss to be seduced by the first handsome gentleman to kiss her, even if he was a master of seduction.

But even as the thought rose to her mind, it was lost beneath the fierce tide of pleasure rushing through her body.

Hands that had risen to push him away instead grasped at his coat as her knees became oddly weak. His lips gently parted her own and a deep sound of satisfaction rumbled in his throat.

Who would have thought a kiss could be so . . . delightful? she wondered fuzzily. Her entire body felt alive with tingles of captivating pleasure.

"Mmm . . ." Guy's mouth reluctantly untangled from her clinging lips. "You taste of spring, Miss Stone," he murmured in husky tones, "sweet and tenderly enticing."

With an absurd amount of difficulty, Bianca lifted her lids to encounter his shimmering black gaze, so dark she could lose herself in the velvet softness. "Oh."

At her tiny exclamation of bewilderment Guy chuckled with rich amusement. "Oh?"

The sudden realization that Guy was in no way as disturbed as she brought Bianca sharply to her senses.

Fool, she chastised herself. Of course he was not disturbed. He had shared such kisses with dozens, perhaps hundreds, of gullible misses. While she . . . she had melted in his arms like the veriest schoolgirl.

Angered as much by her appalling weakness as by his forward behavior, Bianca abruptly jerked out of his grasp.

"Mr. Ravendell, please save your rather tawdry charms for ladies who appreciate being seduced by the Wicked Raven," she retorted in uneven tones, all too aware of the color stinging her cheeks. "Just because I have been forced to take a position does not mean I will endure being taken advantage of."

Guy's dark eyes narrowed at her sudden attack. "Tell me, Miss Stone, are you angry because I kissed you—or because you so evidently enjoyed yourself?"

"Why, you . . ."

"Yes, Miss Stone?"

She glared at him for a long moment. Then, tossing her head, she turned on her heel and marched back up the narrow path. What could she possibly say? That she hadn't enjoyed his kiss? They both knew it would be a lie. There was nothing to do but make as graceful a retreat as possible under the circumstances.

Uncaring of whether Mr. Ravendell was following or not, Bianca made her way to the garden, fully intending to use the servants' entrance to make her way to her room and lock herself in. But with the same ill fortune that had plagued her the entire day, she was a mere step from the door when Miss Windmere abruptly rounded the corner.

"Ah, Bianca, did you have a nice day?"

Nice?

Aggravating, unnerving and earth-shattering, but definitely not nice.

"It was delightful until I encountered Mr. Ravendell," she muttered before she could halt the words.

"Guy?" Ella offered a sympathetic smile. "What has that naughty boy done now?"

"He . . . he is an arrogant, insufferable toad." After making her less-than-tactful pronouncement, she pulled open the door and swept inside.

As she watched Bianca's stormy retreat, Ella's smile widened with a distinct hint of satisfaction. "Yes, I do believe things are progressing nicely."

Five

Ignoring the brooding clouds and sharp breeze, Bianca slipped into the garden. She paid little heed to the realization that their guest had been left on his own in the library. For the moment she could not bear to face the Wicked Raven.

Would the gentleman never leave? She plopped onto a marble bench. For the past three days, she had struggled to maintain her composure—not an easy task when her every thought seemed haunted by the memory of Guy's branding kiss.

Bianca shivered and moaned softly. How could she have humiliated herself in such a fashion? She was no beetle-witted chit ripe for a bit of seduction, especially not with a man renowned as a hardened rake.

She could only presume the strain of the past few months had taken its toll on her staunch defenses. After all, the secret she harbored close to her heart was a heavy burden for any woman to bear on her own, and he might easily have caught her in a moment of weakness.

Unfortunately, her determination to absolve her absurd behavior did not explain her continued awareness of Mr. Ravendell.

He had only to walk into the room for her stomach to tangle into knots, had only to brush her arm for shocking tremors to race through her body. And even in the safety of her bed during the night, he managed to disturb her dreams.

Why, oh why, would he not return to London and leave her in peace?

Heaving an exasperated sigh, Bianca suddenly frowned as she heard a sound from above. With a smooth motion, she rose to her feet and moved toward the nearby tree. Peering into the branches, she soon spotted the source of the noise.

"Zeus, what are you doing?" she demanded, regarding the shivering kitten with stern disapproval. "Come down here at once."

In response, the tiny cat gave another pathetic cry. Bianca shook her head. She should leave the cat to its own devices. It had managed to climb the tree easily enough. It could just as easily find its way down.

But its piteous cry tugged at her soft heart. What if the kitten was genuinely stuck? Could she forgive herself if something terrible occurred?

Cursing her own stupidity, Bianca reached up to a nearby branch and carefully pulled herself upward. She winced as the sharp twigs tugged at the ribbon on the hem of her gown. Just a bit farther, she reassured herself. After balancing herself on a large branch, she inched her way toward the trembling kitten.

Unfortunately, her determination to retrieve the miniature feline made her unaware of the smaller branches that hung down. Not until her spencer was firmly caught upon a stray branch did she realize her danger.

"Blast," she muttered, struggling to reach the stick caught in the midst of her back.

Her efforts did nothing more than make her feet slip in a precarious fashion and the branch give a sudden sway. With a hiss of reproach, the kitten abruptly jumped to a nearby branch before scrambling easily down the tree.

"Traitor," she muttered, angrily wondering what the devil to do now.

The obvious answer was to call out until she attracted the attention of a servant. But the fear she might instead attract the attention of Guy made her hold her tongue. She could not possibly allow him to see her in this absurd predicament.

Still, she could not remain in the tree simply hoping that a servant might stroll past, she reluctantly conceded. Not only might it be hours before a servant entered the private garden, but she was becoming chilled.

On the point of swallowing her pride and calling for help, Bianca abruptly halted as she caught a glimpse of a tall, annoyingly handsome gentleman strolling along the pathway. She sucked in a sharp breath, her heart filling with dismay. Blast! Would her luck never improve?

For an absurd moment, she held herself perfectly still, as if hoping he might not notice a grown woman perched in a tree like an awkward bird, a hope swiftly doused as he glanced upward and came to a startled halt.

"Good God," he drawled, his gaze slowly roaming over her stiff frame and annoyed features. "What the deuce are you doing?"

Bianca could not prevent the heat from crawling beneath her pale skin. She discovered it was inordinately difficult to maintain a cool composure when lodged in a tree.

"I was attempting to rescue Zeus," she retorted in her most lofty tones.

One dark brow slowly rose. "Zeus?"

"Millie's kitten."

"Ah . . . and have you?"

"Have I what?"

"Rescued Zeus."

Her lips thinned. "He jumped down after I had climbed the tree."

He gave a wicked chuckle, strolling to stand directly beneath her. "Typical. No matter how innocent kittens might appear to be, they harbor a devious nature and are not to be trusted."

Bianca gritted her teeth, not missing his subtle reference to the fact he had once likened her to a kitten. Or that she was not to be trusted. Of course, he had also likened her to the spring, sweet and tenderly enticing, a traitorous voice whispered in the back of her mind. It was a voice she swiftly stifled. "I will keep that in mind on the next occasion."

"Are you coming down?"

"In time." She regarded him in a pointed manner. "Please do not let me keep you."

His expression was deceptively mild. "You are not keeping me. Indeed, I am pleased to have a bit of company. Ella and Millie have decided to visit the vicar."

"I fear I am rather occupied this afternoon."

"A pity." He shrugged, moving to settle himself on a nearby bench. "I suppose I shall simply have to find some means of occupying myself."

Her eyes widened. "What are you doing?"

He stretched out his legs and crossed them at the ankle. "Enjoying the fine day."

"It is a ghastly day."

He peered at the ominous clouds. "Perhaps."

If it had not been so dangerous, she would have stomped her feet in exasperation. "Would you please go away?"

"Not until you admit you are stuck in that tree."

Bianca sucked in a sharp breath. "Why, you wretched beast! Just go away."

"And leave you trapped in this damp weather?"

She was unable to prevent her shiver. "What do you care?"

"With my current luck, you would no doubt die of consumption only to return from the netherworld as a sharp-tongued spirit to haunt me through all eternity," he mocked.

"Go away!"

Guy slowly rose to his feet, his expression wry. "Of all your numerous faults, Miss Stone, being a nitwit is not one of them."

She glared down at his finely carved countenance. "Why did it have to be you?"

An odd, almost rueful grimace twisted his features. "It is a question I have asked myself more times than I care to recall, Miss Stone." He walked to stand directly beneath her. "Please scoot to one side."

"Why?"

He heaved a long-suffering sigh. "I cannot very well help you from down here."

Blast her cursed luck. She had no doubt he intended to remain in the garden the entire day unless she gave in to his demands.

"Very well," she muttered, cautiously inching farther along the branch.

With annoying ease, Guy managed to pull himself onto the branch, rise to his feet, and inspect the back of her spencer.

"Hold still."

Bianca sucked in her breath, willing herself not to notice the heat of his body pressed close to her own and the sweet brush of his breath on the back of her neck. "Have you finished?"

"In a moment." His face pressed into her hair. "What is that scent?"

She trembled. "What?"

"I smell . . . honeysuckle."

"Mr. Ravendell, please. Just free me."

His head moved until his lips touched the tip of her ear.

A shock of pure pleasure raced through her body, making Bianca gasp.

"Do you think of our kiss, Miss Stone?" he asked softly.

Bianca closed her eyes, battling the traitorous sensations stirring deep within her. "Mr. Ravendell."

"I do," he continued. "I shut my eyes and I can still feel the softness of your lips and the way your body felt pressed close to mine. Indeed, the memory has haunted my dreams."

No. She could not allow this gentleman to realize how easily he could disturb her. If only she could move from the unnerving heat of his body. "I have told you to save such nonsense for your London flirts."

He gave a low chuckle. "Suppose I tell you my London flirts have never managed to thrust themselves upon my every thought the way an emerald-eyed shrew has managed to do?"

She could feel his lips brush against her ear, smell the faint scent of his soap. It was oddly intimate despite their strange predicament.

"I would tell you I am far too old to be swayed by such Banbury tales," she gritted. "Perhaps if you are searching for entertainment, you should visit the village. There might be one maiden dull-witted enough to succumb to such blatant clankers."

She had intended to wound him with her condemning words. Instead he gave a low laugh. "What a cynic you are, Miss Stone."

"Are you going to help me down or not?" she demanded.

"Wait . . ." His fingers pressed into the center of her back. After what seemed to be an eternity, her spencer was abruptly freed. She breathed a sigh of relief as he easily vaulted back down to the ground. Then he turned about and lifted his hands toward her. "Come along."

Bianca hesitated, having no desire to place herself in his arms once again. But the knowledge he would stand there until they both died of a chill made her thrust aside her alarm. It was best to have the ghastly encounter over and done with.

Holding herself perfectly rigid, she leaned forward until his strong hands encircled her waist. With surprising ease, he plucked her from the branch and swung her to the ground. All too aware of his lingering hands, she forced herself to meet his glittering gaze. "Thank you."

"I am always pleased to aid a damsel in distress." He smiled as he stepped closer. "And, as any gallant hero, I demand a small reward."

Her lips parted in protest at the same moment his dark head swooped downward. He claimed her mouth in a brief, searing kiss. Bianca moaned. Her hands lifted, whether to push him away or tug herself closer she was thankfully never to know, as he abruptly lifted his head to gaze down at her shocked countenance.

"Mr. Ravendell . . ." she breathed unsteadily.

He gave a rather self-derisive laugh. "Do us both a favor, Miss Stone, and stay out of trees."

With that parting shot, he turned on his heel and marched away.

Six

A decidedly restless Guy paced down the long hall. Although he was expected for tea in the front drawing room, he swiftly passed the closed doors without even slowing. Over the past few days, he had discovered more and more reasons to avoid his aunts.

No. He abruptly forced himself to be honest. He was not avoiding his aunts, but Miss Stone.

It was absurd. He was a gentleman who knew everything there was to know about the fairer sex. He knew how to charm them, how to make them melt in his arms, what gifts would please them. Most of all, he knew how to walk away before they managed to stake a claim on his emotions.

But somehow Bianca Stone made him feel as awkward and uncertain as the veriest greenhorn.

Bloody hell, he muttered beneath his breath, heading toward the secluded library.

He was supposed to be shadowing Miss Stone's every movement, watching her with his aunts and discreetly interviewing the neighbors to discover her hidden secrets.

And she did possess secrets, he had no doubt of that. He had seen her expression freeze when questioned about how she had spent her day away from Claremont and when he had casually demanded her plans for the future.

But rather than devoting himself to discovering the

truth, he spent his days avoiding her cold glances and his nights dreaming of her deceptively innocent kisses.

Cork-brained fool.

With an exasperated sigh, Guy shoved open the door to the library and stepped into the vast room. Although it was simply furnished with a mahogany desk and a handful of mahogany trelliswork chairs, Guy found a sense of peace among the leather-bound books. At least he would be assured of privacy with his brooding thoughts. Preparing to cross toward the blazing fire, he came to an abrupt halt as he belatedly noted the tiny woman curled up on the window seat.

He felt a prick of annoyance. Miss Stone was supposed to be with his aunts in the drawing room. He had come here to be free of her disturbing beauty and beguiling scent of honeysuckle.

Then his annoyance hardened to suspicion as she hastily tucked something beneath the pillow beside her.

Narrowing his gaze, he paced across the carpet to tower over her stiff frame. "Good afternoon, Miss Stone."

She eyed him warily. "Mr. Ravendell."

"Am I intruding?"

Faint color stole into her cheeks. "Not at all."

His gaze shifted to the heavy book lying upon the small table near her. "Were you reading?"

"I . . . yes."

His suspicions deepened. "What?"

"I beg your pardon?"

"What were you reading?"

She gave a vague shrug. "Nothing of importance."

Determined to discover the truth, Guy leaned forward. "May I join you?"

"No," she said hastily, even as he reached out to push the pillow aside.

The cushion tumbled to the floor, revealing a heavy sheet of paper with an unmistakable sketch of Claremont.

Guy caught his breath. He was not certain what he had expected. A diary? Love letters? A stash of stolen jewelry? Certainly not the delicate charcoal etching that captured the charming whimsy of the estate.

Lifting his gaze, he met her guarded expression. "What is this?"

For a moment he thought she might refuse to answer. Then she gave a sudden toss of her head. "Millie's birthday is drawing near, and I wished to give her a present. Since my income is limited, I thought she would enjoy this."

An odd pang flared through Guy's heart as he reached down to retrieve the drawing with exquisite care. He had misjudged this woman yet again. "This is beautiful. You are extraordinarily talented."

"My talent is passable at best," she argued.

"That is not true." His gaze lifted to study her pale features. "This could rival any number of works at the Royal Academy."

Embarrassment rippled over her countenance. "Absurd."

"Did you have an art instructor?" he inquired without thought.

She gave a sharp laugh. "My father rarely recalled I was at the estate. His interest certainly did not extend to providing me with art instructors."

That pang returned and an unconscious frown furrowed his brow. "He should have taken better care of you."

She blinked at his sudden growl.

Hardly surprising. He never seemed to know how to react to her. One moment he was suspicious, the next fiercely protective, and always he battled the urge to sweep her into his arms.

He could only wonder if this was how poor souls found their way to Bedlam.

"I have always been able to care for myself."

His gaze probed her wide eyes. "Perhaps it is time someone else did."

Her lips parted, as if he had managed to strike deep in her heart. Then her features abruptly hardened. "Certainly not. Besides, you have made it clear you consider me more than capable of seeing to my own needs."

Guy grimaced. "Perhaps I am beginning to suspect I was wrong."

"Then you trust me?" she suddenly pounced, carefully regarding the mixture of emotions he could not disguise. She gave a wry smile before rising to her feet. "I see."

Realizing she was about to flee, he abruptly reached out to touch her arm.

"Miss Stone . . . Bianca . . ."

She stepped from his touch. "What?"

With an effort he thrust aside his distaste for revealing his private feelings. His grandfather had disliked the mere hint of emotions. A gentleman was expected to remain aloof and in stoic control at all times. "It is not easy for me."

"Indeed?"

"I am accustomed to those who seek to gain something from my acquaintanceship," he retorted, thinking of the grandfather who demanded duty, his friends who expected the freedom of his considerable wealth, and the women who desired him for his position.

"Be assured I want nothing from you, sir," she retorted in cold tones.

"What do you seek, then?"

She frowned in confusion. "Seek?"

"You cannot wish to be a companion to Ella and Millie forever. What do you wish for the future?"

Her tiny features stiffened to an unreadable expression. "Security."

"Nothing more?"

Her soft lips twisted. "That is a great deal."

"And what of love?" The odd question tumbled from his lips before he could halt it.

"I assure you, Mr. Ravendell, my life will be filled with love." Her tone was unexpectedly harsh. "No matter what I have to sacrifice. Excuse me."

This time there was no halting her determined exit. Guy found himself alone in the library. Feeling more disturbed than ever by the unexpected confrontation, he glanced down at the lovely picture.

Would he ever unravel the mysteries surrounding Miss Stone?

Seven

Standing at the bay window in the library, Guy watched the heavy raindrops slide down the foggy panes. His mood was as gray as the day.

He should return to London. After being in Kent for over a month, he no longer suspected Bianca meant any harm to his aunts. No one could be so patient and caring while harboring a scheme to do away with the two old ladies in their sleep or even to sneak away with the Van Dycks. And yet as the days passed, he made one excuse after another to linger.

It was absurd. He could be trading quips with Brummell at his club, eating dinner with Prinny, or even seducing that delectable opera dancer. Instead he was roaming through this house like the veriest mooncalf, all for the simple hope of catching a glimpse of a pale countenance and flashing emerald eyes.

He must be becoming noddy in his old age, he decided with grim humor. Not only had he turned his back on his normal pursuits, but he had wavered between following Miss Stone about on every opportunity and avoiding her for hours on end, as if he were a lad of twelve who did not know whether he wished to kiss a girl or stick a frog in her pocket.

Noddy indeed.

"Pardon me, sir."

Guy gave a small start at the interruption. Turning about,

he discovered the butler standing on the threshold of the library with a faintly apologetic expression.

"Yes, Lowe?"

"You have guests awaiting you in the drawing room."

"Guests?" Guy repeated in startled disbelief. "Thank you."

Lowe bowed slightly before backing out of the room. With a distinct sense of bewilderment, Guy made his way to the hallway and down to the drawing room. There must have been some misunderstanding. He had no acquaintances in the neighborhood besides his aunts.

Pausing to ensure that his pale green coat was smooth and his cravat still stiffly tied, Guy stepped into the drawing room. At the sight of the two elegantly attired gentlemen sprawled on the sofa, he came to a sudden halt.

He readily recognized the flamboyant Lord Scandridge, with his bright red hair, and his constant companion Mr. Bryce. The two were often with Guy when he was in London and were as renowned as himself for their love of high stakes and beautiful women—certainly not the type to travel willingly through the countryside in the midst of winter.

No strangers, he acknowledged with a sinking heart, but a part of his life he oddly wished to forget at the moment.

"Ho, Ravendell," Lord Scandridge called, grinning as he rose to his feet.

"Good God, Scandridge. What the devil are you doing in Kent?" Guy demanded.

"Why, we have come to rescue you, old chap."

"Rescue me?"

Scandridge's grin merely widened at Guy's puzzled frown. "From the perils of country living."

"What perils?"

Scandridge regarded him with surprise. "I assumed

you, above any gentleman, realized that a soul can perish from sheer boredom."

It was precisely the type of comment he would have found vastly amusing a month ago. Now Guy simply wondered how swiftly he could rid himself of his uninvited guests.

"That is very kind of you, Scandridge, but unnecessary, I assure you. I am perfectly content."

"You cannot mean to say you are actually enjoying rusticating in such a fashion?"

Guy shrugged. "It is bearable for the moment."

A growing suspicion glinted in the nobleman's eyes. "By gad, I never thought to live to see the day the Wicked Raven would be content to mold in the country, eh, Bryce?"

"Odd," the broad, dark-haired gentleman announced in blunt tones. "Deuced odd."

"There you have it, Ravendell. Bryce declares it deuced odd."

Guy folded his arms across his chest. "Surely you did not travel all the way to Kent to declare me odd?"

"London was a bit dull," Lord Scandridge confessed, his gaze narrowed in a thoughtful manner. "We were up for a bit of a lark and decided we should come and discover the reason for your sudden fascination with cows and mud and such."

Guy had no doubt the two had come to pry into his long absence from London. He had promised to return within a week when he had left. All the more reason to rid himself of their presence with all speed.

"There is no fascination. I came to visit my aunts. If you wish a lark, I suggest you return to London."

"In such a hurry to be rid of us?" Lord Scandridge slowly turned to regard his companion and gave a wounded sniff. "He doesn't relish our company, Bryce. What do you make of that?"

"Deuced odd."

"All right you two, enough of your foolishness," Guy retorted with a hint of impatience. "I shall take you to the inn and tomorrow you shall return to London."

"Oh, I say, old . . . well, well." The drawling words came to a halt as Scandridge's gaze shifted over Guy's shoulder. "What have we here?"

Exasperated, Guy turned to discover Bianca stepping through the doorway. His expression unconsciously hardened. Little wonder Lord Scandridge looked as if he had been kicked in the head by an ox. Attired in a soft lavender gown, her golden curls tumbling in charming disarray about her porcelain countenance, she was a vision to rattle any normal male.

Clearly startled at discovering a room full of gentlemen, Bianca glanced toward Guy with a faint frown.

"Pardon me. I did not realize you were entertaining guests."

Guy pointedly turned back to his friends. "They were just leaving."

"Do not be absurd," Lord Scandridge denied. "I refuse to leave until I have been introduced to this beauty."

Guy clenched his hands at his sides. "Miss Stone, may I introduce Lord Scandridge and Mr. Bryce? This is Miss Stone, my aunts' companion."

Smoothly crossing the floor, Lord Scandridge raised Bianca's fingers to his lips with practiced charm. "I now understand my friend's reluctance to leave Kent, as well as his hurry to rid himself of our presence. He clearly desires to have you all to himself."

Bianca removed her fingers with a firm motion. "I am merely a companion, my lord."

"An exquisitely beautiful companion."

Guy ground his teeth as he stepped forward. The sight of even his closest friend touching Bianca was making his blood boil. "Were you not leaving, Scandridge?"

"Was I?"

"Yes."

"A pity." Lord Scandridge's gaze never left Bianca's cool expression. "I had rather hoped to spend some time becoming better acquainted with . . . Kent."

Guy snorted. "Fah."

"And it is such dismal weather for traveling."

"Perhaps you should have considered that before leaving London."

With an innocence Guy did not trust for a moment, Scandridge turned toward the silent Bryce. "Well, it seems there is nothing for it, Bryce." He heaved a sigh. "We are clearly unwelcome here."

"Unwelcome?" a new voice protested from the doorway. Guy lifted his eyes heavenward before turning to meet his Aunt Ella's scandalized gaze. "What is this?"

He felt rather as if he had walked into a French farce. Damnation. Could he possess any worse luck?

"My friends were about to leave for the inn, Aunt Ella," he explained, sending a warning glare toward the smirking Scandridge.

"But why?" the older woman demanded. "We have plenty of room here."

Scandridge lifted one hand to his heart. "We should not like to intrude."

"Nonsense. We shall be delighted to have you," Ella insisted. "Indeed, it would be a most welcome pleasure. Millie and I were just commenting on the fact we have been living far too quietly of late. There is nothing a large house needs more than a group of young men and women to liven it up."

A satisfied smile curved Scandridge's mouth. "If you are certain we will not be a burden."

"No burden at all."

Scandridge performed a small bow. "You are too kind."

"In fact, I have just had the most splendid notion," Ella declared. "We shall host a ball."

"What?" Guy regarded his aunt in horror.

"A Valentine's Ball." Ella clapped her hands with a delighted expression. "I must find Millie. How excited she will be!"

A small silence fell as Ella scurried from the room. Guy felt a stab of remorse as Bianca's delicate features paled. There was little doubt the two visitors would sharply remind her of her father and his frivolous companions.

"Excuse me," she muttered as she turned and left the room.

Guy swallowed a curse and hurried after her. He had no concern for what Lord Scandridge or Mr. Bryce might think of his odd behavior. He only wanted to assure Bianca that he had not requested their presence.

"Bianca, please wait." Grasping her arm, Guy firmly turned her about to meet his somber gaze. "I did not invite them here."

Her expression remained stiff. "It is not my place to concern myself with the guests at Claremont."

"Bianca . . ."

Uncertain how to convince her that he would never wish to see her unhappy, Guy was interrupted as Scandridge stepped into the hallway.

"Ravendell, come along," he called gaily. "Bryce and I are about to bet on which raindrop will reach the bottom of the pane first."

An expression of deep distaste twisted Bianca's features as she pulled from his touch. "Go to your friends, Mr. Ravendell. I have better means of occupying my time."

Eight

Bianca knew she was unconscionably late as she reluctantly made her way down the long staircase. She had heard the first guests arriving for the Valentine's Ball nearly half an hour before. But with a cowardice quite uncommon to her nature, she had discovered herself lingering in her bedchamber.

And why shouldn't she be reluctant? The presence of Lord Scandridge and Mr. Bryce had stirred up memories she would have preferred to keep buried, and certainly she had no interest in their persistent flirtations.

But sheer honesty made her concede neither Lord Scandridge nor Mr. Bryce had made her virtually disappear into her bedchamber over the past few days. Quite simply, Guy Ravendell had.

It did not matter how often she chided herself for being a fool or tried to convince herself those unnerving flutters in her stomach were nothing more than irritation. She was undeniably attracted to the Wicked Raven. Thoroughly, illogically, and unwillingly attracted.

With an effort, Bianca squared her shoulders and turned to make the long trek to the east wing and the formal ballroom. She had to put a halt to these ludicrous notions, she told herself sternly. Soon Guy would return to London and she would once again be able to concentrate on the only important thing in her life: sweet, innocent Annie.

Arriving all too swiftly at the double doors to the

ballroom, Bianca glanced about the vast room. In honor of the holiday, the flowers were in shades of red and white. A large cupid chiseled from ice stood in the center of the floor. From a distant balcony, soft strains of music competed with the chatter of numerous guests.

Hoping to sneak her way to a quiet corner, Bianca was almost instantly captured by Ella, who scurried forward, smiling.

"There you are, Bianca." The older woman's gaze ran appreciatively over Bianca's gown of silver netting covering simple white silk. In the candlelight, the material seemed to glitter with stardust. "Do you not look lovely?"

"Thank you, Ella."

"Come along. We are playing the most delightful game."

Bianca glanced toward the cluster of giggling maidens and elegant gentlemen gathered around a table with a large crystal bowl. Her heart sank at the thought of joining in the childish amusements. "Oh, I do not . . ."

Ignoring Bianca's protest, Ella determinedly steered her toward the young guests. "Here we are. Are all the names in the clay?" she demanded. At the unanimous cry of confirmation, she turned to Bianca. "You go first, my dear."

Bianca frowned. "What?"

"Drop the names into the water," Ella explained, waiting for Bianca to gather the balls of clay and dump them into the crystal bowl. "Now we will retrieve the first to the top. Here." Ella quickly snatched one of the small balls as it floated to the top and shoved it into Bianca's reluctant fingers. "Pull off the clay and read the name, dear. It will reveal your true love."

Oh . . . blast! She should have remained in her bedchamber. She could have pleaded a headache. Or the smallpox. Or imminent death. Anything to avoid standing in the center of the ballroom with every eye trained upon her as she was forced to pull the small slip of paper from the wet clay.

With shaking hands she unfolded the paper, thoroughly prepared to discover the boldly scrawled name of Guy Ravendell. The only surprise would have been if there had been any other name.

"Who is it, Bianca?" Ella urged.

Feeling her face flame with embarrassment, Bianca clenched the annoying piece of paper in her fist. "Mr. Bryce."

"Lucky chap!" someone called out.

There was scattered applause before the guests turned back to the bowl for their chance at discovering their true loves. Uncannily conscious of Ella's lingering gaze, Bianca shifted away from the table and headed directly for a large potted plant. Waiting until she was nearly hidden from the other guests, Bianca tossed the paper to the ground. Ridiculous superstition.

"Tut, tut, Miss Stone."

The drawling voice made Bianca spin about in horror. The evening was plunging from bad to worse, she acknowledged as she viewed the dark, towering form of Mr. Ravendell.

Why the devil did he have to be so annoyingly handsome in his precisely cut black jacket and formal knee pants? No woman could be expected to remain immune to such male beauty, especially when it was combined with a smile that could melt a Russian winter.

"You startled me." She lifted a self-conscious hand to her neckline as he made a thorough survey of her gown. Then her breath caught in her throat as he deliberately reached down to retrieve the forgotten paper.

"Not tossing away the name of your true love, are you, Miss Stone?"

She instinctively reached out to grab the paper. "Give me that!"

Easily avoiding her efforts, Guy unfolded the paper, then stabbed her with a strangely glittering gaze. "Well, well, Miss Stone."

Cursing herself for not having burned the absurd piece of paper, she tossed her head. "It is just a foolish superstition."

"Then why did you lie?"

"I must have misread."

He gave a disbelieving chuckle. "Tell me, Miss Stone, who was the first gentleman you saw this morning?"

She frowned in puzzlement until she recalled the superstition that the first gentleman a maiden spotted on Valentine's Day morning was her true love. She also recalled that Mr. Ravendell had been walking down the corridor when she had left her bedchamber this morning and was well aware he would have been the first gentleman she would have seen.

"Why do you not return to your friends?" she demanded.

"I was hoping I was with my friend."

His soft words caught her off guard. "What?"

"Does that surprise you?"

"Considering that you came to Kent because you suspected I was on the point of murdering your aunts, yes, I do find it a bit surprising."

Something that might have been regret rippled over his features. "I have admitted I jumped to conclusions."

She refused to be swayed. He was a practiced rogue with the ability to seduce the most wary female. "I am not a gullible schoolgirl to be blinded by your charm," she informed him. "If you no longer suspected me of wishing to harm your aunts, you would have returned to London."

He met her gaze squarely. "Perhaps it is something besides suspicion that keeps me here."

Her heart gave an unruly jolt, but she sternly subdued

the traitorous excitement. "Yes, there are the joys of placing bets on where a fly might alight, or how many peas Lord Scandridge can balance on a knife."

A surprising flare of color bloomed along his cheekbones. "Bianca, I will admit I have led a frivolous existence. After my grandfather's rigid upbringing, I longed for nothing more than days filled with unfettered pleasure."

She turned away. How easy it would be to allow herself to be swayed by his soft words. "You do not have to explain to me."

"I know, but I wish to explain," he insisted. "I became the Wicked Raven because I thought it would bring me happiness."

Bianca studied her clenched fingers. "And did it?"

"No, it merely allowed me to forget my loneliness."

"Like my father."

"No." He firmly turned her to meet his narrowed gaze. "Your father was not alone. He had you, and how he could ever forget that is beyond all understanding." Guy loosened his grip on her arm to raise his hand and brush it softly against her cheek.

Heat speared through her body.

"I will never forget you."

It was strangely difficult for her to catch her breath. How dark and beautiful his eyes were. As beautiful and entrancing as a night sky. "Mr. Ravendell, this is absurd."

"Why?"

"Because." She struggled for a steadying breath. "You know nothing about me."

His hand gently cupped her chin. "Then let me get to know you. Quit hiding from me."

Sharp, poignant regret pierced her heart—regret that this man was merely trying to prove she was untrustworthy, and regret that even if he were sincere, she could not share her heart. Her secret made such dreams nothing more than dangerous fantasies.

"No. It is impossible."

"Anything is possible," he argued in rasping tones.

"Hey, you two, no hiding in corners." A boisterous voice intruded upon their privacy as Lord Scandridge deliberately moved in their direction.

Suddenly Bianca was vividly aware of the loud chatter of the guests and the strains of music. With a small gasp, she moved from Guy's lingering touch.

"We cannot speak here." Guy shot her a piercing gaze. "Meet me in the garden tomorrow."

Bianca frantically shook her head. It would be the worst sort of lunacy to be alone with this gentleman. "No."

Lord Scandridge stepped beside her, boldly claiming her hand. "Ah, Miss Stone, I believe this dance is mine."

Although Bianca had no desire to join the couples on the dance floor, she allowed herself to be led from the frowning Guy. At the moment she would waltz with the devil himself to be away from the Wicked Raven. It would be safer than losing her heart to a man who could only bring her pain.

When they were nearly on the dance floor, she heard the low, oddly rough voice of Mr. Ravendell. "Tomorrow, Bianca."

She bit her bottom lip. Tomorrow she would ensure she was far away from the gardens of Claremont.

Nine

The house was silent as Bianca slipped out of a side door and through the empty garden. Hardly surprising. The ball had lasted well into the early morning hours. Only the fact that she had not managed to sleep at all had ensured she was up shortly after dawn and warmly attired in a thick gown and woolen cape.

Unconcerned that she might encounter anyone but the servants, Bianca followed the path that would lead her through the parkland of Claremont and into a distant field. She never paused as she maneuvered on the uneven ground and eventually made her way to a small farmhouse. Her footsteps quickened as she crossed the narrow courtyard and knocked on the door. All her inner turmoil was forgotten as an unconscious smile curved her lips.

Within moments, a plump, sweet-faced woman with a neat wool gown and pale brown hair opened the door.

"Miss Stone." Ruth Carter regarded her guest in surprise. "We were not expecting you."

"I am sorry for calling without warning. I wished to see Annie."

"Of course." Stepping back, Ruth waved Bianca into the tidy front parlor. "I just finished feeding her breakfast."

Bianca crossed directly to the toddler quietly playing in the center of the floor. Her heart swelled with love at the soft blond curls and wide emerald eyes that were an exact replica of her own. This tiny bundle of joy was the reason for all her sacrifices, and she would do whatever was necessary to keep her safe.

"There you are, my sweet." Bending down, Bianca swept the child into her arms, giving a laugh as Annie squealed with delight.

"She is always pleased to see you," Ruth commented as she watched the child cling to Bianca.

"I wish I could have her with me." Bianca sighed. "What fun we would have, eh, Annie?"

Stepping forward, Ruth took note of Bianca's pale features. "Is anything wrong, Miss Stone?"

Bianca swallowed a wry laugh. What was *not* wrong? "No. Nothing."

"You look tired."

"I am fine." Bianca had a sudden urge to have Annie to herself. "Do you mind if we go into the garden?"

"Of course not."

Ruth immediately moved to a cabinet, where she pulled out a heavy blanket. With the swift efficiency that had encouraged Bianca to choose her as a surrogate mother for Annie, she wrapped the blanket about the giggling child. "There."

"Thank you, Ruth."

Holding Annie close, Bianca moved toward the far door that opened into the small but sheltered garden. Once alone, she perched on a stone bench and held the child against the warmth of her body.

With a tiny sigh, she deliberately forced her thoughts away from Claremont and the disturbing gentleman no doubt awaiting her to join him. Instead, she led her thoughts back to the moment her life had changed.

It had come without warning. After receiving an abrupt message from her cousin that she was to vacate her home, she had been quite determined to purchase a cottage and enjoy a life of independence. Then one morning a strange woman carrying a small child had appeared on the doorstep. With a sense of shock, Bianca had listened to the woman's claim that the baby belonged to Bianca's father and that without support she would dump the child at the nearby orphanage.

Bianca had only to hold the emerald-eyed child once for her decision to be made. She could not allow the child to be abandoned. Annie was her sister and the only family she possessed.

Unfortunately, her small income would barely cover the necessities of life. How could she possibly see to all the finer luxuries a young girl should possess?

Torn between the desire to have the child with her and sensible to the realization she needed to earn money for the future, Bianca had reluctantly accepted Ella's generous offer and had discovered Bob and Ruth to care for Annie for a small charge.

It had all been thought out so carefully. She had never considered the notion her plans might be shaken by a dark-eyed rogue with the charm of a devil.

Bending her head to gently kiss Annie's golden curls, Bianca was startled by the sound of approaching footsteps. Her heart faltered as she hurriedly set Annie on the soft ground and rose to her feet to shield the child behind her skirts. She had no doubt who the intruder would be. Who else would possess the audacity to thrust his way into her privacy without regard for her feelings?

It took only a moment for her worst fears to be confirmed as, without apology, Guy strode into the garden. Coming to a halt, he regarded her with a dark scowl. "Bianca."

With an effort, she tilted her chin to a defiant angle. "Mr. Ravendell. What are you doing here?"

"Obviously searching for you. If I had not caught a glimpse of you crossing the field, I never should have found you." His handsome features tightened. "I asked you to meet me in the garden this morning."

"And I declined your invitation. We have no reason to meet."

"Liar." Moving forward, he towered over her stiff form. "You are as aware as I am that there is something between us."

Bianca was desperately aware of the child behind her. She had to rid herself of Guy before he discovered her secret.

"You are mistaken, sir."

His gaze narrowed. "Do you mean to tell me you react to every man's kisses in such a manner?"

She could not prevent the heat that darkened her countenance. "You are the only gentleman who forces his kisses upon me, Mr. Ravendell."

"Force?" He sucked in a sharp breath. "Why, you provoking creature."

"Please just go away, Mr. Ravendell," she pleaded. "Go back to London where you belong."

His dark features hardened. "Not until you confess why you push me away."

"I cannot."

"You wished me to trust you," he growled in exasperation. "Now I ask the same of you."

How she wished she could trust him. "It is impossible."

"I told you last night that nothing is impossible." Without warning, he grasped her arms and tugged her toward him. The sudden motion revealed the child behind her, and his dark eyes widened in shock. "What is this?"

Filled with a combination of fear and aching disappointment, Bianca reached down to gather Annie in her arms. "Please, go away."

Guy looked as if he had been smacked in the face. "A baby."

"Yes. Now go away."

He gave a slow shake of his head. "Who lives here?"
"Mr. Carter and his wife."
"Is this their child?"
"No."
His features twisted. "Bianca . . ."
"What?" she breathed.

His dark eyes carefully studied the blond curls and large emerald eyes.

"Does . . . is this child yours?"

Bianca wavered. Her heart demanded that she confess the truth, that she share the heavy burden she carried with this man who had come to mean so much to her.

But years of bearing responsibility on her own and the fear that Annie might be taken away stilled the impetuous desire to confess her secret. "Yes."

He stepped backward, his breath coming in shallow gasps. "My God."

"I told you to leave."

"I knew you were keeping a secret, but not this." He shook his head in disbelief. "How could you have allowed this to occur?"

Although the censure in his tone was no less than she had expected, she could not deny a sense of disappointment. "I do not think that is any of your concern."

"Of course it is my concern," he rasped in sudden anger. "You live with my aunts."

She held Annie closer. "This has nothing to do with them."

"Do they know?"

"No."

"What do you think will happen when the neighborhood learns that their companion has a . . . child?"

She flinched as she realized he had barely prevented himself from calling Annie a bastard. Despite the fact that it was no less than the awful truth, she felt a flare of fury.

How dare he presume to judge her? Heaven only knew

how many illegitimate children he had scattered about England. He had no right to look down upon her or poor Annie. "It will not reflect upon them."

"Of course it will," he snapped. "Their reputations will be irretrievably tarnished."

A stark, nearly unbearable pain raced through her body. "Very well. I will leave." She tossed her head. "You have what you always wanted, Mr. Ravendell. I will be out of Claremont tomorrow."

"It was not what I wanted." After studying her stiff countenance for a long moment, he shook his head. "It was not what I wanted at all."

With oddly jerky movements, Guy turned on his heel and marched out of the garden.

Once alone, Bianca laid her cheek on Annie's head and allowed the waiting tears to trickle down her face.

Ten

Guy waited in the damp gardens of Claremont. He was impervious to the chilled air, the persistent drizzle, and even the fact he had long since missed lunch.

After spending the past few hours raging like a madman through the parkland, he had at last come to a startling, inescapable realization.

He was in love with Bianca Stone.

He loved her courage, her kindness, her gentle nature that masked a will of iron. He loved the way her eyes glowed with the excitement of life and how her lips softened beneath his kiss. He loved her with an intensity he never thought to feel.

He had also come to the conclusion he could not live without her.

No matter what had occurred in her past or what mistakes she might have made, he wanted her at his side. Lord knew he had enough mistakes in his own past.

Nearly numb with cold, Guy paced back across the garden, his heart giving a sudden leap at the sight of Bianca's slender frame moving up the path. With grim determination, he marched to block the path, not surprised when she came to a sudden halt and regarded him as she might a rat in her pantry.

"You," she breathed.

"Please hold a moment, Bianca."

Her eyes flashed with a wounded anger. "What now,

Mr. Ravendell? Have you packed my belongings so I needn't tarnish the sacred ground of Claremont with my presence again?"

His heart twisted with regret at his harsh accusations. It did not matter he had been striking out in pain. It had been unforgivable. "No, I wish to speak with you."

She pressed one hand to her heart. "For God's sake, haven't you said enough?"

He smiled with rueful amusement. "No doubt, but I haven't yet said the correct things."

She eyed him with open suspicion. "What do you mean by that?"

With a restless shrug, he shoved his hands into the pockets of his greatcoat. "I will not say I wasn't shocked when I discovered you possessed a child."

She seemed to flinch. "You made that obvious."

"And I questioned whether or not I had allowed myself to be deceived by your seeming innocence," he forced himself to confess. Honesty was a quality that had been sadly lacking between them.

"I have never tried to deceive you."

He ignored her obvious lie. "I told myself I had been a fool, that what I felt for you was based on an illusion of the woman I thought you to be."

Her eyes darkened with a hint of the vulnerability she struggled so hard to hide. "Please, do not."

He stepped forward, his voice urgent. "But the truth is that the only illusion is thinking I do not love you."

"Mr. Ravendell . . ."

"I came here to rid my aunts of a scheming jade and instead discovered the one woman who could fill the emptiness in my life."

She faltered back a step, her expression one of stark disbelief. "You know nothing of me."

"Perhaps I do not know your favorite food or if you prefer Plato to Socrates, but I know you are kind and loyal and extraordinarily vulnerable beneath all that prickly independence."

She blinked back the threat of tears. "Why are you doing this?"

He reached out a hand to stroke the satin skin of her cheek. "Because I love you. And I hope very much you love me in return."

"And what if I did?" she burst out in ragged tones. "Then what?"

"Then I would marry you."

A shocked silence fell as she struggled to accept his blunt words. "Marry me?"

His fingers moved to push aside a stray golden curl. "Is that not what usually happens between a gentleman and maiden in love?"

"That is absurd."

"Why?"

"Because." She shook her head. "What of my family? You know better than anyone that I can never rid myself of the scandal attached to my name."

His expression became wry. "My own name is hardly free of scandal. As you so justly pointed out, I was a hypocrite to presume I was in a position to judge others."

She stilled at his confession, her expression unreadable. "And Annie?"

"I will claim Annie as my own," he said without hesitation. It was a decision he had made hours ago. "My position and wealth will help protect her."

She trembled, her eyes wide with wary disbelief. "You would do that?"

"Yes."

"But why?" Her gaze probed deep into his own, as if seeking whether or not he could be trusted. "You hate responsibility. Why would you take on a wife and child who can only bring harm?"

"Because I love you," he said simply. "After I left my

grandfather's, I promised myself I would never be trapped by responsibility again. He made my life a misery. But since meeting you, I have never felt so wondrous." He cupped her chin to tilt her face upward, his heart sinking at the tears shimmering in her eyes. "What have I said?"

"You love me?" she whispered.

"With all my heart."

"And you will never leave me?"

He abruptly wrapped his arms about her and pulled her into his arms. She felt so right curved next to his hard form, her head snuggled against his shoulder. "Nothing could drag me away."

"Oh, Mr. Ravendell."

He softly chuckled as he brushed his cheek against the silky softness of her hair. "I think we have progressed to Guy, have we not?"

"Yes . . . Guy."

"And you will marry me?"

With a hint of reluctance, Bianca pulled back to regard his softened features. "First I must tell you of Annie."

"There is no need."

"But I wish you to know," she insisted. "Annie is not mine."

Guy stiffened in shock. "What?"

Pulling out of his arms, she lifted her hands in a helpless motion. "After my father died, I discovered I had only a small income. Then my cousin returned to England and I was forced to leave my home. At first I did not mind. I intended to purchase a small cottage and live quietly. Then a woman showed up at the manor with Annie. She claimed my father had been supporting them, and without that support she would have to put Annie in an orphanage so she could return to London and the stage."

After hours of adjusting to the notion that Bianca possessed a child, Guy struggled to accept the fact the baby belonged to her father and an out-of-work actress. "Annie is not yours?"

"No. She is my half sister."

Guy regarded her pale features for a long moment, caught between a rather guilty sense of relief and a rising anger. "Why did you let me think she was your daughter?"

She possessed the grace to blush as she shifted uneasily beneath his unwavering gaze. "I have been terrified someone would try to take her from me," she attempted to explain. "That is why I have her hidden with the Carters and why I never told your aunts. Besides"—she gave a sudden shrug—"I have grown up having others think the worst of me. I suppose it has become habit to pretend as if I do not care."

His brief anger instantly died. How difficult it must have been for her to take responsibility for the child. What other woman would have taken in her father's illegitimate child, especially when it meant only sacrifice and hardship for herself?

"My poor darling. Is that why you took the position with my aunts?"

She gave a slow nod of her head. "Yes. I hoped to save enough so Annie could have all the things a young lady requires."

Unable to prevent himself, Guy once again swept her into his arms. He wanted to hold her and never let her go. "You are a most astonishing young lady."

As she tilted back her head, a slow smile curved her soft lips. "You did not think so when you arrived. You wished me in Hades."

He gave a mock shudder. "Do not remind me. I was an arrogant fool, although you soon had me as uncertain as a moonling."

"And you had me behaving as a giddy schoolgirl."

"So you will marry me." His words were a statement

of fact rather than a question. He had no intention of allowing her to slip away.

"What of Annie?"

"We will tell the world she is a distant cousin who has lost her parents. It would be natural for us to take her in and raise her."

"And you will not regret the burdens of a wife and child?"

"My only regret is that we did not meet sooner."

Having waited long enough to taste the sweet temptation of her lips, Guy lowered his head with an unwavering determination.

The Wicked Raven had been thoroughly tamed at last.

Far above the garden, Ella and Millie watched the couple with a shared smile of satisfaction.

"I did tell you, Ella, that Bianca would be precisely right for our dear Guy."

"You?" Ella gave a small snort. "The notion was entirely mine."

"Absurd. I have always possessed the most marvelous talent for matchmaking."

Ella gave a tinkling laugh. "Well, whoever thought up the scheme, it worked to perfection. Such a nice touch to change the will, do you not think?"

"Oh, yes." Millie nodded her head. "Guy might not have come to Kent for ages if not for Mr. Stanton."

Ella raised a cup of tea to her lips. "Perhaps we should thank Mr. Stanton in person."

"You mean invite him to Kent?"

"Yes."

A sudden glint entered Millie's dark eyes. "What a splendid notion. And perhaps we should also invite Cousin Kate. Such a pity she never wed."

Ella tilted her head in a thoughtful manner. "Or perhaps Mrs. Greaves. Her first husband was a lawyer, you know."

"Or perhaps . . ."

The two unlikely cupids put their heads together as they happily considered the fate of the hapless Mr. Stanton.

Wild Honey

by
Donna Simpson

One

Valentine's Day Ball, London
February, 1808

Lord Bron Alvarice circled Lord and Lady Never's ballroom. They were holding their annual pre-Season Valentine's extravaganza, and he had attended out of sheer boredom. He could think of no other reason why he was dressed in his best blue coat and gazing stupidly at a lot of chits in pretty white frocks as they danced with a collection of London's bucks and beaux, floating about the red and white decorated room in a cotillion dance.

But the usual round of London excitements for a young man of means had become a dead bore. Mills, races, cockfights, gambling hells, opera dancers . . . he was twenty-four and bored to death with it all. He had a fund of excess energy that he had no idea what to do with. None of his other friends seemed to be suffering this dreadful ennui.

He spotted a friend, Derrick Laughton. He was doing the pretty to the chit his mother had chosen as his bride. Fairly sanguine about it he seemed, too. She was well enough looking, but had a tendency to bray when she laughed, and had a thick waist. Maxwell Prosper was in attendance as well, squiring an heiress who would be on the shelf if she did not find a husband this season. Her besetting sins were a face like an Arabian horse and a shrewish manner. One or the other could be ignored, thought Bron, but together . . . he shuddered.

Well, not for him. He was the future Viscount Blackthorne, but right now he was just Lord Bron Alvarice, and he intended to enjoy himself thoroughly before settling down to a life in leg shackles. So why did everything seem so devilish flat?

He saw a crowd near the row of chairs on the west end of the ballroom. There was a palpable air of excitement emanating from the knot of young gentlemen, and Bron wondered if some announcement about the war had been made and was being discussed. His pulse quickening, he advanced, only to see the knot separate and one young man lead a girl onto the floor.

She was breathtaking. There was no other word for the vision in palest peach muslin, her honey-colored hair dressed high in a coronet with a circlet of white roses atop it, her swanlike neck circled in glowing pearls. She was slim and graceful, and the lucky man, one of Bron's acquaintances, William Conroy, led her into the dance. It was a quadrille, and she gracefully walked through the steps with William, his face beaming red by the end of the dance, for he was stout and even the gentle pace of such a dance was usually beyond him.

Bron's curiosity was raised, for William never danced. He watched them, and as his friend took the girl back to her seat, the crowd of young men descended upon her again, like drones to the queen in a hive. She was irresistible, it seemed, and was casting every other girl in the place into the shade.

The next dance was a country dance, and she was led out by a stranger to Bron, but her effect on him was just the same as it had been on Will. Drawn by curiosity, Bron circled and drew near to the crowd of her admirers.

"Like an angel," one young man breathed as he gazed at the girl who spiritedly moved through the country dance, one honey lock of hair dancing and bouncing on her pale shoulders.

"Exquisite," his boon companion agreed. "And absolutely unspoiled. D'you know, she has danced with poor Dobbs, and he ain't got a penny and is homely as they come from the pox. Gives a fellow a chance, not like some o' these nose in th'air types, I say."

"A perfect angel," the other young man breathed again, as he watched the object of his admiration.

Bron rolled his eyes. What gudgeons! No girl was so unspoiled if she was that beautiful. Straight out of the schoolroom she looked, though he had to admit she seemed to have more address than most schoolroom misses. He began to watch to criticize, intent on finding her fatal flaw, for certainly she must have one. All women did.

But as the evening progressed and she stood up with any young man who asked, and treated them one and all to the same sweet smile, he wondered if her only fault would be that she was a simpleton. Broodingly, he wondered if he should ask her to dance, just to confirm his guess, for she was beginning to prey on his mind.

He had found out her name, Miss Honoria Stillwell, and her age, just eighteen that very day, her birthday. He had even found out her nickname . . . Honey, of all things. It was enough to gag one with cloying sweetness. Even the society dragons, who could usually be depended on to find something wrong with each girl, seemed enamored of her. One of the most severe, Lady Benton, pronounced her to be a "well-behaved, pretty sort of gel." From her that was high praise indeed, she who found fault even with Princess Charlotte, damning her as a little hoyden.

William Conroy moved ponderously toward him, a smile beaming on his red face. "I say, Bron, well met!"

"Well met, Will. Did my eyes deceive me, or did I see you dancing earlier?"

Will flushed even redder, if that was possible. He snagged a glass of champagne from the refreshment table behind Bron and gulped it down, sighing afterward and wiping his mouth delicately with a kerchief. "You did see me dancing. How could one miss me?" he joked with his usual good humor.

"And I thought you never danced. What is so different about this chit?"

Both men glanced toward the floor as Honey Stillwell floated by in the figures of another country dance with an older man they both recognized as a confirmed bachelor. The look in his eyes, though, as he gazed down at his pretty partner and laughed at some remark of hers was bemused interest.

"She's a stunner," William sighed.

"Lots of pretty girls every year," Bron said. "What's so different about this one?"

Frowning in concentration, his friend gave it some thought. "Makes a fellow feel ten feet tall when he is with her," he finally said. "And it is not just that she is so demmed pretty. Nice, too. And smart! Heard her talkin' about the war with Major Jenkins. Seemed to know what she was talking of, too. But it's more than that."

Cynically, Bron said, "So she's perfect, is that it? A paragon. Flawless looks, smart, nice . . . what else do you need? You sound as if you are halfway in love with her. Should ask her to wed now."

William rounded on his friend with an angry look in his usually placid eyes. "See here, Bron, know how demmed cynical you are, but Miss Stillwell is off limits for that kind of talk."

One brow raised in as much surprise as he would allow himself to show, Bron gazed down at his hefty friend. Will never troubled himself to become enthused or angry about anything, but one would almost think he was willing to come to blows over this girl. "Come, Will, she is just a girl! Lots more of them every year. Sort of like roses, new crop every spring."

The angry light died, and something wistful floated through the other man's gray gaze. "Not like Miss Stillwell. I know I don't have a chance with her . . . look at her! Surrounded by men so thick if you shot a cannon you would kill half of London's young bloods. But somehow, when we were dancing, she made me feel like I was the only man in the room. Never took her eyes from mine—you know how some of the girls use the dance to check out every man in the place, eyes wandering constantly. Not her. Got the feeling she was really interested in me."

Bron made his adieus to his friend and strolled away. Will still watched her like a lovesick moonling from the edge of the floor, and Bron wondered if that was his own fate. He could not seem to take his eyes from her, and yet she had not even noticed him yet. That was a blow, for he was used, at six feet tall, to standing out among other men. Women generally made a fuss over him, sighing over his black hair and blue eyes as if no other man had ever had those assets.

But Miss Stillwell was too engaged in her partner's conversation. Maybe she was just nearsighted—couldn't see past the tip of her delectable nose. But no, her look did not have that vacancy in it. The dance ended and her partner squired her back to her place by an older woman of faded beauty—her mother, perhaps, by their similar looks. And then the crowd closed in again.

Not for him that jostling good-natured competition, though. Still, he could not keep his eyes from her, and waited with a thumping in the region of his heart as a new partner led her out for a mazurka. Her step was light and her joy in the dance infectious.

"You seem as bloody infatuated as we all are," came a deep voice at Bron's side.

It was a good friend, Percy Scott, and he and Bron shook hands.

"She has a rare beauty," Bron admitted grudgingly.

Percy gazed at him with curiosity. "Never seen you stare at anyone quite like that. And yet you haven't joined her court, nor asked her to dance yet."

Bron shrugged. "Two reasons. I'm afraid if I get too close, I will find something to disapprove—no one can be so bloody perfect—and you know what the society dragons are like! One false move on my part, and they'll have me leg-shackled to the chit."

"Worse fates than that to be suffered," Scott mused. "Still, she's worth the danger, my friend. She's a rare 'un, and I say that who never goes for the chits in their first Season. But her father's in dun territory. She'll be auctioned off to the highest bidder, I don't doubt. Sad but true."

"Still," Bron said, "the Season has not even officially started yet. He won't do anything until the Season is underway. A girl like that, even saddled with a poor family, should make a good match." Even as he said it, there was a sick feeling in the pit of Bron's stomach at the thought of her with any man but him. It surprised him, and he admitted to a jolt of fear. Perhaps he should make himself known to the girl. But he was not in the market for a wife. He was too young, only twenty-four, and had a lot of living to do before putting his neck in the marital noose. Still . . .

"Is she going to be at the Stoddarts' ball in two weeks? The one that opens the Season?"

"She is," Percy said. "I tried to bespeak a dance, but she very prettily said she did not want to fill her dance card before the actual night. You going to go?"

Bron made his mind up swiftly. He nodded. "I am. If I have not forgotten her face before then, I will dance with her."

"Awfully good of you, old sport, to give her a chance like that," Percy said, sarcasm dripping from his cultured voice.

But Bron didn't answer, for at that minute his gaze met with a pair of eyes the color of a summer sky, and he felt as if all the air had been sucked from his body. *Miss Honey Stillwell,* he thought, *I look forward to our dance in two weeks' time as I never thought I could look forward to anything.*

Two weeks later, the Stoddarts' ball found him pacing anxiously by the entrance, waiting for a girl he had not been able to forget. The two weeks had dragged, even though he had filled it with mills, races, and a trip to a friend's in Brighton.

His memory of her had become an obsession, his dreams at night filled with fantasy meetings between them, sometimes in a London ballroom, but more often on a wild heath somewhere in the middle of nowhere. He did not recognize the surroundings, but it was a wild place, rocky and hilly, and he saw her standing on a hilltop, with the wind lifting her honey-colored hair and tousling it. He would, in his dream, approach her, and she would come into his arms as if she belonged there. He would hold her close to his heart and whisper, "Forever," and then awaken with a jolt.

He had decided that it was a brain fever that would likely be healed the moment he danced with her and found her to be just an ordinary young lady. His obsession was being fueled by the mystery of her and that last, long look—and the awareness in her eyes as she had gazed at him.

"Percy," he cried, seeing his friend, one of the few he could look directly in the eye. They clasped hands, but Bron's eyes returned to the entrance.

"What ails you, my friend?" Percy asked.

"Nothing," Bron said, jolted from his vigil. He hoped he was not making a cake of himself. "I am just . . . I am looking out for Miss Stillwell. I wish to sign her dance card before it is filled."

Percy looked at him curiously. "You must have been out of town this last week. Did you not hear the latest?"

"What latest?"

"Miss Stillwell is no more."

Bron felt a jolt of pain streak through him. "She died!" he cried. "No! That is not possible. What happened?"

"Not dead, old man, merely wed. Her father sold her off to the highest bidder, old Abner Hockley, saving himself the cost of a Season. Clever, hmmm?"

"That glowing girl wed that horrible little wine merchant Hockley?"

"Not willingly, gudgeon! Her father announced her fate to her, so the tale goes, and she ran from the city to some aunt in Bath. Father dragged her back and shackled her to Hockley right and tight. Don't know what he did, but it is said that the girl did say 'I do' right enough."

Bron felt a deep sadness for the lively, sweet girl who had promised to take the *ton* by storm. "What a fool of a father," he said, his voice harsh. "Hockley is rich, but she could have had a duke! Money *and* title, she was that lovely."

"It's whispered that Hockley held the old man's debts. Bought them up, then traded them for Miss Stillwell."

All of the joy had gone out of the Season for Bron. He never saw her again, and heard that Hockley had taken his prize immediately to his home, somewhere up north.

In some way, the jolt of that shock made Bron sick of himself. Poor Miss Stillwell did not have much choice in her life. Women didn't, it seemed to him, as unfair as that was. But he was a man, and his life could be whatever he wanted. And he wanted to do something with it.

So he bought a commission in the cavalry, advanced through the years to a captaincy, was decorated twice, saw action on the Peninsula, was wounded and invalided home, but recovered in time to have a hand at Waterloo beside old Nosey himself. With Napoleon safely secured on his island, Bron sold out in 1816, after the death of his father and his ascension to the title, and returned to the life of a London gentleman—wine and women, gambling and carousing.

Men called him Blackthorne now, for his title was Viscount Blackthorne, but among the young ladies of the *ton,* he had become known as Blackheart for his tendency to raise a young lady's hopes only to dash them time and time again. It was noted, though, that he had a soft spot for young ladies running away from marriages that they were being forced into, or in which they were unhappy.

And it was that chivalrous impulse that led to his trouble in late 1819, and the necessity to get out of town shortly after he spent Christmas with his mother in Bath.

Two

Yorkshire
January, 1820

Thirty. In two weeks, on Valentine's Day, she would be thirty years old, Honey Hockley thought as she sat by her parlor window mending some household linens. It was the kind of job a housekeeper could be expected to take care of, but her last had been pensioned off after Mr. Hockley died three years ago, and Honey had decided not to replace her.

After all, what did a woman who lived alone need with a large staff? She did not even keep a butler, preferring the informality of a maid answering the door. And since Abner died she had much more free time, time that used to be taken up with her nursing duties to him. It was good to keep busy, she had learned, through the long cold Yorkshire winters.

But still, mending a tear in a bedsheet did not keep her mind occupied, and it returned, as it often did, to that long ago time laughingly referred to as her Season.

One ball. That was the entirety of her recollection. She gazed out the window at the snow-covered landscape, the hills behind dotted with sheep, outcroppings of gray rock the only relief to a harsh view. Life since that night had taken on a monotonous quality that made that one night a shining beacon and an unalloyed pleasure.

That night she had not known her father's intentions. That night she had believed that yes, she would need to marry, but that she would be able to engage someone's affection—someone kind, someone good—and live a happy life away from her father's house.

Instead her hand had been given to a hunched, evil-smelling old man who even then was ill, though he refused to admit it. She had endured five years of his meanness before he became bedridden. Even then, her sense of what was owed to the man who raised her family from penury was too strong to abandon him to a hired nurse. She did it herself for four long years, until one night as she sat at his bedside he just faded from life. She had no children.

And for three years now she had sat at this window, watching the life of the moors and heaths of Yorkshire pass by. She snipped a thread, then rethreaded the needle, holding it up to the gray light that came in the window.

Again her mind returned to that ball, the Valentine's Day Ball where she had celebrated her eighteenth birthday. She had been besieged by admirers, to her surprise. She had never expected such success, and it had heartened her. The evening had flown by. So many kind, nice men! William Conroy, stout and out of breath, but so gentle and complimentary. He would have made an exemplary husband, she thought. And in vulgar cant, he was well to grass, rich enough even for her father's avarice. She had thought that though her father intended to choose her husband for her, it would be from among men who had shown interest in her.

But the very next morning, after an extraordinary dream of a pair of cobalt blue eyes that burned in a pale face—she remembered those eyes still, though she would not be able to place the man in a crowd—her father had announced his decision.

"No point in all this Season folderol. Going to hitch you with Abner Hockley. Got plenty of blunt, and willing to spend it to buy a pretty trinket to decorate his home and look after his collections."

She hadn't understood at first. The full horror of what her father had done did not sink in until later that day, when all of her admirers from the previous night were turned away and their offerings of flowers tossed after them. He had already signed the marriage settlements, he told her, and she would be married within the week.

She had rebelled. Never before had she refused to do anything her father had told her, but she did this time. And when he commanded her to comply, she had run away to her aunt in Bath, her mother's sister. Her mother had helped her pack, horrified by what her father was doing.

But he learned where she was and came after her, hauling her unceremoniously back to their rented rooms in London. For two days she was locked in her room with no food, a guard at her door. Her father would alternately badger and wheedle, but still she refused. Finally, though, he lost what little patience he had ever possessed. If she refused to follow his orders, she would be sent to an uncle of his in Scotland. Never again would she be allowed to see her mother, nor her younger sister or brother. Nor would she be allowed to correspond with them.

At eighteen, knowing her father was capable of such a deed, she had felt the full sting of that threat. Her family was all she had, and to be sent from them, never allowed to see them again . . .

She had capitulated. Two days later, on a dreary, snowy February day, she was married in a dismal chapel to a man who collected her as he did his enamel snuffboxes. He took her immediately north, not wanting anyone else to see her, hiding her away as he did his collection, for his own greedy perusal. So dismal and frugal was his household that she rarely saw her family anyway. And Lockworth, where Mr. Hockley made his home, was almost at the Scottish border. Perhaps she should have held firm and risked her father's sentence, for life was not so very different after her marriage than in his dreadful edict.

But there was no point in moping. Her marriage and the money that came to her family had allowed her brother to study at Oxford and her sister to marry decently. Nine years after her marriage she was widowed at last, and felt the perfect hypocrite in black, for she did not mourn. It was a kind of freedom that she looked forward to, freedom from the petty tyranny Abner had practiced even from his bed.

Her father was dead, too, having died even before the frail Abner Hockley—the result of too much wine, his doctor said. Her mother now lived in Bath with her sister, Honey's aunt, the one she had run to twelve years before. Her brother, Roderick, had become a respected cleric and scholar, and Nellie, her younger sister, had been married for six years now.

So good had come from bad after all, and she could not regret that long ago decision she had been forced to make. But still, Honey felt restless, like there was some kind of change coming, something she could not control. She loved her village, Lockworth, and Lockworth Moor, the long, wild hill that rose above it. Her own home, the finest in the small community, was at the high end of the village, so she had a view of the village from her breakfast room and of the moors from her parlor. Her delight was her rose garden in the summer. But winter had set in, and it would be long, she knew from experience. *There must be more than this* hummed through her brain like the refrain from a song. She sighed and broke off her thread after setting the final, fine stitch.

At least there was still dancing, Honey thought the next night, her toes tapping to a lively mazurka as she stood arm-in-arm with her sister, Nellie, who had arrived unexpectedly that very morning for what she promised would be an extended visit. Maybe this was the change she had foreseen, she thought, glancing over at her sister's pretty face.

Nell, as blond as Honey and five years younger, was gazing around at the gathering, the monthly assembly at the Lockworth Ballroom, though the grandiose title was overwhelming for the humble space occupied by three fiddlers and a piano player. "Not exactly a *tonnish* gathering," Nell said, her pert nose held high.

"It does fine for us," Honey said, cheerfully. "We are not *tonnish* people." She knew her sister, living in London as she did, was used to more elegant surroundings, but she had always suspected that Nell exaggerated the company she kept. Her husband, John, was a nice fellow and not badly off, but he had no aristocratic pretensions, nor did he move in those circles.

The dancers were a democratic mix of farmers, lawyers, the local doctor, landowners, and whoever else desired to attend. They drank punch, ate sandwiches, danced, talked, and played cards, all to the tune of the only locals who could play instruments.

Honey accepted the outstretched hand of Mr. Fold, the draper, and stepped into the line of dancers with a merry smile. She returned after the tune out of breath and laughing, to find herself the object of a steady gaze from across the room. A tall, lean man with brown skin and eyes that started out of the dark like azure fire stood next to a local landowner, Sir Gordon Tern. Breathless now from more than the dance, Honey returned to Nell's side.

"Who is that very good-looking man?" Nell asked, nudging and pointing toward Sir Gordon and his friend.

"I . . . I don't know. I've never seen him before." She didn't for a moment think her sister spoke of Sir Gordon, not when the other man was next to him.

"He is staring at me in the most familiar way," Nell giggled. "P'raps he shall ask me for a dance."

Honey did not mention that it seemed to her that the gentleman was staring at *her*, not Nell. But maybe her sister was right, for she was very pretty, as well as being more modishly dressed, and, living in London, must be more used to the attention of men. The two gentlemen started toward them, circling the energetic dancers, who had started up a polonaise.

Finally, Sir Gordon bowed before the two women.

Honey was always uneasy with Sir Gordon, for the man had, on more than one occasion, intimated he would like to take the widow Hockley as a mistress. He had stayed within the bounds of civility, but the implication was there, and no amount of snubbing by Honey had turned him away.

"Mrs. Hockley, charmed to see you looking so festive," Sir Gordon said, eyeing the bosom of her dress, a rosy confection that was daringly low cut for Yorkshire society.

Honey flushed, wishing she had not worn this new gown.

"Introduce us to your friend, and I will return the favor," he continued, bowing over Nell's hand.

"This is my sister, Mrs. Jordan," Honey said.

"And this is *my* friend, Mr. Black," Sir Gordon said.

The taller man bowed and took Honey's hand in his own, holding it over long, then laying a kiss on the rose satin of her glove. The candlelight glinted off his hair, giving blue lights to its darkness, echoed by the deep blue of his eyes. He was very tall, broad-shouldered, and with a bearing that could only mean he was a military man.

Nell shouldered past Honey and smiled up at the handsome stranger. "Mr. Black! How appropriate your name, given your handsome hair."

Honey's eyes widened in surprise. Nell spoke familiarly, as if she knew the gentleman, and with a flirtatious lilt in her voice. At that moment Mr. Touley, the barrister's clerk, came toward them and bowed low.

"Pardon the interruption, ladies, gentlemen." He turned to Honey. "May I have this dance, Mrs. Hockley?"

"Certainly, Mr. Touley," she said, with a sigh of relief.

As the dance progressed, she saw that the two gentlemen had left Nell standing alone, pouting, while they ambled around the dance floor. But every time she looked in their direction, she could not help but see Mr. Black's eyes on her, and it made her extremely uncomfortable. Why did he stare? She could no longer believe he was looking at Nell, for his eyes followed her, burning into her even when her back was turned in the figures of the dance.

She returned to Nell, who had recovered from her fit of pique after a very young man had made a cake of himself over her. They drifted to the refreshment table, with Nell chattering at a brisk pace.

"The latest scandal," Nell whispered about London society gossip, her favorite topic of conversation, "is about one of London's premier rakes—Viscount Blackthorne." She sighed. "It is said he can seduce the most virtuous young lady just by looking deep into her eyes. It is rumored he mesmerizes them! The latest *on-dit* is that he has seduced and then abandoned a very virtuous young Spanish lady. She was to marry Prince Schtuckhauser—you know, that German prince. She was awaiting his arrival, and attended a ball. Blackthorne spoke to her but once, during a dance, and three days later she ran away with him!" Nell looked around and lowered her voice. "Some say he abducted her. And now she is carrying his child!"

"Nell! I do not believe in ill-natured gossip."

"He promised her marriage, and after he got what he wanted, he deserted her!"

"Nell!"

"He had to escape London or be hanged by an angry mob, it is said. He was pelted in the street with clods of mud. Isn't that exciting? But the girl, Doña Isabella Asuncion, will not see him prosecuted! Perhaps she still loves him."

Honey sighed and turned to her sister. "Nell, I meant what I said. I do not believe in gossip."

"But just think," Nell said, hanging on to her sister's arm with a tight grip. Her voice was hushed but held an edge of thrilled excitement. "How black his heart must be for him to do such a dreadful thing! That is his name in London: Blackheart."

Honey picked up a glass of ratafia for her sister and one for herself. She hoped the drink would cool her sister's vivid imagination and lust for scandal. "I told you I do not believe in gossip, and I have more than one reason for that. Things become so twisted in the telling that there is no saying what the truth of the matter is. And even if things are just as they have been told, there could be an explanation for it all, one to which the public is not privy. Why would the girl not allow him to be prosecuted if he abducted and . . . and forced himself on her?"

"Why, because she fell in love with him! It is said that he is irresistible. No woman is proof against his charm."

"Rubbish," Honey said, forcefully. "I will not believe that any woman, young or otherwise, could be so foolish as to fall in love with a man who would treat her so ill! We are not such irrational creatures as that."

Nell, her nose in the air, said, "Anyone can see you have never been in love. You know nothing, living in this . . . this backwater! Dancing with law clerks and drapers! Peasants!"

But Honey did not answer, for she saw, with alarm, that Mr. Black, whose gaze had never left her, was walking her way, and he had the most determined gleam in his blue eyes. She looked around for an escape, but then realized how idiotic that was. She had just said how rational women were, and now she would stand by that judgment and not be scared off like a silly rabbit eyeing a fox. Calmly she turned and watched him approach.

Three

Was it really her? He couldn't bring himself to believe that after all these years, the woman who had haunted his dreams would be found in a rustic backwater, and that he would find her while running from scandal in London.

That he had been forced from the city was bad enough, but the fact that he had almost been trapped into marriage by that little trollop was unthinkable. He still did not know if that was her plan all along, or whether there was something else afoot with Doña Isabella. So now he traveled as Mr. Black, living with friends along the way. He had been wondering if he ought to leave England altogether, go someplace sunny and warm, away from dreary January in this cold and, at the moment, inhospitable country.

After all, he was a man of means, rich, respectable—well, not entirely so at the moment; in fact, his reputation as a rake was well established even without this last trouble—and . . . and bored out of his mind with his life of debauchery. He shook off that thought as a dog does rainwater.

He gazed at the object of his dreams, the woman who haunted him. Twelve long years had intervened to make his memory fuzzy, and his recollection had been tampered with by time and sorrow and trouble, through a long war and Seasons on the town, wooing and bedding more women than he cared to remember. Was it really her?

As Mrs. Hockley was returned to her sister's side by

her dance partner, he found himself leaving Gordon behind and moving across the floor with single-minded determination. He saw her start, and her blue eyes widened as she saw him approach. How could a woman who must be . . . well, if it was his own Wild Honey, as she had come to be in his memory, she must be thirty, or almost thirty . . . how could a woman of that age, and who had been married for many years before her widowhood, according to Gordon, be so shy?

Finally he stood in front of her. "Mrs. Hockley," he said, bowing. The sister was moving restlessly, trying to get his attention, but he had no time for flighty, flirtatious chits. "Would you do me the honor of saving me the next dance, the one after this just starting?"

She glanced at the programme in her hand and nodded, wordlessly. He bowed again and walked away toward the steward of the ballroom. He could hardly wait to touch her, to hold her, even if it was only to dance. He needed to find out what it was about her, a woman he had only now exchanged fewer than half a dozen words with, that had stayed with him through many years and many more women. And to that end—to have her as close as he wanted—he took the steward aside and pressed some gold into the man's palm, whispering to him.

As the music played on, he watched from across the room the woman he thought was his Wild Honey. If it was her, she was even more beautiful now. She had been a slender, sylph-like girl—little more than a child, it had seemed to him at the time—just out of the schoolroom. Now she was a lovely widow, mature, voluptuous, with a soft seductive light in her blue eyes and still the same honey-colored hair and delicate, blooming skin. And the cut of her dress, though high by London standards, gave him a thrilling view of a lovely womanly bosom. His fingers itched to touch her skin, her hair, her body.

Was that all it was? A male need to sample her charms, devour her sweetness?

As the music for the current dance wound to a halt, he made his way to his partner and claimed her, taking her trembling hand in his own and moving out to the dance floor with the aplomb of many Seasons on the town.

The steward hopped up on the dais where the musicians sat and waved his hand to get everyone's attention. He whispered to the musicians, one of them nodded, and then he cleared his throat.

"We have a special request from a stranger in our midst. Mr. Black has requested that this dance be changed from a mazurka to a waltz, and I have agreed."

Bron felt the woman start, and she gazed up in alarm.

"I . . . I don't know how to waltz," she said, panic tingeing her soft voice. "The year of my come out it was not yet done in London, and I . . . I have never . . . they do not have the waltz here . . ."

"But you know the steps?" he asked, placing his hand at her waist and taking her other in his.

"I . . . yes, no . . . oh, I don't know."

"Follow me," he said, as the music started.

The musicians were just as uncertain, and it took a few bars to get the rhythm, but soon they caught on, and Bron swept Mrs. Hockley into the steps. She followed his lead, and alone on the dance floor, they whirled.

It was her. He knew it, even though all those years ago he had never heard her voice nor held her in his arms. Time halted and then spun backward, taking him back to 1808, before he had become a soldier, before he had seen the horrors of war, before Honey was taken out of his life forever after the barest glimpse into her eyes. He gazed down at her, but she would not raise her face to meet his eyes.

"May I call you Honey?" he asked. *Ah, that did the trick.*

She glanced up, startled. "No, sir, you certainly may not!"

Her voice trembled with indignation, and perhaps with something else. Fear? Agitation?

"We have barely been introduced," she continued.

Ah, but, Honey, you have lived in my heart these past twelve years! He longed to say the words out loud, but it was absurd. She had not even known he existed until this moment, even though their eyes had once met across a crowded ballroom. And what he felt for her was surely just curiosity, unsated lust, or interest piqued by her sad story so many years past. Would things have turned out differently for them both if he had just taken the chance and engaged her to dance that night?

Honey could not even think at first, for Mr. Black's strong hand held her waist firmly, burning her through the fabric as if she wore nothing at all. Why did he affect her this way? Or was it just the dance? The waltz *was* considered dangerous—not for the immorality of it, but for the swift turns, so dangerous for a woman's delicate constitution. But she began to think it was dangerous more for the closeness of man and woman together, especially when that man was so desperately attractive, his voice so low and masculine, his height and breadth blocking everything and everyone from her vision.

They were alone on the floor at first, but soon some young people, encouraged by the example of their elders, stepped out on the floor and tried it, whirling joyfully in great sweeping motions across the polished hardwood. But still she felt utterly alone, and she stole a glance at her partner to find Mr. Black gazing steadily down at her.

How dare he ask to call her by her first name? That must have been Sir Gordon's doing, for he persisted in calling her Honey when they were dancing, and he always made it sound like a lover's endearment rather than her name.

But if this man called her Honey in that way it would be her undoing, she feared. And yet how ridiculous that was! This man was just amusing himself at a rustic ball while he visited his friend for a few days. He would soon become bored and move on, back to London, back to his natural milieu, which was certainly the ballrooms and bedrooms of London's elite.

What a shocking thought. What had brought that into her mind, about bedrooms?

"You are blushing," he said.

She looked back up into his eyes. They were familiar, almost, in their deep blue color, and she was reminded of a pair of blue eyes that had long ago scorched her across a ballroom. But she had never formed an impression of the man to whom those eyes belonged; she had no time before her dance partner swept her away. She did know that they were set in a pale face, though, and Mr. Black was bronzed to a tawny golden color.

"Tell me what made you blush," he whispered, holding her gaze.

"I . . . it is nothing, just a wayward thought."

"I would give much to know what that wayward thought was. I would give more if it had to do with me."

"Mr. Black," Honey whispered, "you must not . . . you shouldn't . . ." Her pulse hammered and she became conscious of every point of contact between them—his hand on her waist, her hand in his, her other hand on his shoulder, his muscles flexing and knotting as he directed her through the sweeping steps.

He pulled her closer, and they danced so close she could feel his thighs brush hers occasionally. In one turn, he pulled her close enough that he brushed her breasts with his chest, setting up a tingling that would not go away. She didn't understand these strange feelings. What was wrong with her? Was she ill? She was certainly dizzy.

The music slowed and finally ended, but he did not

return her to her sister's side. Instead he pulled her into an alcove off the ballroom.

"Where are we going?"

"Here," he whispered, and pulled her behind a thick pillar.

She gasped but could make no other sound, for he covered her mouth with his that instant.

And then she was lost. *Struggle*. She ought to struggle, some part of her brain told her. She ought to tear herself away. She should hit him. He was being impossibly, scandalously impertinent. She should . . .

But oh, my . . . what was he doing with his lips and his hands and . . . and his tongue? Her eyes closed and she felt her heart pound against the muscled wall of his chest, hard even through layers of cloth. His lips were soft and yet firm and clung to her own with a moist pressure that made her head whirl and her knees go weak.

She had read romance novels but never understood the silly heroines who allowed a man to take such liberties. Now she lost all train of thought and gave herself up for a few precious seconds to the new sensations that threaded, wound, *jolted* through her body, setting every inch of her tingling. Her hands crept up around his neck and her fingers threaded through silky hair that curled possessively around her fingers, beckoning her further.

What was happening to her?

With that frightened thought, she pulled away from him. He released her almost the moment she struggled, and she staggered away from him. His blue eyes glittered in the dim light and his breathing was raspy.

She covered her lips with one shaking hand and shook her head, unable to speak. With tears clouding her eyes, she stumbled away from him. She must leave. She went to find Nell so she could escape to the sanctuary of her calm, cool, safe home.

Four

Bron leaned back against the pillar and touched his lips, tasting her there still, shaken by how sweet she felt in his arms and with his lips pressed to hers. He felt like a man who had been starving, only to have honey fresh from the comb dripped into his mouth. The few drops left him ravenous for more.

And yet . . .

He would have sworn when she pulled away from him she was frightened, that there were even tears in her lovely eyes! They were in a public ballroom. Surely she knew he would go no further than that kiss, when just feet away were a hundred or more people. But she had backed away from him, shaking like a child in a thunderstorm, bewildered by the power, trembling with excitement and yet fear.

But she had liked it, of that he was sure. She had enjoyed that kiss almost as much as he had—almost, but not quite. A passionate madness had welled up in him when her slender fingers threaded through his hair, caressing the nape of his neck and sending him wild with desire. It had been a very long time since just the touch of a woman's fingers had done that.

Perhaps she had not had a lover since her husband passed away. It had been three years, Gordon had said. And her husband was infirm before that. Who knew how long it had been since a man had touched her that way?

She might be shaken by fear of her own desire for that reason.

But she was a widow now. He had not truly thought of that until this moment. He had not thought beyond dancing with her; the kiss had been the inspiration of the moment. As a widow, she was allowed so much more freedom than the young girl she had been when first he saw her. She could indulge her carnal hungers, and no one need know.

It was a new thought, and a very welcome one. He need not confine himself to a stolen kiss, but could dip into this honey and savor the sweet taste all through the night, and mayhap through the day.

But from her startled reaction to his ardor, she would need to be wooed. That was not a problem. He thought he might enjoy pressing his skills into use when the reward would be heaven on earth. For she was not indifferent to him. Far from it. She had trembled with desire and molded to his body as if she hungered for him.

Once more in control of his body's ardent response to the delicious widow, he walked out of the alcove only to see Honey leaving, pulling her sister toward the door, their cloaks and bonnets in hand. He swore under his breath. He did not want to rush—it was unseemly—but neither did he want to lose this opportunity. He bolted across the ballroom, slipping between the dancers that circled the floor.

"Hon . . . Mrs. Hockley," he called.

The sister stopped and whirled at his voice, smiling sweetly. Honey would not turn. But she was forced to look at him as he called her name again. He stepped toward her and she drew back, as if he were aflame and she in danger of being burned. And her expression! She was repulsed, if he was not mistaken.

He frowned, but was wise enough to keep his distance.

He bowed to both ladies. "Good evening, ladies. Charming to meet you both. May I call on you?"

Mrs. Jordan spoke immediately. "Oh, please do, sir! Lockworth Manor! Anyone in town can direct you. It is the largest house in town, at the head of the main street. Call tomorrow!"

He looked for encouragement to Honey, but her eyes were downturned and her cheeks flushed, probably in reaction to her sister's bold speech. It could not end this way, he vowed. One way or another, she would be his. He would bend her to his will and have her begging for his love, or he was not the man some women had called Blackheart.

"I look forward to it, Mrs. Jordan. Your servant, Mrs. Hockley."

Honey was mortified. "Nell, how could you be so encouraging? The man is a rake and a scoundrel, I just know it."

"I hope so," Nell said, gasping as the cold Yorkshire wind whipped them as they exited to their carriage.

"Nell!" Honey spoke not another word as the ancient carriage took them up the sloping street to Lockworth Manor, her home since her marriage to Abner Hockley. At one time it had belonged to a knight of the realm, but when the man gambled away his last farthing, the thrifty wine merchant had bought it and all of its furniture.

And she was thinking of such rubbish to avoid contemplating that scandalous kiss. How could he have abused her that way? What kind of man would do that? Of course, they knew nothing about Mr. Black but that he was a friend of Sir Gordon. The baron's home was some miles away, but he was a gregarious sort, and was known throughout the district as something of a rake. Clearly his friend was of the same ilk.

And yet all through the long, cold night, the memory of Mr. Black's terrifying kiss kept her warmer than she had been for many a winter.

The next day dawned frosty and overcast, the kind of day that could mean a heavy snow would set in and not let up all day. Honey hoped so. It would keep Mr. Black and Sir Gordon away, with any luck. After breakfast, Honey and Nell retired to the morning parlor. Honey settled on her favorite chair with another stack of household mending.

"How is John?" Honey asked of her sister's husband, squinting at her needle and threading it in the weak light that filtered through the lace curtains. Sighing, she set her mending aside and got up, pulling the curtains open and then resuming her seat. She needed all the light she could get to thread her needle and set stitches, but also she hated blocking the view of Lockworth Moor, the long rise behind the manor house that swept up, broken only by hedgerows and rocky outcroppings. Snow lay lightly on the grassy moor, and blackfaced sheep nosed past the thin coating to the green underneath.

Realizing Nell had not answered her, she glanced up at her sister. "Nell? I asked how John was."

Nell, her slender figure shown to advantage in a cream morning gown with rose net over the skirt, paced to the window and laid her cheek to the pane.

Troubled by her loquacious sister's silence, Honey once more laid her sewing aside. "Dear? Is something wrong between you and your husband?"

Turning away from the window, her smile bright, Nell said, "Why ever would you say that? John adores me; you know that. Do you know what he said when he asked me to marry him? He said . . . he said he had never known anyone with so beautiful a smile, and he wanted to make sure I smiled forever."

Alerted by the brittle tone, Honey considered her next

words carefully. "And so why have you come to visit me, dear? And for a long visit, I think you said. Not that I do not want you here. You will never know how much I appreciate your company, but with your anniversary coming up . . ."

"La, but we cannot be in each other's pockets forever," Nell said. She flitted around the room and gaily laughed. "I thought it would be amusing to come up for a visit this time of year."

To Yorkshire? Nell, who needed a constant round of balls and card parties and routs and musicales to be happy, in lonely Yorkshire in the dead of winter? There *was* something wrong, but for the moment she would leave it alone, for Nell was clearly not ready to talk about it.

They sat for a while in amicable silence, then had luncheon, and still the snow had not come. After luncheon, Honey again suggested sitting in the morning parlor, but Nell condemned the view as dreary, and restlessly demanded that they do something, anything!

"Well," Honey said, doubtfully, "I promised to take some treats to old Mrs. Landers down at the bottom of the hill. If you would like to take the walk with me . . ."

"I suppose that will have to do," Nell said, ungraciously.

And so they bundled themselves up in cloaks and bonnets, Honey adding a bright red scarf over hers, for the air was frosty, and set out down the slanted street toward Mrs. Landers's small cottage. Lockworth was a tiny village, not much more than one short row of cottages and shops. In the dreary stretch of winter after Christmas and New Year's, the villagers settled in to hearth and home, with only the monthly assemblies to break up the routine.

Mrs. Landers was an elderly widow, formerly the schoolteacher of the dame school in Lockworth. She inhabited a small corner cottage next to the bakery and around the corner from the tobacconist, and, though too proud to admit it, had not nearly enough money to live on. She was ninety, and had no family left alive. She lived on the goodwill of the parish—the vicar was very good to her—and what little she had left from a long ago inheritance from a husband who had been dead for half a century.

Honey had for years taken it upon herself to make sure that anyone in the village who was struggling did not struggle in vain. She had given much through the years, but had found that Mrs. Landers had become a favorite. Now she visited not just to bring the old lady luxuries she could not afford for herself, but also for the salty wisdom of nearly a century of life.

She tapped on the door, and she and Nell were let in by the cheeky little maid Honey had sent from her own household to be "trained" by Mrs. Landers. It was one of the many ruses she used to provide the old lady with help without appearing to give charity.

The nonagenarian was snoozing by the fire, her plain white cap neatly perched atop a coronet formed by her braided white hair. Nell glanced around, sighed deeply at the plain aspect of the small cottage parlor, and took a seat in the shadows.

"Mrs. Landers," Honey said gently, kneeling beside the old woman's chair. She put her hand on the older woman's shoulder.

"Eh? What?" The woman awoke and glanced up at Honey. She covered the younger woman's gloved hand with her own, which was gnarled and blue-veined and crooked with arthritis. "Honey!" Her voice, the thin, querulous sound of old age, nevertheless held a note of affection.

"I brought some treats for our tea," Honey said, placing her large covered basket on the stone hearth, "and my sister to visit!" She beckoned Nell, who moved into the firelight reluctantly.

Mrs. Landers squinted up at Nellie and put her spectacles on her nose. She looked from one young woman to the other. "I see the resemblance," she said. "But she don't have your eyes, child. You've got kind eyes. She doesn't!"

Honey flushed with embarrassment and glanced anxiously at Nellie, who had drawn back, offended by the older woman's plain speaking.

"But she is so much prettier than I," Honey said, and laughed.

"Not so," Mrs. Landers said. She gazed steadily at Nellie. "Come here, child," she said, holding out her hands to Honey's sister.

Her lips set in a prim line, Nellie moved forward and knelt reluctantly in front of the old woman. Mrs. Landers grasped her hands, pulled her into the firelight, and squinted at the younger woman. "Not happy. You're not happy. Man trouble?"

Nellie gasped. "Not at all," she exclaimed. "I am married!"

"Doesn't mean you haven't any man trouble." The woman laughed, a thin, reedy chuckle that ended in a coughing fit.

Honey rushed to get her a glass of sherry and held it to her lips. After the restorative, the old woman sat back in her low chair near the hearth.

"Just because I am an old woman and my husband died nearly a half century ago does not mean I do not remember what being married is like." She cast a shrewd glance Nellie's way. "Humphrey was the best of men in many ways, but all men have their peccadilloes, and we women spend the better part of our lives trying to correct them. Which is our mistake. Take them as they are, young woman. Take your husband as he is."

Her lecture over, she turned her attention eagerly to the basket Honey had brought and looked through the contents while Honey cast Nell a questioning glance. But Nell would not meet her eye and the maid, Mary, bustled in with a tray of tea.

Honey laid out the fresh scones she had brought down, still warm from the oven, and a pot of her own rose hip jelly. They had worked their way halfway through the simple but sumptuous feast when Mary bobbed a curtsy in the doorway.

"Begging your pardon, ma'am," she said to Mrs. Landers. "More comp'ny, ma'am." Her face was flushed and her eyes suspiciously bright as she ushered in Sir Gordon and his friend Mr. Black.

They bowed, and Sir Gordon advanced to take the old woman's hand and bow low over it, murmuring a hello. Nellie had moved forward from her seat in the corner.

"You gentlemen are just in time for tea," Mrs. Landers said after she had been introduced to Sir Gordon's friend. Her pale eyes twinkling, she indicated a low settle near the wall. "Pull that over, gentlemen, and let Honey . . . Mrs. Hockley serve you some tea and scones. The jelly is her own, if I am not mistaken, and is delicious."

Honey had not yet met Mr. Black's gaze, though she felt it on herself. "Mrs. Landers, I am sure the gentlemen are just stopping on their way somewhere. They are dressed for riding."

"On the contrary, Mrs. Hockley," Mr. Black said. "I can think of nothing I would rather do than take tea with such a bevy of beautiful ladies."

Mrs. Landers chuckled delightedly. "Ah, a flatterer. Watch out for this one, Honey. His tongue is dipped in sugar, surely."

For the next half hour, the gentlemen kept up a steady stream of entertaining chatter. Nellie sat down on the settle between them, to Honey's shock. Her sister had come alive the moment the men entered the room, and was laughing gaily at something Sir Gordon had said, all the while throwing languishing glances at Mr. Black.

But Mr. Black was looking at her, she could feel it. Honey glanced up cautiously and was riveted by the warmth of his expression.

Under cover of the chatter from the others, he said, leaning over and speaking softly, "How beautiful you are, Mrs. Hockley. I thought so last night in the ballroom, but you are shown to even more advantage by these humble surroundings and the firelight. The light dances off your golden hair."

"Mr. Black! You should not say such things." Honey was shaken by the compliment, and by his intimate manner while delivering it. His voice drew her, and she felt herself sway toward him, his words like a siren song.

"I must. It is only the truth."

She stared at his handsome face, the hard planes carved into hollows and shadows by the dancing firelight in the dim cottage. His hair was coal black and tousled, falling in artless disarray across a high forehead. "Is it?" she whispered.

A smile tugged at the corner of his mouth. "Only a small fraction of the truth, actually. I . . . I wanted to apologize for alarming you last night, after the dance. I have no excuse."

She tried to stop herself, but she felt the thawing of her fear and wariness. She did not want to be angry with him, and his words sounded sincere. "I accept your apology, Mr. Black."

Nellie cast a jealous glance over at them. "What are you two whispering about?"

Sir Gordon laid his arm over the back of the settle and said something in her ear that made her laugh. Then he pinched her cheek. Honey frowned. That her sister would allow such liberties was shocking, yet she did not seem to just allow them, but to encourage them. Mrs. Landers was watching the pair, her pale eyes hooded, her expression neutral.

"We are not whispering," Mr. Black said, straightening. "I was just asking Mrs. Hockley if we could escort her and her sister back to Lockworth Manor, if that is where they are headed after this visit."

"I am ready to go now," Nellie said, leaping to her feet.

"Nell!" Honey was shocked yet again. Her sister had been raised as strictly as she had as far as courtesy went, and to appear too eager to leave was unseemly.

"You children run along," Mrs. Landers said. "This has been pleasant, but I am an old woman, and I need a nap. Thank you for visiting once again, Sir Gordon. It is always a pleasure to see you. And Mr. Black? Is that your name?"

The man stood and bowed.

The old woman examined the tall man. She shook her head and glanced over at Honey. "May I speak to you, dear, before you go?"

Honey looked down into the pale gray eyes and nodded. "I will meet the rest of you outside in one moment," she said, "after I have gathered my things together."

After proper good-byes were exchanged, Honey was alone with her old friend. "What was it you wanted to say?" she asked, kneeling at Mrs. Landers's side.

One gnarled hand stretched out and caressed a golden curl. "Be careful, my dear, with that . . . that Mr. Black, if that is his real name."

"I will," Honey said, laying a kiss on a pale cheek that felt like wrinkled old silk under her lips. "I do not think he is to be trusted either," she added.

"I did not say he was not to be trusted," the old woman said. "I think he is concealing something, but it does not mean it may not all turn out for the best." She turned back to the fire and closed her eyes. "You are too good to be so alone," she whispered, and nodded off to sleep.

Five

Over the next few days, Sir Gordon and his houseguest were frequent visitors to Lockworth Manor. The weather held, and an unseasonably warm spell descended on the valley, melting the snow on the moor with bright, thin sunshine. Honey longed to deny the men occasionally for respite from her desperate yearning to feel Mr. Black's arms around her once more, but Nellie would not hear of it. Honey could not explain without revealing his scandalous kiss the night of the ball.

"Deny such attractive and entertaining gentlemen? Fie, sister!" Nellie hummed a little tune and danced across the floor. "What harm is there in such society? You have buried yourself away in Yorkshire for far too long. You should come to London this season and find a husband. But in the meantime, I think Sir Gordon and his devastatingly attractive friend are quite smitten with us and I, for one, intend to enjoy every minute of their admiration."

And that was part of what worried Honey so very much. Nellie would not speak of her husband and cast dark looks Honey's way when she brought him up in conversation with their two callers around. Nellie had her share of Mr. Black's attention, but Honey felt the intensity shift from lighthearted flirtation when it was aimed at Nellie to a more serious and intent pursuit when the man neared Honey. And though she admitted her immoral longings to herself, she would show no sign of them to Mr. Black.

She was bewildered by the flush of heat she felt whenever he was near. It could not be wholesome, this hold he had over her senses. And so she compensated with a frostiness that seemed to entertain him.

"What lovely hands you have, Mrs. Hockley," he said one afternoon as the two men sat in the morning parlor with the ladies. "I think there is no sight prettier—well, almost no sight prettier—than a lady's naked hands engaged in some activity."

Honey was sewing, and she bent her head over her work so he would not see the flush he brought to her cheeks with such outrageous words. When she had command over herself, she gave him a quelling glance. "Mr. Black, you are impertinent."

"And you, Mrs. Hockley, are adorable when you snipe at me like that," he said, giving her a wicked grin. He glanced over at Nellie and Sir Gordon, who had strolled to the end of the room and whispered together like conspirators. Seeing them occupied, he grasped her hand and laid a kiss on the palm, lingering with it cupped against his mouth for far too long.

Honey pulled her hand away and gasped, her heart hammering with a sick kind of dread at her own wanton reaction. For she hadn't wanted to pull her hand away; she had wanted to stroke his hair and let him hold her hand for as long as he desired, laying heated kisses on her palm and wrist or even the soft skin of her arm.

He was dangerous. Her mind told her to stay away from him and the strange feelings he induced in her, to push him away if she would keep her safe, sane world intact. Some instinct told her he could be the death of her peace.

And so she did deny him the door one day. She had her chambermaid answer that the ladies were "not at home" to visitors that day. It would have been a lovely day of peace, except for what she saw a few minutes later. Nellie, who was supposed to be in her room resting from a slight cold, slipped out when she thought her sister did not notice, and Honey watched her hasten down the road in front of Lockworth Manor to meet a tall man in a caped greatcoat. Honey knew in an instant he was Mr. Black.

Where did they go? What did they do? Wretched feelings twisted through Honey in the long afternoon that followed. Nellie was gone for two hours, and though Honey's common sense told her they were likely just walking, darker suspicions reared their heads and demanded notice.

She might not like his attention, but she dreaded having him turn his skillful wooing toward Nellie, whom she feared was vulnerable from some kind of rift with her husband.

And so in the days that followed, she did not deny the gentlemen again. Sir Gordon and Mr. Black came nearly every day, and soon Honey relaxed in their presence. Mr. Black maintained a respectful distance from her most of the time and showed no signs of pursuing a dalliance with Nellie, though the young woman pouted and flirted with him whenever she could. And Nell *never* let a visit end without an invitation to the men to come back the next day.

Bron, for his part, was puzzled by the beautiful Mrs. Hockley. He had met women of many nationalities, all classes, and many degrees of morality. He knew a scared virgin from an experienced courtesan and understood the subtle signs women used to signal availability for an affair. But Honey gave such a mixed array of responses that she had him completely mystified.

Sometimes she was cool, almost as if he had offended her in some way. But when she forgot to act the part, she would laugh with him in the most natural way—until he made some physical move toward her. Then she would freeze up again into an ice maiden.

And yet she was not cold. Quite the opposite. Warmth radiated from her in waves that bathed him like soft summer rain. February turned to July when he was near her and his blood heated to boiling, her merest movement intoxicating him.

Not one of the contradictions in her character had dissipated his intent to take her into his bed. A passionate fire burned within her somewhere, and he longed to plunder her molten depths. If only he could get her alone!

If she had been her sister, it would have been easy. Nellie Jordan was pathetically eager to offer herself to him, even though she was married. He was tempted just because she was pretty and willing, but ultimately he denied himself that treacle tart for the mead of Honey's delicious love. The sharpness of his hunger would make the final satisfying of it all the more luscious.

And so, with Gordon's help, he plotted Honey Hockley's downfall, though surely what he had planned for her was no sad end. All he wanted was for her to surrender to the inevitable and join him for a while in the delights of love. They would both enjoy the affair. When he was able to return to London after the scandal died down, he would leave Yorkshire sated.

"My friend has a special reason for visiting with me today," he said to the ladies one afternoon during the first week of February. He glanced over at Gordon. "Why don't you tell them the treat you have in store for everyone, Gord?"

His handsome friend, his red-brown brows high on his freckled forehead, smiled and glanced from Honey to Nellie. The latter eagerly sat to attention, but Honey stared down at her ever-present mending.

"Do tell us, Sir Gordon," Nellie said, flirting with the man with a drop of her long lashes. "I vow I am all aflutter, waiting."

Gordon smiled. "Valentine's Day is in one week. I am

having a ball to celebrate the most loving time of year, and I would like you two ladies to come."

Nellie clapped her hands together. "What a delight!"

"My concern, though, is that the weather threatens to close in."

Honey glanced up and looked out the window. Sir Gordon was right. The mild spell was over, and a bitter cold had swept down from the moors. Heavy, snow-laden clouds hovered threateningly above the high fells.

Nellie pouted, her eyes downcast. "How mean you are! To dangle such a pretty treat before me . . . er, us, and then snatch it away."

Sir Gordon laughed and took her hand. "What a saucy child you are," he said indulgently, lacing his fingers through hers. "I have the solution to our little problem, though."

Nell's eyes lit up.

"There, that has solved your sulks," Sir Gordon said. "You and your sister must come and stay at Longmoor Abbey for the week until the ball. That way if the snow comes, you will not miss the fun."

Honey opened her mouth to say that in no way could they impose themselves on his household for a week, for numerous reasons. Surely it was improper, with Sir Gordon a bachelor, and she would not like to abuse his kindness that way. But before she got a chance to state her objections, Nellie spoke, carefully avoiding her sister's eyes.

"We would be delighted. It sounds just the thing! I am entranced by the idea, and you must allow us to help with the decorations."

"Nellie, wait," Honey said, throwing her a warning glance. "We cannot impose on your goodness that way," she told Sir Gordon. "Better to take the chance that the weather will hold and come for the ball."

Bron saw her agitation, and since he was beginning to

understand her after more than a week of visiting every day, he spoke to calm her worries. "Gordon should have mentioned that there will be others in the house party, including his sister, a widow of two years with a small son."

"There," Nellie said. "So you needn't go all prune-faced, Honey, and deny me this fun as you always do."

Honey's cheeks reddened and she looked down at her hands twisted together on her lap.

Has no one ever taught the little featherbrain manners? Bron thought. He flashed an angry look at Mrs. Jordan and she subsided, her high spirits dying down just a little.

"I . . . I did not mean that, my dear sister, but I do so want to go," Nell pleaded. "Say that we might, please?"

"It is partly in your honor," Bron said, gazing steadily at the soft pink of Honey's cheeks and pretty blue of her eyes, barely visible under long lashes. "It is a birthday party for you as well, Mrs. Hockley," he said.

She looked startled and glanced at Nellie, who was unconscious of the questioning look. Bron realized that he had given himself away with that, but hoped she would forget it. He had not told her about his first sight of her all those years ago, and that he knew that that night was her eighteenth birthday. He wasn't sure why he kept it a secret, but he had tucked that away within himself and told no one.

"I . . . I guess . . ."

"Then it is settled," Nellie gushed, bouncing in her seat like an anxious child. "We would be delighted to be the guests of honor at your ball." She cast Bron a languishing glance full of meaning.

He sighed. She was going to be trouble before the week was out, he was sure of it, but if he persuaded Honey to succumb to her obvious feelings for him, he cared not about having to fend off the importunate girl. He would handle Nellie. He would handle a dozen Nellies to get close to his Wild Honey.

Six

Honey had to admit that Sir Gordon's home, Longmoor Abbey, was beautiful and comfortable to a degree she was not used to. She and Nellie had brought only Honey's abigail, Virtue, but the Abbey staff was competent and met every need even before it was expressed. Sir Gordon's widowed sister, Eleanor, ran his home with quiet efficiency, and acted as his hostess with aplomb. There were seven other adult guests, and a few children besides her own son Nathaniel, so the Abbey was cheerful and lively at every hour of the day and night.

After two days, Honey found herself happily settling into the routine of a house party as though she were used to such things, even though she had lived a solitary life until now.

"How is it that we have never met, Mrs. Hockley?" Eleanor asked as both women sat with sewing baskets open, stitching where the light was best in a south-facing parlor.

"Please call me Honey! My late husband was an invalid for many years. And even when he was well, we did not socialize."

Eleanor glanced at her over the rim of the spectacles she used to see the fine stitches. "That is too bad," she murmured. "And you say you were married for nine years and have been widowed for three? How young you must have been when you married. I hear Mr. Hockley was in his mid seventies when he died."

"I . . . I was not overly young. Eighteen. It is the usual age for a woman to marry, is it not?" Honey did not answer the unspoken question, which was how she had come to marry such an old man.

"Not for someone as beautiful as you, perhaps. I was full thirty years of age before I married, and then I was widowed so few years later." She sighed. "I miss Charles more than I can say, though I fear my dowry more than myself attracted him at first."

"Oh, no!" Honey exclaimed, looking up at the other woman. She was unused to such plain speaking. Eleanor was not unattractive, but her skin was pitted from the pox, and the ravages of the disease had left her sallow and frail. But her voice and an aura of goodness that exuded from her more than made up for any lack of personal endowments. Honey longed to say that, but knew not how to without offending. She had had few female friends other than her sister, and Nellie never spoke on serious subjects.

"Do not think me bitter," Eleanor said, seeing Honey's shocked expression. "We learned to deal very well together, and before my husband died, I think he even loved me a little. He was very good to me."

Honey did not need to be told that on Eleanor's side it was *always* a love match.

"May a bored gentleman interrupt your gossip for a while?"

Honey looked up to see Mr. Black standing in the doorway, leaning negligently against the frame, one booted foot crossed over the other. He was dressed for riding in buckskin breeches.

"We are not gossiping, Bron, merely talking quietly about important topics," Eleanor said, snipping a thread. "You would be bored senseless in two minutes."

The woman spoke sharply, and Honey wondered at her

tone. In the two days she had been there she had noted an antagonism between Sir Gordon's sister and his friend, but it remained unexplained.

"Claws, Eleanor, claws," he murmured. He strolled into the room and, his eyes on Honey, circled to stand near the window.

"Where are the others? Why are you not out riding with Gordon and the other men?"

"May I not prefer the company of ladies?" he returned.

She paused in her sewing and cast him a darkling look. "You usually do."

He chuckled and sat down next to Honey. She was so very aware of him, his physical presence, an aura of barely restrained vitality that clung to him almost like a virile scent. He and Eleanor spoke quietly for a few minutes, and Honey used the time to gather her wits. The past two days had been remarkable for his restraint, she thought. He had stayed close to her, but had not overtly pressed his suit, if that was what it was. He flirted with Nellie, but not with her, and she was grateful.

Occasionally he proved to be a witty and entertaining companion. They had talked about books, finding that they both enjoyed the work of Miss Austen and had mourned her death most earnestly three years past. He was an advocate of the works of Sir Walter Scott, and had come to her door just the previous night with a copy of *Guy Mannering,* which she had confessed she had not read.

She had been in her nightdress and uncomfortable standing at her door talking to him, but he had not flirted, nor had he by any move or word made her nervousness worse, but simply bid her a good night and left her with an echoing "Sweet dreams," his words drifting down the hall to her from his own bedroom doorway.

She was even more confused about him than she had been when he was merely a visitor to her home. The stolen kiss at the ball seemed like an aberration now, and she would almost think it was all in her imagination if there wasn't something still, just beneath the surface of his everyday conversation with her.

"Do you not think so, Mrs. Hockley?"

With a start, Honey realized she was meant to respond to something Mr. Black was saying.

"I . . . I am sorry. I was not attending; what was the question?"

Mr. Black smiled at her, his tanned face creasing in attractive lines. "I was just saying that I thought the Valentine's Ball need not be a masquerade, even though that was Gord's suggestion."

"I suppose I agree. Would it not put people to a great deal of trouble to come up with masquerade dress at a country ball?"

"My thought exactly," he said.

They sat side by side on a brocade settee, but he never let his leg touch hers, nor did he gaze at her too warmly. Honey noticed, though, that Eleanor was watching him with skepticism in her brown eyes.

"I, too, agree," she said. "And so I will tell my brother that the majority rules in this case. We shall have an American-style democracy just this once."

"Or, since I outrank him, I will just claim my right to precedence!" he said glibly and laughed.

Honey stared at him, puzzled. Whatever did he mean he outranked Sir Gordon, who was a baron? Mr. Black was just "Mr.," without even an "Honourable" in front of his name. She opened her mouth to ask, but just then Eleanor spoke up.

"I rather think democratic principles should rule just now," she said, sending him a warning glance.

His blue eyes widened. "I could not agree more. Now, as to the theme of the ball, I think the obvious, hearts and flowers, is so trite, and I was wondering if . . ."

They spoke on in amicable conversation, and she passed off his strange comment as some kind of joke, the details to which she was not privy. When she forgot to be afraid of him, Honey found Mr. Black an ideal companion in conversation. He was intelligent and yet not bookish, opinionated but not overly stubborn, and had a ready wit that had her laughing before long.

It was after some absurd comment of his that had both Honey and Eleanor giggling that a querulous voice in the doorway made them all start.

"So this is where you are, Bron!"

It was Nellie, and Honey's laughter died in light of her sister's odd usage of Mr. Black's first name and her possessive manner. Nellie took a seat on the settee on the other side of him and laid one hand on his thigh. "I have been looking for you all morning, and was told you had gone out riding with Gordon and the other men, and then I find you holed up here in the ladies' parlor!"

Eleanor glared at Nellie and looked pointedly at her small hand resting on Mr. Black's muscular, buckskin sheathed limb, but Nellie did not move. Honey was horribly embarrassed by her sister's outrageous behavior, but there was not a thing she could do. In the past two days, Nellie had become fretful and agitated, and Honey could only think it was because she was not receiving what she felt was her share of Mr. Black's attention.

He shifted slightly, enough that her hand fell away from his leg.

The silly chit, he thought angrily. His campaign to win Honey's confidence was advancing day by day with encouraging results, but this could be a blow to it. He found, to his surprise, that he not only wanted Honey, but he liked her, too. He wondered if she would consider, once he had tempted her into his bed, making the arrangement more permanent. He had never in his life kept a mistress, finding fleeting affairs less entangling, but for the first time he found himself wondering if Honey would consent to an arrangement that would bring them both pleasure on a long-term basis.

But at the moment he had to deflect the amorous intentions of her younger sister. He had met—and bedded—women like Nellie Jordan before. She had a husband, probably one of the plodding, unexciting, faithful types who doted on his wife and allowed her far too much freedom. Now that she had security, she wanted excitement in and out of bed, and looked to Bron to provide it.

Any other time he would not be averse to taking her to bed, for she was very pretty, and if she kept her mouth shut might be entertaining for a few hours under the covers, but he had no intention of damaging his pursuit of Honey with an ill-considered tumble with her younger sister. He would have to tell Nellie Jordan once and for all that he was not interested in her and never would be.

And yet . . .

The women chatted and he glanced over at Honey, who sat in a pool of golden light from a lamp, lit to dispel the darkness of a coming snowstorm. Her honey-blond hair glowed with a soft sheen and he itched to touch it. Soon. Soon it would be spilled across his pillow rather than bound tightly in a bun. He considered his dilemma. If he rejected Nellie out of hand, she might be so humiliated she would talk Honey into leaving before he had obtained his objective.

To that end he joined the conversation, without giving Nellie Jordan the set down she deserved for that whorish display she had just made. No woman staked ownership of him in such a public way without a reprimand, but this once he would be forced to forget it.

Two more days passed in pleasant conversation and happy socializing. Honey found she was enjoying herself.

She looked back on her fears before they came and realized how outrageously silly they were. She had foreseen some kind of debauched reveling with Sir Gordon, Mr. Black, and other bachelor friends. Instead, there was a comfortable mix of married couples and single people and children, and the Abbey was alive with preparations for the Valentine's Ball. Nellie had found a friend from London among the other guests, and was content to spend most of each day with Mrs. Smythe.

Mr. Black became simply "Bron" to Honey, and he was often at her side, with only occasional warm glances and fleeting touches to indicate he thought of her as anything but a friend. Paradoxically, she found herself longing for his touch and finding excuses to brush his hand with her own.

Only a few days before the Valentine's Eve Ball, Honey and Bron were working together on the decorations for the ballroom that the women had been busily making since the beginning of the house party. She climbed a ladder to affix a lace heart over the ballroom doorway, but she slipped, and with a cry felt herself falling. Bron caught her up in his arms.

"Honey, are you all right?"

It was a thrilling moment. She couldn't find her voice to answer. The blue of his eyes deepened, and she lost all awareness that others were near. His strong arms held her as if she weighed no more than a child. She was breathless with anticipation as he leaned over her, his mouth no more than five inches from hers. But a strange look crossed his face. He stared into her eyes, his jaw flexed, and he set her gently onto her feet.

"Thank you," she said, breathlessly.

He swallowed and bowed, then turned and left the ballroom. It was unaccountable, and she could not figure him out. Her upturned face and her expression must have been an invitation to kiss her, and yet he had resisted. Her heart throbbed. Did that mean he was no longer pursuing her, or had it only ever been a light flirtation on his side? She had so little experience of social flirting, for her own Season had consisted of just the one ball before she was married and whisked away to Yorkshire. His behavior might be just usual for an unmarried man.

But later he found her alone in the library, entered, and shut the door behind him. "I'm sorry for leaving you like that earlier," he said. "In the ballroom."

He crossed the floor to where she sat ensconced in a large leather chair, reading a fascinating old tome on ancient courting traditions. She gazed up at him and was puzzled by the uncertainty of his expression.

"Why did you?" she asked.

He knelt beside her chair and took her hand in his. "I am only human, Honey. You are so very beautiful, and I am a mortal man, after all. I wanted . . . I wanted to kiss you, but I have been so afraid since the village assembly of giving you a disgust of me."

"Oh." She could say no more while staring into his mesmerizing blue eyes, which pierced her so deeply she felt as though they caressed her very soul.

"Do I disgust you?" He rubbed his thumb against her palm and she felt her body tremble to life, as if she were a rose asleep under a thick coating of snow and the first soft caress of spring sunshine was bringing her to life.

"No. Oh, no," she whispered.

The library was dark with the early afternoon twilight of February, and his face was shadowed. He stood and pulled her to her feet. "I am so glad I do not disgust you. I . . . I couldn't bear it, Honey."

Like a puppet with no will of her own, she stood and allowed him to pull her into his arms. He cradled her securely against him and she felt the vigor that pulsated through his powerful body. Never had she been held so close by a man, and her skin prickled with awareness.

"Honey," he whispered as he tilted her face back and cupped it in one large hand.

Before she realized his intentions—he always seemed to be taking her by surprise—he lowered his face close to hers and kissed her, softly, gently, until a shudder passed through his body and the kiss deepened into a fierce possession of her mouth. Her outcry of startled fear was smothered and disappeared as he surged into her mouth.

For a few sweet seconds she succumbed utterly to the spell he wove with his body and his hands and his mouth. She clung to him and felt his embrace tighten. And then an icy thrill of fear pierced her and she ripped herself away from his grasp. She pushed against his chest and twisted from his arms.

"What are you doing?" she cried in the stillness of the dim library.

His breathing was ragged. "I am making love to you. Honey, I want to . . ."

"No!" She held up one shaking hand. "You are playing off your rake's tricks on me! I know what you are. I have heard how you London men work your wiles. I must go."

"No! Honey . . ." He grabbed her arm and pulled her back to him.

Instinctively she fought him, hammering his arm with her fist until he let go of her and stared at her in puzzlement, rubbing his arm where she had hit him.

"What is wrong with you? I'm not going to rape you! I only want to make love to you."

Wordlessly, she turned and fled the room, not stopping until she reached the safety of her chamber.

Seven

He had pushed too far too fast, Bron thought, clenching his fists against the frustrated ardor that still pulsed through his body. She had been on the precipice of surrender, had melted into his arms and nestled against his body like the sweetest little turtledove when he held back the full passion of his desire. But his lust unleashed had frightened her.

He was haunted by the fear in her eyes, the unmistakable panic in her movements. Lord, but he did not want to scare her! And why should she be so frightened? As a widow, she knew all that could happen between a woman and a man. Surely there was nothing to terrify an experienced woman in a man's desire for her. He should be a welcome change from the dried up old prune of a husband she had been forced to wed.

He paced to the dark window and gazed at his own reflection. For a moment he thought back to Honey as she had been twelve years before. He still had not told her of his first glimpse of her. It was so precious a memory to him he had told no one. She had been so fresh, so untouched, so sweetly innocent. By some miracle, twelve years later she still carried with her that air of untouched loveliness.

Was that the attraction for him? Was that what made him so eager to have her for himself? He had been a soldier for years, killed more men than he cared to remember, laid with Spanish women of easy virtue and French courtesans, and then after the war spent years bedding the most delectable London widows and unsatisfied wives.

In all that time, the only good he actually felt he did was when he, in the name of Honey Stillwell, as she had been when he first saw her, helped some girl escape a forced marriage, or aided a broken and beaten wife to flee the clutches of a husband who was no better than an animal.

His soul felt old and soiled to him, like his battle uniform after Waterloo, grimed with the filth and blood of a day of more pain and death than glory and victory.

But Honey . . .

He remembered in the midst of that bloody day at Waterloo, the longest day of his life, one single moment stood out. He was resting near a farmhouse, trying desperately to think of a way to get a message to his regiment, from which he had been separated. Out of a crack near the foundation of the old stone house there had bloomed one small, perfect flower. He was no plant expert, but it looked like a buttercup, a pale creamy yellow with delicate petals and feathery foliage.

He had stared at it and realized he had a choice. He could pluck it to carry with him as a reminder of one sweet, fragile part of a horrible day, or he could leave it to bloom and live on, untouched by his grimy hands. He had left it behind, to remain a memory.

Bron sat down in the chair Honey had vacated and buried his face in his hands. Honey was that buttercup, fragile and sweet and somehow untouched by her awful marriage, for it could not have been good with that money-grubbing old man as a husband. Should he now, with hands soiled by the memory of a hundred women or more, pluck her and keep her with him, or should he leave her to bloom on, unnoticed?

* * *

Honey stayed in her room that evening with what she told Eleanor was a headache. Eventually, after trying to figure out her own reactions to Mr. Bron Black, she fulfilled her own lie by developing a throbbing headache in truth.

The next morning she decided it was all foolishness. She had overreacted, that was all. Bron had proved himself to be a friend, and if she was firm, he would be content to leave it at that. He could do nothing to her that she did not agree to, and she had proved that despite a physical temptation the previous night, she was strong enough to push him away.

She left her room and took the servants' stairs, for she wished to thank the housekeeper personally for making and bringing her a tisane the previous night. She could hear Mrs. Wedge's strident voice as she slipped down the back hall. The housekeeper was evidently speaking with the butler about some matter, so she would just hang back and wait until their conference was through.

"I tell you, Mr. Dennis, I refuse to send my girls into that monster's room. I said nothing when I heard we wasn't to call him by his rightful title, even though such havey-cavey goings-on I have never heard of in this household. I held my tongue. But after the story I heard about what he done in London . . . well, I ain't sending my girls into his room."

Honey frowned. Havey-cavey goings on? Someone concealing a title? This was the kind of thing she should not be listening to. She started to slip back down the hall on quiet slippers, but the butler's words arrested her movement.

"Sir Gordon made this request, and it is none of our business if Lord Blackthorne wishes to masquerade as Mr. Black. I have instructed . . ."

"I know all this, Mr. Dennis," the housekeeper's voice boomed again. "An' if it were just the gent's title we was concealing, I would not care. What the quality does is no concern of mine, nor of my girls. But I will not send innocent maids into the room of a man who done what he done to that poor foreign girl. She might be Spanish, and popish, too, likely, but it don't mean an English lord can kidnap her and take her innocence like he done!"

Honey staggered and leaned against the wall. A dozen questions coursed through her mind. Bron, a kidnapper? And did the housekeeper really mean he took the girl's innocence by force? It was the same story Nellie had related with such relish, but now, to hear that Bron was the man . . . She did not hear the butler's reply, nor did she want to hear another word.

Ultimately, she thought, as she crept back up the stairs and to her own room, it did not matter what part of all that was true. That he was concealing his identity clearly showed he had done something wrong, even in his own estimation. She must tell Nellie as soon as possible so they could leave.

"What a villain," Nellie gasped, after hearing her sister's tale.

Her reaction should have been satisfactory to Honey, but Nellie's eyes were wide and her lips curved up in a smile. Her blue eyes sparkled with excitement.

"Nell, this is a serious charge!" Honey paced to the window of her chamber and glanced out at the weather, wondering if it would be possible to pack, say her good-byes, and escape Longmoor Abbey by that very afternoon. "What a rogue he must be! I have never seen Lord Blackthorne in person, and so did not recognize him, but I told you this very piece of gossip, did I not? He is called

Blackheart for the number of women he has bedded and the number of girls' hearts he has broken."

Honey did not like the thrilled accents of her sister's voice. She eyed Nellie, who sat up on Honey's high full-testered bed and now clutched the thick walnut post, hugging it and stroking the red velvet curtains.

"Then we must leave immediately!" Honey said. "I will call Virtue, and she can begin packing my things. Do you think you can be ready by afternoon?"

Nellie's gaze slewed to her sister and sharpened. "Go? Why would we go?"

"We can't stay in the same household as Blackthorne!"

"What do you think he is going to do, rape you?" Nellie asked.

Shocked by her sister's offensive mockery, Honey gazed at her steadily.

Nell rose and twirled on the pale rose carpeting beneath her feet. "I am not leaving until after the Valentine's Ball. You can do what you want."

She flitted from the room, and Honey heard her skip down the stairs.

Somehow, by that afternoon, everyone had openly admitted Blackthorne's identity. He suspected that somehow a servant had let it slip, for he knew the housekeeper had voiced her disapproval of the charade. Eleanor, although she had made her disagreement known to him on several occasions, would not stoop to tattling no matter how much she disliked going along with his little ruse.

Perhaps it had never been necessary so far north, but in the months following that debacle with Doña Isabella, he had rather gotten used to being plain Mr. Black, except for that slip in conversation with Eleanor and Honey when he had talked about outranking his friend's barony. As

Viscount Blackthorne he did, but as Mr. Black he most certainly did not. How one became used to a title!

Perhaps Honey would be impressed by his title. Did he hope so, or did he hope he would have to win her favor just as diligently as poor Mr. Black did? Either way, he set himself to be charming.

But she was even colder to him than before. He had gone a long way toward conquering her distrust of him, but as the company gathered that evening, he could see she meant to avoid him.

"What is wrong with your sister tonight?" he asked Nellie, who always seemed to be hovering at his elbow.

"She disapproves of you, my lord," she said, gazing up at him and fluttering her lashes. She took his arm and stroked, squeezing the muscled swell above his elbow and moving closer to him.

"And why is that?" he asked, dreading the answer.

"Oh, you know how some people listen to gossip! She fears you are an unrepentant rake and a rogue, sir. She doesn't know how to appreciate a man of your . . . quality."

In other circumstances, Bron might have been entertained by her childlike attempts at seduction. But, disturbed by what she had said, he pulled away from her and made his way across the room to Honey.

She was standing next to Eleanor, listening to a redhaired young woman tell a comic story of her "tragic" first Season, but he grasped her bare arm and pulled her away. Eleanor glanced at them and raised her eyebrows, but Honey shook her head and turned to face Bron.

"What do you think you are doing handling me like that, sir? Or should I say, my lord?"

"Honey," he said, lowering his tone and moving closer to her, "is that what has upset you, my concealing my identity? Or is it that earth-shattering kiss we shared yesterday in the library? I have been able to think of nothing else all night and day."

The fire blazed in the deep hearth near them, and it was the only thing Bron could think of to explain the heat he felt when he moved closer to her. He stared into her eyes, and felt something within him twist at the sadness he read, the disappointment expressed in the droop of her lids and the downturn at the corners of her sweet mouth.

"Lord Blackthorne, I . . ."

"Call me Bron," he said impatiently. "We are friends."

"Bron," she said. "I have heard things I don't care to repeat, nor do I believe everything I have heard. But I would ask you one thing. Please do not repeat that very improper embrace from yesterday. I did not like it, and I would ask that you do not use me that way again. As a friend, please heed my request."

In the face of such gentle remonstrance, he was helpless. He gazed down into the loveliest blue eyes he had ever seen, eyes that reminded him of summer skies and the days when he was a carefree boy, and nodded. "I will do what I can to respect your wishes, my dear. But please believe I am not guilty of everything I may have been accused of. For reasons I cannot divulge, I am not free to exonerate myself, and that was my only reason for traveling incognito. I . . . I would not have you think ill of me."

"I think I understand you for what you are, Bron, truly."

And with that ambiguous response he had to be satisfied, for Eleanor moved toward them at that minute, a worried look on her plain face, to invite them to sit down for cards.

The rest of that day and the next passed in harmless pastimes. Bron, an ache in his heart, watched Honey's laughter and her smile, her pensive moments and her frequent periods of calm reflection. She was a delight, he thought. Why had she never remarried? She would be a prize for any marriage-minded male. Even in the wilds of Yorkshire one would think some man would have seen her blossoming unnoticed and plucked her for himself.

When asked, Gordon merely shrugged and suggested that maybe she didn't want to marry. Some women were just cold by nature and did not want a man in their life, especially if they were independently wealthy, as she was. But Bron knew differently. She was neither cold nor passionless, which made her single state a puzzle.

He found himself enjoying her company. He relaxed with her, and found that when he did not pursue her, she sought his company on her own. He liked that. She was simply, quietly, uniquely irresistible, and the moments he spent with her were the sweetest hours he had ever experienced. There was no ulterior motive with Honey, no hidden, secret plan.

Unlike her sister. He was aware that Nellie watched him constantly now that his identity was out in the open. She was antagonistic toward her sister and boldly inviting toward him, but for Honey's sake, he did not give her the set down she deserved.

Until the company started to part for the night.

It was still fairly early by party standards, but the next night was the Valentine's Eve Ball and most wanted to get a good sleep. Honey was just about to ascend the stairs when he stopped her.

"Will you save me the first dance tomorrow night?"

She blushed.

"I don't ask for the waltz. I promise I will not make you uncomfortable. Just say that I may have one dance. Or two." He looked down at her, the chandelier light glinting off her hair, the soft curve of her cheek beckoning his hand. But he restrained himself. If he would achieve his object, restraint was necessary.

"I will save you the first dance," she whispered, gazing up at him.

"Sweet dreams, then, and good night. I will count the hours until our dance."

She smiled, then turned and gracefully ascended the stairs.

He watched her go up.

"She will never come to your bed, you know," a voice behind him said.

He turned to find himself alone with Nellie. His expression hardened. It was time the little baggage learned a thing or two about men. "But you would, am I right?"

Hope lit her eyes, so like Honey's in color and yet so unlike them in expression. She swept close to him and pressed herself against him shamelessly. "I would."

He took one of her blond curls in his hand and twined it around his finger. "What a difference between two sisters," he said.

"I know," she said, smugly. "She doesn't like men; I do."

Nellie rubbed herself against him, and he was reminded vividly of a cat in season. Would he feel differently if this was Honey so shamelessly beckoning him into her bed? Was part of the elder sister's charm her elusiveness? Perhaps. But he rather thought that if Honey was rubbing up against him, he would already have picked her up and carried her to his bed. As it was . . .

He pushed Nellie away. "Go to bed. I am not interested in cuckolding your poor husband." He turned and took the stairs two at a time and strode to his bedroom.

It was the early hours of the morning. The household was silent and slumbering when a sudden hoarse shout followed by a thumping awoke everyone on the third floor.

Honey pulled on her wrapper and stumbled into the hall, worried that someone was hurt. Much of the company stood blinking sleepily at each other in the dim light afforded by a night lamp in a wall sconce.

"What the devil was that?" Sir Gordon shouted.

"It came from Bron's room," Eleanor said. Her room was right next to his.

"Maybe he has fallen," the baron said, and strode to the viscount's door, pushing it open with one thrust. He stopped in the doorway and made not another move.

But the others were curious and Honey followed as they surged forward, spilling into the room. A collective gasp echoed in the chamber, and Honey looked toward the large bed in the center of the room.

Nellie, clad in only a flimsy shift, knelt in the middle of the bed, and Bron stood next to it. A buzzing sounded in Honey's ears, and she felt lightheaded. Bron had turned to the crowd. His eyes locked with hers.

"It is not . . . we weren't . . ." He stopped and shrugged helplessly.

Nellie scrambled from the bed and pushed past the crowd, head down, her cheeks a flaming red.

After the initial shock, Honey felt a surge of fury course through her, and then, to her surprise, an even darker emotion swept the anger away. Jealousy turned and roiled in her stomach, jealousy that Bron would say sweet words to her and then bed her sister. She gave him one long, silent look, and then turned and went back to her room.

Eight

"Where is she?" Bron pulled the frightened abigail toward him by the front of her dress.

"Sh-she said she was not staying another minute in this house, sir, and first light saw her a-tearin' down t'the stables to fetch a ridin' horse."

"Damn and blast the little puritan!" he swore, releasing the woman.

He had awakened at first light hoping it had all been a nightmare, but it was true. That little tramp Nellie Jordan had slipped into his room after the rest of the household was abed and was under his covers running her hands over his body when he awoke. For one fevered moment he had thought it was Honey who pressed herself to him and whispered that she would make him forget every other woman he had ever been with, but as he pulled her to him and felt her body, he knew it wasn't her.

He had leaped from the bed, lit a taper from the smoldering embers of his fire, and found Nellie Jordan blinking up at him from under his covers. He had lost his temper in that one moment, yelled at her to get out, and tried to pull her from his bed, but she had screeched, shaken off his hand, and he had fallen with a thump onto the floor. Just as he had stood and was about to try again to get her out of his room, Gordon burst in, and then the whole damned company was in his doorway gaping and staring.

He would be the butt of gossip yet again, but that would not have mattered a bit if he hadn't seen the look on Honey's face as someone moved and she caught sight of the scene. Fury was quickly chased off her face by hurt, and then . . . was it jealousy?

Maybe, but he would not refine on that too much. She would never forgive him, even if she had been coming close to succumbing to his blandishments.

But still, he felt compelled to explain. And so he had tapped on her chamber door, only to find that her abigail was packing her mistress's things, intending to follow her home.

She had taken a horse out in this weather? During the night the snow that was already on the ground had been coated by a thick covering of frost and treacherous ice. She would not make it two yards in this!

He raced down the steps and out into the bitter cold, down to the stable. Mrs. Hockley had indeed been there, demanding one of her carriage horses be saddled, a stable boy said. She would not even wait for her carriage, she'd said; she must leave immediately.

The head groom shrugged when castigated about letting her go, saying there was no reasoning with her. His lordship surely knew what women were like once they had gotten a bee in their bonnet.

Blackthorne demanded his own horse be saddled, for he would never rest until he was sure Honey was safe at home.

He was right to be concerned. He had gone only a mile down the slippery, icy road, when he heard a faint cry. He leaped from his horse and promptly fell on the ice, picked himself up, and climbed over a snowdrift.

It was Honey! With a jolt of fear, he saw her cloaked form in a snowbank, and every angry word he had been about to say to her for her foolishness fled in the face of that terror. He scrambled over the deep drift to find she had been thrown.

"My darling, are you all right?" he cried, pulling her onto his lap as the ice melted and soaked into his breeches. He wore no greatcoat, so hurried had he been, and he was freezing, but one word from her would make all well again.

There were tears in her eyes. "This is terribly embarrassing," she sobbed. "I . . . I have been thrown."

"Do you hurt? Is there anything you cannot move?" he asked, gently running his hands over her limbs.

"I . . . I think my bottom hurts from hitting the ground, but there was a cushion of snow, so it is not too bad." Her face was pale and she trembled all over. Tears froze on her lashes.

"What were you thinking?" he said. Then, pulling her against him, he muttered a silent prayer of thanks to God for protecting her. She could have died, and somewhere deep within himself he knew he would never have been the same if he had killed her, for it would have been his fault, even though he could not have foreseen her silly sister climbing into his bed.

"I only wanted to go home," she said, her voice muffled by his chest.

He stood, picking her up as well as he could, and waded through the drift with her firmly in his arms.

"I . . . I can walk," she said, struggling to get down.

He held her even more securely. "You are not getting down," he said, his voice harsh with emotion. His horse had wandered, but moved back toward them. Bron set her up in the saddle, bade her hold on, and led the horse back up to the house.

The alarm had gone up, and all of Longmoor Abbey was roused. Eleanor was on the front step and gave a cry of alarm when she saw them coming, but then calmed when she saw Honey was well. She and Mrs. Wedge, the housekeeper, followed Bron as he lifted her off the horse and carried her into the Abbey and directly up to her room.

She would be all right, Eleanor had informed him, her lips tight with anger as if he himself were to blame for her idiotic flight from Longmoor. Well, perhaps he was to blame. Bron paced back and forth in the library, having escaped from the company of the other men with difficulty. He was being treated as the hero of the day for having saved "poor Mrs. Hockley."

But he was the reason she had been running in the first place. What did it mean that the scene from the previous night had shocked her so much she could not bear to stay? Had he read her expression right? A look of purest jealousy had twisted her pretty face when she saw a woman in his bed, and that woman her own sister.

Perhaps he had been close to tempting her into an affair, but he rather thought all hope of that was over. She would never come to him now. He would never hold her in his arms again, never talk to her in the soft flickering glow of candlelight, admiring her loveliness, savoring her intelligence, enjoying her company. He had taken for granted all the wonderful moments when they just conversed, or played cards, or were simply in the same room, and he could look over and see her there, knowing she would be there tomorrow, and the next day . . .

He stopped in his pacing. *Knowing she would be there tomorrow and the next day.* Those were his exact thoughts! In truth, he could no longer imagine each day starting and ending without seeing her, talking to her, touching her. Twelve years ago he had stopped still in a London ballroom and gazed at the sweetest, prettiest girl he had ever seen, and he knew, instinctively, she was someone special to him.

If he had followed his heart that night and asked her to

dance, he might have understood himself better and made a push to make her his own. Instead, he had let his head rule his heart, had tried to push away the thought of her, only to find out she was married to someone else and it was already too late for that dance, that single dance.

And now twelve years later he had not learned a thing. He had never forgotten her, because she was the one. She was the one woman to whom he could give his heart and soul and know it to be safe and cherished. Instead he had tried to seduce her, had tried to take her sweetness cheaply, as if it could be discarded after a sample, like Haymarket ware.

Honey was it for him. She was the love of his life and had been from his first glimpse of her at a crowded Valentine's Ball. His physical passion for her remained unabated, but there was so much more to it than mere lust. He had recognized that she held a power over his senses no other woman ever had, but he had passed it off, and now had lost his chance.

Was it truly hopeless? Could she ever forgive him for the way he had treated her? He could do nothing about Nellie's infatuation for him. That was the result, he rather thought, of his reputation, for some women found it titillating to make love to a rake. That kind of woman was either convinced she could make him over with her love or was willing to take the experience of lovemaking with him as a feather in her cap.

More serious to him was that he had pursued Honey with no serious intentions, willing to bed her and discard her—although he rather thought if he had been able to woo her into his bed, he would have discovered the secrets his heart held from him. How could he make love to her without discovering he was *in* love with her?

But what could he ever say now to convince her of that love?

Nine

Honey gazed at herself in the cheval glass as Virtue bustled around behind her, putting things away and bringing order back to the room. In the mirror she saw a pale young woman, her honey-blond hair piled high, with long tendrils framing her oval face. Her eyes looked huge in the dim lamplight.

She worn an aqua dress of sheer floating material over an ivory satin underslip. A train of ivory and silver lace floated behind her from two diamond clips at her shoulders, and her pale arms were encased in ivory satin gloves above the elbow. She hadn't wanted to go to the ball, but some stubborn pride made her determine she had done nothing wrong. Let Nellie hide away, or Bron, but she would not.

As she descended the stairs alone, she could hear the crowd of people who had been arriving for an hour or more. An invitation to Longmoor Abbey was unusual enough that people had gone to great lengths to accept, traveling through the afternoon with servants and luggage, for the Abbey was prepared to offer them hospitality for the night.

She had not spoken to Nellie all day, but knew from Virtue that her sister intended to go to the ball. The abigail had said, through stiff lips, that Nellie was boldly unrepentant and called Honey a prude and a puritan. Honey suspected that something very bad indeed must have happened between Nell and her husband for the girl to act in such a way. She was spoiled, but not licentious—or at least she had not been in the past. Once she had been in love with her husband.

Honey braced herself as she neared the public rooms and took a deep breath before nodding to the waiting footmen to open the doors for her.

A dazzling spectacle greeted her eyes. The ballroom was actually three rooms—the withdrawing room, a formal parlor, and the largest dining room—with adjoining pocket doors slid open to make it into one long room. It was filled with brilliantly gowned ladies and dark-clad gentlemen, and the babble was a wave of sound that washed over Honey and almost physically pulled her in.

Eleanor, her pockmarked face lit by a kindly expression, moved toward her from a circle of young ladies whom she was greeting.

"Honey," she said, and put her arms around the other woman. "I am so glad you decided to come down. I was afraid that after your tumble you would not feel up to it."

Honey gazed down at the aqua satin toe of her dancing shoes. "I almost decided not to come. Did . . . has my sister come down?"

"She did," Eleanor said, then clamped her lips tightly together. Her eyes said much more, though.

"I am sorry for all of the trouble we have caused you. That scene last night was . . . was . . ."

"My dear," Eleanor said, taking Honey's arm and steering her into the room, "none of this is your fault." She spoke as well as she could over the noise. "I have seen how Bron has made a dead set for you, and then to take your sister to bed . . . it is below what I thought him capable of."

"I have been thinking about that," Honey said, glancing around, relieved not to see Bron anywhere. Maybe he had decided to stay away. "It was a strange scene, and I cannot help but think Bron did not expect my sister to come into his room. I have a feeling she crept in there when he was not aware, perhaps even while he was sleeping, and that . . . that he was trying to throw her out."

Eleanor gave her a pitying look. "Bron throwing someone out of his bed? My dear, if that is what you need to tell yourself . . ."

They became separated, as Eleanor needed to see to some emergency related to her by a footman. Honey, overwhelmed by the sight of so many people all together at one time, wondered if she had made the right decision. The orchestra, on a dais in the middle of the ballroom along one wall, warmed up, adding to the cacophony of voices, and lines formed for the dance.

"Miss?"

The voice made her whirl. Bron was bowing before her. He straightened and there was an odd light in his bright blue eyes. Honey tried to harden her heart to him, but found her soul would be truthful. He was a sight to gladden her heart. But why did he call her "miss"?

Bron gazed into her wide, startled eyes and felt his heart throb and his gut ache with longing. Self-discovery had been very painful, he found, for he had to admit he was within a day or two at the most of losing what had become so very precious to him. What were the chances that she felt for him the deep love he had discovered in himself for her? But he had determined that all he could do was to enjoy the moment, the sight of her in lovely aqua, the color of her eyes, and perhaps the feel of her in his arms. He had decided to go back in time to twelve years before, when he'd had the chance of a lifetime and had wasted it on caution. He *had* been cautious as a young man. He would learn to take his chances now that he was older.

"Miss, I was wondering if your first dance was spoken for."

He smiled inside to see her puzzlement. She remembered promising him the first dance what seemed a lifetime ago now, but was less than twenty-four hours in reality.

"It is," she whispered, staring into his eyes. "I am promised for this dance."

"And has your partner shown up, or may I hope you will be free to dance with me?"

She frowned, and he felt a rush of love and desire for her as he begged her with his eyes for the chance to dance with her.

"I . . . I suppose . . ."

"Good," he said, and swept her into the line. She was silent through the dance, and he knew she had not forgiven him. How could she when she didn't know the whole story? And how could he ever tell her that without impugning the character of her sister, whom she must love? But he had sworn not to plague himself with all of the things that would never be and just enjoy her company if ever he had the chance again.

Nellie was there, too, her head held high, avoiding both his and her sister's eyes. But her composure was brittle, Bron thought, and more than once a tear glistened in the corner of her eye. He and Honey had just rejoined for a figure of the dance when a commotion rippled through the line of dancers.

Honey gasped and looked down the line at where her sister stood, furiously arguing with a man in water-stained traveling garb, their voices audible over the strains of the orchestra. "Oh, no!"

"What is it?" Bron pulled her to his side. The rest of the dancers had stopped and the orchestra trailed off, sensing something was amiss.

"It is Nellie's husband, John! And they are quarreling. I think something happened between them, and that is why she came running up here from London, even though she has not said anything to me about it. I think that is why she . . . why she came into your room and tried to seduce you."

Bron felt like a bolt of lightning had struck him. He twirled Honey around to face him, though she was tugging at his arms, trying to go to her sister. "You mean you know that was not me? That I did not invite her into my room?"

"I . . . I suspected. Nellie has not been right since she came here, and she acted so . . . so differently. I think she needed to prove something to herself, and that is why she so blatantly . . ." She shook her head and tried to twist away from him. "I must go to her!"

"We'll go together." Bron took her arm, and they marched down the room to the arguing couple.

The dancers had formed a circle and avidly watched the combatants, for there is nothing more exciting than a good fight between married people or lovers to fuel gossip, and Mrs. Smythe was busily whispering in people's ears the whole story.

". . . how you could run off from me in this manner I do not know! Just because that idiot Lovell threw you over for another woman?"

"John Jordan, how can you say such a thing, as if you don't even care," Nellie screeched. "You never challenged Lovell, never even showed any anger or jealousy . . ."

"Because I thought that was what you wanted. A 'civilized' marriage, you said. Like other couples, free to go your own way." The young man took her shoulders in his gloved hands, snow dripping off his greatcoat and onto the marble ballroom floor.

Honey approached on Bron's arm and worriedly circled the couple, who did not even notice her in their heated anger.

"I wanted you to care," Nellie screamed, wrenching one hand free and beating her husband's shoulder with it. "You don't care anymore! You don't love me! You are always working, and you go away on trips without me, and you . . ."

John Jordan yanked his wife to him and planted a hard kiss somewhere near her mouth while she struggled. Then he kissed her again and she calmed, swaying to him with a little moan. He put her from him and stood, darkly furious, before her. "Is that the kiss of a man who doesn't care? It killed me to see you flirting with that fop, Lovell, and to know you were going to his bed. I paid him to discard you, you little idiot—told him I'd kill him if he didn't—because I couldn't stand to see you with him any more!"

"Then you were a fool, because I was never in his bed! I would go to Sally Becket's place and stay, just to make you think I was cheating, but you—never—cared!" She punctuated the last three words with more blows to her husband's shoulder.

"You weren't cheating?"

"You threatened to kill him?"

First John and then Nellie realized what the other had said. They rushed at each other and threw their arms around each other. Like the denouement of any good theater piece, the audience broke into applause, and the two sheepish lovers fell apart.

Nellie saw Honey and Bron nearby, and shamefacedly said, "Oh, Honey, I am so sorry about last night! I didn't really want . . . I went to his room, but Lord . . ."

"I say," John Jordan said, staring at Bron. "Aren't you Blackheart . . . er, Viscount Blackthorne?"

"In the flesh," Bron said, suppressing his laughter over this strange couple's manner of fighting and making up.

"Most amazing gossip about you in town right now!" the young man said, his square face lighting up.

"I know the gossip," Bron growled. "And if you would keep your head attached to your body, I would not repeat it!"

"Oh, I say! But this is good! That Spanish girl, whatever her name is, has confessed all! Seems the man of the hour was her English tutor, randy young fella, and the father of the chick she is incubating. Her da, a right fierce old gent, Don Pedro de something or other, had her in seclusion and was goin' to send her back to Spain if he couldn't find you, but the girly confessed. Seems she and the tutor fella had a brief courtship, anticipated the vows, and then he was dismissed. He's the Earl of Cramdenshire's grandson, or such."

Bron gazed steadily at the ruddy young man's open countenance and felt a surge of relief. The end he had been hoping for, and had hoped to ensure by escaping London and forcing the girl to be honest, had come about. He was glad she was not trying to entrap him, but it seemed she had merely been using him to escape from the forced marriage she was to enter with the elderly German prince. Once again he had come to the rescue of a girl in the name of Wild Honey, but this time it had turned very, very bad. Though not so bad in reality, for it had sent him from London and straight to Honey's arms. If only . . .

"And so what is going to happen?" he asked.

John shrugged. "Don Pedro is allowing the marriage, s'long as the fella converts to their popish religion. Seems he doesn't mind, and they're set to wed before her . . . er, condition shows too much."

Gordon, who had been nearby and heard everything, clapped him on the back and pulled him into an embrace. As his friend led him away to the refreshment table to stand him a drink, Bron saw Nellie and Honey embrace. Then Honey went with her sister toward the stairs.

The ball continued, though the conversation was equally divided between buzzing about Nellie and John's very public quarrel and reconciliation and Bron's return to grace. Eleanor danced with Bron, a waltz.

"I am sorry I misjudged you, but when you came here not wanting to go by your real name and title, and then I heard the story, I thought you had finally stepped over the line. I should have known it was just one of your quixotic turns."

He easily forgave her, but then she gazed up at him steadily again, and said, "That does not explain, though, what you have been doing with Honey. Are you pursuing her? And for what reason?"

"Are you her guardian of a sudden, my dear?" he asked.

"I feel . . . responsible for her for some reason, yes."

"She is a grown woman, a widow, and does not need a guardian."

"And yet she still seems so . . . oh, untouched. Don't you think?"

He gazed down into her intelligent gray eyes. They were waltzing past the doorway into the great hall, which was flung open, and he saw Honey hugging a cloaked Nellie and the tall form of her brother-in-law, John Jordan. The married couple left, and Honey, with one swift glance into the ballroom, fled down the hall.

"She does," Bron said.

The dance ended, and Eleanor was claimed by her next partner. Bron had not committed himself to any other dances, and slipped from the ballroom. After the revelation that his exile was over, he felt curiously light and free. He approached a footman and whispered a question. The man nodded toward the library down the hall, and went back to his duties.

Bron made his way to the library, which was lit with lamps and candles in case anyone needed a quiet retreat for a few minutes. He entered and closed the door behind him. She was in the same big armchair she had been in a few nights before when he had found her alone. But oh, how different his intentions were now.

She looked up at him, her pale skin glowing in the candlelight. She was not surprised to see him, he thought.

He knelt beside her chair and gazed up at her, taking her hand in his. She had removed her gloves, and her hand felt small and soft and cold. He chafed it and laid a kiss on the palm, then curled her fingers around his thumb.

"I . . . I have an apology to make to you," she said.

"And I to you."

"I . . . I misjudged you. I don't know what happened with that Spanish girl . . ."

"Briefly, she was being forced into a marriage with an older man and was desperately unhappy. I tried to help her out of it, but she was using me to break it off irrevocably."

"Oh. She must have been very frightened and very desperate. When you are young, your family can use so many pressures to make you fall in with their plans. That is what happened to me. My father said I would never see my mother again if I did not marry Abner Hockley. He needed the settlement money to cover our debts."

"You poor sweet. I wish I had known. I wish . . ."

"But you didn't know me. You couldn't have helped me."

Their voices were a whispery echo in the dim library. In his heart, Bron was saying *Ah, but I could have,* but it was not the moment. "But I know you now," he said, instead. "Honey, I have come to understand so much more about myself this week than I ever have before. Enough to know I want you. I need you."

She shuddered. He stood and gathered her up into his arms and held her close, warming her cold, bare arms with his big hands. He pulled her to him and lifted her chin. "Honey," he whispered. "I . . ." There were no words for what he was feeling, and so he claimed her lips, his body quivering with love and desire as her slender arms threaded around his neck and her slim fingers jammed into his hair. Icy chills went down his back and he released her lips, gasping with suppressed ardor.

Her sweet face was a mask of confusion, and she tried to pull away from him.

"Don't you want me, too?" he murmured into her ear, pulling her back to him and holding her firmly.

Tears trembled in her lovely aqua eyes. "I do," she sobbed. "That is the trouble!"

He thought he understood and cursed himself for a clumsy dolt. She still didn't know his intentions!

"Then marry me, my sweet Wild Honey! I have fallen deeply in love with you, and I never thought I could love any woman. Marry me!"

A clock ticked on the mantel and a cinder popped in the grate, making a log fall. He didn't dare take a breath as he held her back and gazed down into her eyes.

"Please, Honey, marry me!" he repeated, fear making his voice harsh. He was gambling the rest of his life on this one moment.

"I can't," she cried.

Ten

"No? Honey, don't you love me? You said you wanted me!"

"I . . . I don't know how I feel!"

"But you said you wanted me!"

"I do!" Honey pulled away from Bron and retreated behind the big armchair.

"Then what is wrong?"

"I don't know. I . . . I just don't know!"

"But, Honey . . ."

Bron started to advance around the armchair, but Honey raced around the chair, across the room, and into the hall. As the door shut behind her, he saw a pack of guests and servants, some leaving to go out into the fearfully cold night. He slumped down into the chair, just as he had the last time she ran from him. Was this his destiny? To always send her fleeing from his arms?

He would talk to her in the morning, when she was rested. Perhaps this scene with her sister and all of the new information was overwhelming her. He was anxious, so very anxious, but he would give her time, the time she wasn't given the last time someone sought her hand in marriage.

It was very late. Midnight had chimed long before, and as Honey paced in her room she realized it was Valentine's

Day, her thirtieth birthday. She had vowed, sitting in her calm, quiet parlor at Lockworth Manor, to come to some decisions by her thirtieth birthday—decisions about what she wanted to do with the rest of her life.

And now she was more confused than ever.

Bron Alvarice, Viscount Blackthorne, had asked her to *marry* him! He had said he loved her and seemed so very sure of himself! But then, he had so much experience he must know when what he was feeling was love.

But Honey hadn't a clue. All she knew was that he could make her melt as if she were a statue of butter with the merest touch of his hand, and his kiss turned her into a hissing cauldron of desires that churned and bubbled inside her until she thought her whole body would burst into flames.

But what did that mean? Those feelings were purely physical, as was the pull she felt to him, the need to be at his side. Was that all it was, man's inexorable draw for a woman? Was what she craved to be found between the covers of his bed?

What was love? Was it separate from those feelings, or a part of them?

She tiptoed to her door and pulled it open, peeking out into the hallway. The household had long ago settled into slumber, after an unprecedented amount of rushing here and there, servants summoned, more guests to be settled into their rooms. But now all was quiet. She slipped into the hall and down toward Bron's door, pausing before it.

Go to him! It was a whisper in her brain. *Go to him and make love with him. Find out if all you want is his magnificent body on yours.*

But no! What kind of brazen female went to a man's room and begged him to make love to her? Nellie had done that, and she had seen fury and scorn on his face. That was what had convinced her it wasn't his idea, that look on his face.

Go to him!

It was different between them, that voice whispered. He had asked her to marry him. Surely that meant he wanted her. How would she ever know the truth if she didn't? And when would she ever get another chance? The house party was breaking up on the morrow.

Her heart throbbing, she slipped his door open and slid in. His curtains were open, but it was a cloudy night. There was just enough light to see the figure on the bed.

It was him, she thought with relief, as she approached the bed. Now what? Wake him up and say, *Make love to me so I can find out if I love you or only want you?*

She shivered in the chill air of the room, and as she gazed down at him, he half turned and opened his eyes, starting back but restraining himself before he cried out.

"Honey!" he whispered.

"Bron, I . . ."

"You poor thing, you look half frozen! I will stir up the fire. Why did you not bring a wrap?"

He was about to slip from the bed but she put out a hand, and then, making up her mind, slipped under the covers beside him. He gasped.

"Honey, this is not a good idea, my love."

"Why not?" she asked.

Bron gazed down at her face, glowing palely in the weak light from the window. She wore only a nightrail of flimsy cambric, and it had settled over her curves in a way that set his pulse to hammering. "Why not?" he croaked. "Honey, I want you too badly. This is only torture, having you here and not being able to touch you in the ways I want to."

"Then touch me," she whispered, sliding her arms around his neck.

She was close, so close he could feel her slim hip against him, and his body throbbed in awareness. She pulled his head down and he covered her lips in a kiss, but pulled away from her and stared at her intensely.

"Honey, I want no mistakes here. I want to make love to you. Do you understand that?"

"Bron," she said, smiling up at him, "it is Valentine's Day, and my birthday. I think this is fitting, do you not?"

"Oh, Lord. Honey!"

He buried his face in her neck and groaned, then ran his eager hands down over her body, feeling her quivering to life from his touch. If this was a dream, then it was the most delightful, marvelous, wonderful . . . and he hoped he never woke up! She met his questing lips and arched up to meet his fingers when he cupped her breast, gasped against his mouth when he took liberties he had dreamed of ever since he first laid his eyes on her.

Twelve years! Always he had known who the woman in his dreams was, the woman who haunted him as he chased her through endless corridors and across battlefields and through meadows, the woman to whom he whispered "Forever," as they stood together on a windy hilltop. He had wanted Honey, dreamed of Honey, and now he had her.

But there was something different about the reality. His body was ready for her, but he had waited for this night so long, he was going to spend time on bringing her to fulfillment. But in the meantime he could ease his poor body's desire. He pulled up her nightrail and pressed himself to her naked thigh.

He expected her to react, but her cry of fear and the way she bolted from him was totally unexpected.

"Honey?"

"What is that?"

"It's just . . . just me," he said, panting.

"You?"

"Me." He took her small hand and guided it down to the physical evidence of his arousal.

"What? *Oh!*"

Her eyes were wide and round with amazement, and her whole body trembled.

"I want you, my love, so very badly."

"Is that what that means?"

Her question took him totally by surprise, and at first he thought she must be teasing, but the look on her face was a mixture of fear and curiosity. His mind tried to reconcile her long marriage and the fear and innocence more befitting an eighteen-year-old virgin . . .

Virgin?

He pulled away from her, but her hand remained where it was, resting against him, as she swallowed hard and forced herself to touch him. Some of the fear dissipated from her face, but as his arousal burgeoned under her questing hand, her eyes became rounder.

He yanked her hand away. "Honey, I think you ought to tell me a few facts about your marriage."

"My marriage? Bron," she said, moving closer to him again, "I don't want to talk about Abner right now. I want to talk about us. You say you love me. How do you know?"

He gazed down at her and touched her cheek. "Because I can't imagine spending every day for the rest of my life without you. But do not change the subject. How can you have been married for so many years and still be so innocent of the most elementary of male . . . Honey, did you never . . . sleep with your husband?"

"No. We had separate chambers."

"I did not mean sleep. Did you never . . ."

A deep rosy red mantled her cheeks. He was enchanted, and could not restrain himself from dropping one kiss on the end of her nose. Her unique combination of a mature woman's body and speech and soul mixed with her sweet innocence was driving him to the brink once again, but he would know the answer.

"Did you never consummate your marriage with Abner Hockley?"

"No," she said shyly. "He was unable, though I did not know that until after the marriage. He had been sick and wasn't able, he said."

"But he married you?"

"I was . . . Abner collected pretty things. I guess I was part of his collection," she said. She shrugged, and her breasts rose and fell under the flimsy nightrail.

His mind awhirl, Bron gazed down at her. She was ready to give him her innocence! "Honey, why me? Why tonight, this . . . why did you come to me tonight?"

Even as he asked, he realized he would never receive a more precious gift, and he knew, as he never had known before, that he loved Honey Hockley deeply and completely.

"I . . . I want you. I have the most incredible physical feelings through my body, and when you are near me, I want more than just to be held by you. I want you to love me."

"I want you to love me, too, Honey, but with your mind and soul and heart as well as your body."

"But I don't know what I feel!" she cried, her lips quivering. She sat up and covered her eyes. "I may never know if I love you or just want you. I don't know how to tell the difference. People make love all the time and they are not in love. How do you know when you really are *in* love with someone?"

"I love you. I know it because I have never felt this way about any other woman before. It makes me want to spend the rest of my life making you happy."

She took her hands away from her damp eyes and cupped his face. "I . . . I think I might love you, but I am not sure."

His heart throbbed with joy at her timid declaration.

"Give me a chance to show you that you want more from me than just passion."

"How will you do that? Will you make love to me?"

"In a manner of speaking. Honey, do you trust me?"

She nodded and gazed up at him, her light blue eyes brilliant in the clear beam of a shaft of moonlight that had escaped the cloud cover.

"Then come to me," he said, pulling her to him and covering her mouth with his.

Eleven

Filmed with perspiration, Honey clung to Bron, her whole body shuddering after the incredible experience she had just gone through. "Bron, oh, Bron!"

Aching with unfulfilled desire, Bron still felt a heady triumph and deep satisfaction flood his being. She had been sweetly ardent, and as he touched her and stroked her, giving her her first experience of passion, she had cried out his name repeatedly until he was very tempted to lay her back on the bed and take the love she had offered him. But this was *her* night of discovery, and he would rein in his galloping passion for her in the name of love, *eternal* love.

He bundled her up in his arms and held her as she wept. Her arms were wound around his neck and she laid damp kisses on his collarbone and finally stilled in his arms.

In the silence of his room, her voice trembling, her words coming out on a sigh, she said, "Is it always like that for a woman? Is that what . . . if you . . ."

She could not say the words, but she reached down and touched him, and he knew what she asked. His body jolted at the touch of her delicate warm hand, but he kept himself rigidly under control.

"It is only like that when you are deeply in love. And lovemaking, real lovemaking, will be even better, because you love me. We'll make children together with that kind of love. I know what I'm talking about, Honey, because I have never felt like this before with any woman."

He positioned her so he could look down into her eyes. "Honey, I love you. I have always loved you. I saw you twelve years ago in a ballroom and fell in love across the room, though I was too stupid to ask you to dance. And then you were married, and I had lost my only . . . I thought it was my only chance."

She gasped. "I remember you," she said, reaching up and gently touching the crinkled lines beside his eyes. "The Valentine's Ball, my eighteenth birthday, the entirety of my London Season. You looked at me like I was the only woman in the room, and you took my breath away! If only . . ."

"No 'if onlys,' Honey. I was so young and stupid. I wasn't ready to recognize what was right in front of me. I wasn't sure then, my own Wild Honey, but I am now. I love you and only you forever. Will you marry me?"

It was barely three days later. What was there to wait for? Honey and Bron married by special license, and then traveled directly to Blackthorne Hall, two days travel away. In a tiny inn late on the first night, Honey learned what marriage really meant, and how much the joining of two hearts could be sweetened by the joining of two bodies. She was a real wife at last, and she felt completely and thoroughly married.

Bron leaped down from the carriage in front of Blackthorne Hall and lifted his bride out. He carried her through a light drizzle, up the steps, into the huge hall, and, with a cheerful word to his assembled staff, directly up the stairs to their elegant bedchamber.

She laughingly protested. "Bron, I have not even had a chance to meet the staff or see the house. What will the servants think?"

"They'll understand. You see, there is this old tradition that any Blackthorne groom must initiate his wife properly into her duties as viscountess." He laid her on the bed, flung off his coat, and yanked at his cravat. "Her feet must not touch the floor of Blackthorne Hall before she has been thoroughly and completely ravished by her husband. Only then will it ensure good luck to their marriage and fertility. You do want children, don't you?"

"I do," she giggled. "And I suppose now is as good a time as any to start on that old tradition! Or I may never get out of this bed."

"Don't count on it for the next few days anyway, my Lady Blackthorne. I intend to keep you quite busy seeing to the tradition and ensuring our future."

"My lord," she cried, in pretended shock. "Whatever will the servants think if you keep me locked up in this room?"

"Damn the servants. Your only duty is to see to my happiness, my sweet."

"Then by all means, I intend to do my duty." She laughed shyly, tossing her bonnet aside as Bron leaned over and undid the buttons of her pelisse.

As he did that, she undid his vest and pulled his shirt from his breeches, then reached up and pulled him down beside her on the bed.

"We wouldn't want to take any risks by flouting tradition." She wound her arms around his neck and threaded her fingers through his hair. "Kiss me, husband."

He obliged.

More Zebra Regency Romances

__A Noble Pursuit__ by Sara Blayne $4.99US/$6.50CAN
0-8217-5756-3

__Crossed Quills__ by Carola Dunn $4.99US/$6.50CAN
0-8217-6007-6

__A Poet's Kiss__ by Valerie King $4.99US/$6.50CAN
0-8217-5789-X

__Exquisite__ by Joan Overfield $5.99US/$7.50CAN
0-8217-5894-2

__The Reluctant Lord__ by Teresa Desjardien $4.99US/$6.50CAN
0-8217-5646-X

__A Dangerous Affair__ by Mona Gedney $4.50US/$5.50CAN
0-8217-5294-4

__Love's Masquerade__ by Violet Hamilton $4.99US/$6.50CAN
0-8217-5409-2

__Rake's Gambit__ by Meg-Lynn Roberts $4.99US/$6.50CAN
0-8217-5687-7

__Cupid's Challenge__ by Jeanne Savery $4.50US/$5.50CAN
0-8217-5240-5

__A Deceptive Bequest__ by Olivia Sumner $4.50US/$5.50CAN
0-8217-5380-0

__A Taste for Love__ by Donna Bell $4.99US/$6.50CAN
0-8217-6104-8

Call toll free **1-888-345-BOOK** to order by phone or use this coupon to order by mail.
Name_____
Address_____
City _____ State _____ Zip_____
Please send me the books I have checked above.
I am enclosing $_____
Plus postage and handling* $_____
Sales tax (in New York and Tennessee only) $_____
Total amount enclosed $_____
*Add $2.50 for the first book and $.50 for each additional book.
Send check or money order (no cash or CODs) to:
Kensington Publishing Corp., 850 Third Avenue, New York, NY 10022
Prices and Numbers subject to change without notice.
All orders subject to availability.
Check out our website at **www.kensingtonbooks.com**